Whispering Lake

Written by Jessica Coulter Smith

*To Katy —
Best wishes &
Happy Reading!
JCSmith*

Printed in the United States of America

Originally released by Hearts on Fire Books
Release date: August 2008 (e-book)
Release date: November 2008 (Lg. paperback)

Second Edition released by Wild Horse Press
Extended Version: August 2009 (e-book & trade paperback)

ALL RIGHTS RESERVED.
No part of this book may be reproduced, stored in a retrieval system, or transmitted, in any form or by any means, without the prior permission in writing of the publisher, nor be otherwise circulated in any form of binding or cover other than that in which it is published and without a similar condition including this condition being imposed on the subsequent purchaser.

Publisher's Note:
This is a work of fiction. All characters, places, businesses, and incidents are from the author's imagination. Any resemblance to actual places, people, or events is purely coincidental. Any trademarks mentioned herein are not authorized by the trademark owners and do not in any way mean the work is sponsored by or associated with the trademark owners. Any trademarks used are specifically in a descriptive capacity.

Cover Artist: J. Smith
Editor: Shannon Perry

2nd Edition

©2008, Jessica Coulter Smith

Wild Horse Press
www.wildhorsepress.webs.com

Acknowledgements

The extended version of Whispering Lake wouldn't be possible without the support of my family and friends. First, thank you to my husband and children for putting up with me when I zone out and become obsessed with whatever book I'm writing at the time. Second, thanks to Charlene and Shannon for putting up with my endless revisions and getting the book edited and perfected. The finished product wouldn't be the same without you two! I would also like to thank John for his fabulous ideas. It's always nice to have a male perspective on my stories. ☺

Other Titles by Jessica Coulter Smith

Ashton Grove Werewolves
Moonlight Protector, Book 1
Moonlight Hero, Book 2
Moonlight Guardian, Book 3 (Oct 2009)

Stand Alone Books
Magnolia Magick
Vicus Luna (Dec 2009)

Short Stories
For Now and Always
A Love for All Nights
Dreams by Moonlight (A Quart of Blood Anthology)

Prologue

Cassie woke up in a cold sweat, heart pounding and gasping for breath. She'd been gifted with the sight – able to see ghosts and occasionally she would get premonitions through her dreams. This one had scared her more than most did.

"Shhh, it's okay. You just had a bad dream," a deep masculine voice soothed, strong arms wrapping around her body.

Cassie looked up into Matt's strong, handsome face. How many nights had he helped her through horrifying dreams? He was her best friend and she wasn't sure what she would do without him.

"It seemed so real," she whispered, resting her head on his shoulder, enjoying the comfort his strength lent her.

"I'm sure it did, but you're safe and sound in your bed at home. Nothing is going to harm you," he assured her softly.

Cassie nodded her head, but wasn't quite ready to go back to sleep worried the dream would return. Having Matt's arms around her was something of a dream come true and she wanted to revel in it just a moment longer.

"Thank you for being here," she murmured.

Matt chuckled softly in her ear. "Where else would I go? I can think of no one I'd rather haunt."

Closing her eyes, Cassie laid back down with a slight smile on her face. Opening her eyes, she realized Matt had disappeared. Sighing, she rolled to her side and tried to go back to sleep, ignoring the ache she felt inside whenever he was near.

Being in love with a ghost sucked.

Chapter One

Cassie woke the next morning to sunlight streaming through the window. It looked like it was going to be a beautiful autumn day. She stretched and glanced at the clock, a gasp escaping her lips as she noticed the time. She'd over slept and was going to be late. Jumping out of the bed, she showered and dressed in record time.

Today was the beginning of an adventure. She was going out of town with two of her best friends. Whispering Lake, North Carolina seemed like the perfect get away vacation. A girls only trip that Cassie hoped would include a hot guy or two.

Pulling her suitcase out from under the bed, she threw clothes into it left and right. Grabbing a small bag out of her clothes, she gathered her bathroom essentials. She glanced around the room to make sure she hadn't missed anything when she spotted her pink sweater sticking out of a drawer. She quickly threw her favorite pink sweater and jeans into the suitcase and zipped it up.

Cassie caught her reflection in the mirror across the room and walked over to it. Her hair was a mess as always. The long chestnut waves hung down almost to her waist. She had green eyes and a peaches and cream complexion that people had always admired. The only thing she hated about herself was her freckles and her weight. She was five-feet-two-inches tall with an hour glass figure. Her hour glass was a little more pronounced than most with her thirty-six DD bust and wide hips. Her waist wasn't big exactly, but she wasn't exactly skinny either. She had more of a Botticelli figure. Cassie was sure she would have been a hit with the guys a hundred years or so ago, but in modern times she was on the plump side.

She turned around and headed toward the bedroom door. She picked up her bags and started to leave when she felt a sudden chill in the air. Looking over her shoulder, she saw Matt sitting on her bed. He looked gorgeous like he always did; one of the perks of being a ghost, perpetual youth and good looks.

Matthew Spencer had been about six years older than Cassie when he died, which made him twenty-seven years old for an eternity even though he had been dead for over fifty years. Cassie had tried to get him to talk about his life many times. Every now and then he would let something slip about his past, but other than his name and his age she didn't know very much about him. He had been a very nice looking guy, standing at over six feet tall and having a muscular build. Not the kind modern guys had from going to the gym all the time, but one that was earned by physical labor and hard work. It somehow made him more masculine. His sandy hair was slightly tousled and his blue eyes gleamed. It had apparently been late in the day when he had died because he always had a five o'clock shadow on his jaw, which in Cassie's opinion just made him even sexier. Since Matt had first met her when she was about fifteen she was fairly certain he saw her as more of a pesky sister than date material... not that they would be dating since he was dead and all. Lord knew that she'd had her fair share of fantasies though. She only hoped that she didn't talk in her sleep!

Ever since Cassie was a little girl, she had been able to see, speak to, and touch ghosts. When she was little, her parents had just called them her imaginary friends. When she had gotten older, she had learned that her ghostly friends needed to remain a secret. Her parents had often looked at her with worried expressions when they caught her talking to a ghost. To everyone else, it just looked like Cassie was having a conversation with herself, which isn't a good thing if you want to stay out of the psychiatric ward. It also made it rather difficult to have a boyfriend.

"Leaving without saying goodbye?" Matt had a wounded expression on his face.

"It's easier to say goodbye when you're here. I thought you had forgotten that I was leaving today," Cassie said with a grin.

She put her bags down and walked over to Matt. Sitting on his lap, she threw her arms around him in a big bear hug. This was one of the times Cassie didn't mind her gift so much. While she had trouble speaking with most living guys, she was able to be herself with Matt and could talk to him about anything. They had been best friends since the day they met five years before.

Cassie and Matt had gotten to know one another very well over the years. They were so comfortable with each other that many mornings Cassie would wake up to find Matthew in bed with her. He never did anything inappropriate, much to her chagrin. While she knew they could never be together as a couple, she sometimes wished he would take advantage of her. They hadn't even shared so much as one kiss, not unless you counted a kiss on the cheek.

"I didn't forget, but I had hoped you would change your mind. I don't like the idea of you being gone for a week," Matt told her with a worried expression.

"You're just afraid that you'll miss me and be lonely." Cassie looked at him and grinned.

"I already know that I'll miss you, but that isn't why I wish you would stay here. I just have a bad feeling about this trip of yours." Matt sighed and buried his face in her neck. "I wish that I could go with you."

Cassie sighed and snuggled closer to him. She would love nothing more than to have Matt with her over the next week, but they had both researched the matter extensively and hadn't found a way for him to leave

Ashton Grove. Well, that wasn't entirely true. Cassie knew that she could bind Matt to her with magick, but she didn't want to take away his free will. What Cassie couldn't figure out was what kept Matt in Ashton Grove. He had told her on more than one occasion that he wasn't from Ashton Grove and he hadn't died in her small hometown. If he had been able to leave the place of his death, why was he stuck in Ashton Grove now? It didn't make any sense.

"I wish you could come with me too, but we haven't been able to find anything on the subject of ghosts traveling from one place to another. I know there has to be a way, but we're out of time. My friends are leaving in less than two hours."

Matt took Cassie's hand in his. He had grown very fond of her over the past few years and would hate for anything bad to happen to her. When Matt had been alive, he'd had the ability to sense danger coming to those he cared about. His ability seemed to have followed him into the after-life. But what good was this gift if it didn't tell him exactly what Cassie would be facing? If he couldn't protect the one person who had come to mean so much to him, what good was his gift? If he were completely honest with himself, he would just admit that he loved her and be done with it.

There had been many nights that Matt had lain beside Cassie on her bed, just watching her sleep. He would love to take her in his arms and kiss her senseless, but he knew they couldn't have a future together. She deserved someone alive that she could grow old with and have children with. Matt was obviously not that guy, so he'd tried to keep his distance. Yet he found himself drawn to her side over and over again.

Cassie kissed Matt on the cheek and stood up. "I have to go. I'll miss you!"

"I'll miss you too. If I find a way out of Ashton Grove, I'll come and find you."

Cassie smiled at Matt one last time and picked up her bags. She headed downstairs and sat her suitcase and small bag in the entry hall. As she walked toward the kitchen, she could smell breakfast cooking. One of the advantages of living at home was free home cooked meals. The downside was little to no privacy.

"Good morning, Mom," Cassie said as she walked into the kitchen. She plopped down in her favorite spot at the kitchen table. Her mother brought pancakes and sausage over to her along with a glass of orange juice.

"Good morning, sweetie. Are you all packed?" her mother asked.

"Yep, all set to go. I'm meeting Kari at Amber's house. Amber said we could ride with her since we'll have more room in her car."

"Well, eat your breakfast. You don't want to be hungry before you get there."

"I'll be fine, Mom." Just the same, Cassie tried to eat a little extra that morning just to make her mother happy. Cassie was lucky enough to have a high metabolism so she never gained weight. She could probably eat an entire cake and not gain a pound. Of course, she couldn't seem to lose weight either.

When Cassie was finished with her breakfast, she got up from the kitchen table and went to get her bags. She loaded them into the trunk of her little blue Jetta and drove to Amber's house. Small towns in Northeast Georgia tended to have winding roads, which meant that Cassie had a beautiful drive. She drove through the heart of Ashton Grove and looked at the beautiful old homes. Every house in this area was at least fifty years old.

Every time Cassie drove through this part of town, she wondered if any of this had been around when Matt was alive. She was really going to miss him! There had seldom been a day in the last six years they hadn't been together.

Cassie pulled into Amber's driveway and drove around to the back of the house. Kari's red Honda was already parked beside the garage. Cassie parked next to the Honda and got out of the car. She pulled her bags out of the trunk and walked up the back stairs of Amber's house.

Amber's parents had died in a car accident a year ago. She had inherited the house and their new Ford Explorer. The house was beautiful. It was a two-story red brick home built in the nineteen forties. The inside of the house was spectacular with hardwood floors, oriental carpets, stained glass windows in various locations throughout the house, and french doors. It had a homey, old world feel to it.

"Hey guys!" Cassie called as she entered the house through the back door.

"Hey Cass!" Kari replied. "All set for the trip?"

"You bet! It will be nice to get away from the house for a while," Cassie said with a smile.

Kari Matthews was about four inches taller than Cassie and had medium length straight blonde hair and blue eyes. Kari had a willow thin model's figure. The girls had met in Ms. Robinson's kindergarten room and had become fast friends. No one had been able to tear them apart ever since.

Kari was more popular than Cassie, especially with the guys, but that had never bothered Cassie. As far as Kari was concerned, Cassie's dating status and popularity rating, or rather lack-thereof, made her the perfect friend. She could never be friends with someone she saw as competition. Kari had always been one of those girls who always had to be the center of attention, especially when guys were around. Even though she was about to graduate from college, she hadn't changed much. Some people grew as they got older, but Kari seemed to be frozen in time, personality wise anyway.

Amber Tyler was about the same height as Kari, but she was a little heavier than her two friends. Her long red hair frizzed if she didn't straighten it and she had pretty green eyes. She wasn't what most would call beautiful, but she was pretty. While she didn't date as much as Kari did, she had been on her fair share of dates and had one or two serious boyfriends over the years, which was more than Cassie could claim.

Amber had been friends with Kari and Cassie since she moved to Ashton Grove six years ago. The three girls were almost inseparable. If you saw Cassie at the mall, you were sure to see Kari and Amber as well. Each of the young women had a special gift. Kari would catch glimpses of the future in her dreams and Amber was an empath. The three of them very seldom spoke of their unusual gifts unless they were alone. Cassie and Kari were also Wiccans. Amber knew of their beliefs, but no one else in town did. In a small southern rural town, being anything other than Christian was a death sentence of sorts. The south wasn't considered the Bible belt for nothing.

Kari and Cassie were both solitary practitioners of Wicca, but that is where the similarities in their beliefs ended. Cassie followed the Druidic tradition, based in nature and the elements, while Kari practiced the Dianic tradition, based more on feminism. Both women cast spells, but Cassie only did so when she had no other recourse. Cassie felt that the God and Goddess would want her to try and solve things on her own before asking for their help and wisdom. Kari had a tendency to cast spells on a more regular basis, taking the easy way out when possible. The threefold law apparently didn't mean much to her. Cassie on the other hand tried her best to follow the Rede.

The three women talked as they loaded Amber's SUV with their bags. They had a four hour drive to Whispering Lake from Ashton Grove, Georgia. Whispering Lake consisted of a fifty acre lake, about thirty cabins, a ten mile wooded hiking trail, and an assortment of activities and wildlife. The lake was surrounded by mountains, which gave it a secluded feeling. The interstate was a good hour away from the lake so it was a peaceful setting. No horns honking, no cars speeding by ... it was going to be a nice relaxing week. The only thing that could have made it better would be Matt.

Cassie really wished that he could have gone on the trip. It felt strange knowing he wouldn't be by her side for the next seven or eight days. Whenever she needed an opinion on something, Matt was the one she asked. If she needed help with a class project, she would ask Matt. She relied on him a lot and felt truly comfortable with him. If he were alive, she could easily see herself spending the rest of her life with him.

Ashton Grove, Georgia, her hometown, only boasted a population of 875. Cassie loved the quaint feel of small-town life, but she also enjoyed going to bigger cities like Atlanta or Knoxville when she had the opportunity. The one downfall of being in a small town was not having a decent mall. The Ashton Grove mall definitely could not compare to Phipps Plaza in Atlanta; and what girl didn't love to shop? Still, she was looking forward to their week at the lake. It would be nice to get away from it all.

"What kind of activities did the brochure say they have at the lake?" Cassie asked. She knew Amber would have practically memorized the brochure they received in the mail a few weeks before. Amber had been so excited that she had talked of little else for the past week.

Amber smiled and started rattling off activities that would be available, "They have boating, fishing, hiking, and tennis. It said they also have special activity nights in the main lodge, like karaoke night." Amber knew that Cassie loved to sing, but Cassie wasn't sure she wanted to sing in front of everyone. Singing in front of her family or her closest friends was one thing, but to embarrass herself in front of complete strangers was another matter entirely.

"Maybe we can go for a hike this afternoon. I bet the woods there are really pretty," Cassie said. She tried to spend as much time in nature as possible. She always felt the most balanced after she had been in the woods, by a lake, or just outside in general. She loved going to the local park and tried to go at least once a week.

"That sounds like a good idea to me. Do you know who you're rooming with yet," Amber asked.

Cassie shook her head. "I just hope I end up with nice roommates. Or maybe even absent ones."

"At least the cabins each have two bedrooms. I think I read that a few of the cabins had three or four bedrooms," Amber told her.

"I guess if I'm stuck with people I don't know, I can hope they are either quiet or will be out of the cabin a lot," Cassie replied. Being around strangers made her nervous. She was always afraid someone would discover her hidden talents, exposing her as a freak.

"It's too bad they ran out of three bedroom cabins before we made our reservations. It would have been great if all three of us could have stayed together," Amber said.

Cassie agreed. She would have preferred staying with her two friends than staying with people she had never met.

Amber turned the radio on and the three of them settled in for the four hour drive. Kari was flipping through a magazine and Amber was concentrating on driving. Cassie pulled out her iPod and closed her eyes. As she listened to Aimee Mann, Avenged Sevenfold, Green

Day, and her other favorite artists, she thought of what this week could bring to her life.

When Cassie had called to reserve her room, she had been told the only available room was in a four bedroom cabin. The other three rooms had already been booked. The lady said she couldn't tell her who would be staying in the cabin, confidentiality or something like that.

Amber pulled the car to a stop in front of the lodge at Whispering Lake. The three women got out of the car and gathered their belongings. They went into the lodge to get their cabin keys from the lodge manager. Amber and Kari were sharing cabin number eleven. Cassie was going to be staying in cabin number six with her mystery roommates.

As they walked toward their cabins, they made plans to meet for lunch in an hour at the lodge. Cassie arrived at her cabin first. She went up the steps and paused, taking a deep breath to settle her nerves. Opening the door, she stepped inside and found herself standing in a small living room. There was a fireplace, couch, coffee table and small TV. A small kitchen was to their left and the bathroom was to the right. There was a bedroom off the kitchen, and three others off the living room.

"Hello? Is anyone home," Cassie called as she closed the front door.

She didn't get a response and figured her cabin-mates were out. She would just have to find the empty room by process of elimination. She started with the room off the kitchen, but saw a duffel bag on the floor. She went back to the living room and entered the first bedroom she came to. She didn't see a bag anywhere, but when she opened the dresser drawer she saw men's clothing folded neatly. At least she knew the gender of one of her roommates.

As Cassie closed the bedroom door behind her, the front door opened and three guys walked in. Uh oh ... this wasn't looking good. She was sharing a cabin with three men? There had to be a mistake! She could barely speak to men, much less live with three of them for a week.

"Hi, I'm Michael." One of the guys stepped forward with his hand outstretched.

Cassie reached over and shook his hand. "I'm Cassie."

Michael hadn't expected their fourth roommate to be a woman, but he wasn't complaining. She was beautiful! "These are my brothers, Cole and Gabriel."

"It's nice to meet all of you. I wasn't sure which room was vacant," Cassie replied.

"Oh, here, let me help you with those." Michael reached over and took her bags from her. "The empty bedroom is back here." He walked toward the back of the cabin and pushed open the last bedroom door. He walked in and set her bags on the bed.

"I'll let you unpack," he said, backing toward the door.

After Michael left the room, Cassie closed the door behind him and leaned against it. Whoa! Three gorgeous brothers all in one cabin... with her! Each of them had been tall, almost as tall as Matt, and had coal black hair. Two of them had blue eyes and one had steel gray eyes. She was *so* in trouble! Cassie was usually tongue-tied and clumsy around cute guys and these three were dazzling. They looked like fallen angels with that thick, black, wavy hair. She absently wiped her hand across her chin to make sure she wasn't drooling.

On the other side of the door, all three brothers were looking at each other with dazed expressions. Michael and Cole were twins. They were both six-foot-one and were twenty-two years old, but they weren't identical twins. Cole had gray eyes while Michael's were blue, and their noses were a little different.

Gabriel, at twenty-four, was the oldest and the tallest. He was six-foot-two and very broad shouldered. All three brothers worked out on a regular basis, and it showed.

Cole was still in college, but Michael and Gabriel had forgone college to work in their garage as mechanics. Cole worked there part-time when he wasn't in class.

The garage had been their dad's, but now they each owned an equal share. Cole planned on selling his share to his brothers once he was finished with college. He could technically still keep his share and just work there on weekends, but he didn't see the point. His brothers would need the income from those hours more than he would.

Michael was the first to speak. "Can I just say 'Wow'! She is *hot*!"

Gabriel looked at his brother with disgust. "Is that all you can think of? Did you not notice that she seemed a little nervous around us? I'm betting the manager never told her she was staying with three guys."

Michael gave him a blank look. "Why would she be nervous about staying with us?"

Gabriel looked at him like he had a screw loose – or two. "I don't know, maybe she's heard of your reputation? Any woman with half a brain would be nervous to share a cabin with you!"

Michael rolled his eyes. "Oh please, as if those women didn't *want* to sleep with me!"

Gabriel shook his head. Michael was hopeless when it came to women. He thought he was God's gift to women. Unfortunately, most women fell over themselves for a chance to date any of the brothers, so it was hard to convince Michael otherwise. It would be nice if just once a woman actually told Michael no.

Cole walked over to Cassie's room and knocked on the door. He heard a faint response that he took as consent to enter. He opened the door and peeked in her room. She was still unpacking her suitcase.

"When you're done, would you like to see if they have anything left for lunch over at the lodge? Or did you grab a bite to eat on the way here?" he asked.

"No, I haven't eaten yet. Lunch sounds great," Cassie said quietly.

Cole smiled at her. "I'll just be in the living room waiting for you."

When Cole left, Cassie smiled to herself. He seemed like a nice guy. Maybe it wouldn't be so horrible sharing a cabin with the brothers after all. They were definitely nice to look at, even if they weren't Matt. Cassie sighed to herself. Was she ever going to get over Matt? She knew she couldn't have a relationship with a dead guy, but she couldn't seem to get him out of her mind. Even when she had first seen her roommates, she had automatically compared them to Matt. It was a habit she needed to break, and she couldn't think of a better way than to have lunch with Cole.

Cassie put the last of her clothes away and left her bedroom. Cole was talking to his brothers in the living room. "Are you ready?"

"Sure." Cole motioned for her to go ahead of him.

"Aren't your brothers coming, too?" she asked.

"No, they ate earlier."

They left the cabin and walked in companionable silence. When they reached the lodge, Cole held the door open for her. Inside, Cassie could see a buffet set up for lunch. She didn't see Kari or Amber anywhere. Cassie followed Cole over to the buffet and started fixing her plate. She grabbed a sandwich and some chips and turned to search for a table.

"Wait up. I'm almost done," Cole said as he put a few cookies on his plate, to go with the two sandwiches and ton of chips already there. They walked over to a table near the large picture window and sat down. Cassie hadn't expected for him to sit with her. Most guys like Cole never gave her a second look. Even the few who had didn't stick around once she started talking to ghosts.

As they ate, Cole asked Cassie some basic questions... where was she from; was she in college; etc. They found out that they both lived in Ashton Grove and went to the same college. Cassie was a psychology student and Cole was studying biology so they didn't have any classes together. It was funny what a small world they lived in. Imagine meeting people four hours away from home who lived in the same town. Even though they had attended the same high school, Cassie didn't remember seeing Michael or Cole before. She wasn't sure how she could have missed them! Granted, they were a little older than her, but she still would have seen them in the halls.

They ate the rest of their lunch in silence. When they were done, Cassie's friends walked in. Cassie could tell that Kari was just dying to know who she was sitting with. Wait until they heard about her sleeping arrangements! She was never going to hear the end of this.

Cole got up when he noticed her friends were approaching. He didn't want to intrude, but he definitely wanted to get to know Cassie better... just being near her made him feel more alive than he had all year. The week was definitely starting to look up.

"I'll see you back at the cabin," Cole said as he walked away, wanting to avoid her friends for the moment.

Kari and Amber sat down with wide eyes. It wasn't exactly the norm for Cassie to hang out with hot guys.

"Who was that and what did he mean he would see you at the cabin later?" Kari demanded.

"Remember how I made my reservation a little late? And the manager said I was sharing a cabin with three other people? Well, Cole and his two brothers are those other people," Cassie explained.

"Oh my god! You're sharing a cabin with three guys?! Are they all that hot?" Kari was in complete shock, not to mention completely jealous.

"Shh. Keep it down would you?"

Kari rolled her eyes. "Good grief, Cassie. You'd think we lived in the dark ages or something. No one here could care less that you're sharing a cabin with three guys."

Cassie knew Kari was right, but being around Matt had rubbed off on her. He had been born in a time when chivalry wasn't dead. He also had certain opinions of what men and women should and shouldn't do before marriage. Good thing he wasn't here! She had a feeling she was going to break a rule or two this week.

They talked a bit more while Kari and Amber ate their lunch. When they were done, they went outside and decided to take a hike in the woods. They passed by Cassie's cabin on the way to the trail. Cole was sitting on the front porch and watched them walk by.

The woods were really pretty and the women walked in silence at first, just admiring the trees and wildlife. They saw squirrels, raccoons and even a few deer. Cassie felt completely at peace.

About thirty minutes into their hike, Kari decided to break the silence. "Cass, can I ask you something?"

"What is it Kari?"

"As far as I know, you've never dated anyone seriously. Since you don't have a boyfriend at the moment, are you going to take advantage of your current living arrangements?" Kari asked.

Cassie stopped and looked at her friend. "What do you mean by that?"

"Well, if I were the one in a cabin with three gorgeous guys, I think I'd be more than a little tempted to take at least one of them for a test drive." Kari gave her a wicked grin.

"Kari! I can't believe you just said that."

"What? It's true. We're adults and they're adults. What's the big deal?" Kari demanded.

"The big deal is that I don't sleep around," Cassie told her indignantly.

Kari snorted. "Far as I can tell, you don't sleep with anyone period."

Cassie was blushing. She had told her friends before how difficult it was to have a boyfriend when you had ghosts popping up at all hours of the day. Kari had been snippy with her a lot lately. She made it sound like it was a terrible thing to be a virgin. Granted, Cassie didn't know too many women her age that were still virgins, but that just made her unique. Who was she kidding? It made her even more of a freak and she knew it.

"So what if I haven't? You know how hard it is for me to date. How many guys do you know that would be tolerant of me stopping to talk to ghosts at any given time? At least your gift is something you can keep hidden," Cassie told Kari.

Kari rolled her eyes at her. "Whatever, Cassie. All I know is that if you don't plan on taking advantage of that hunky guy you had lunch with, the least you could do is introduce me to him."

Kari stomped back down the trail. Cassie looked at Amber. "What's with her?"

Amber shook her head. "I don't know. She's been different this past year. I think her popularity with the guys has gone to her head."

"I guess so. We'd better catch up with her," Cassie said as she followed in Kari's wake.

As Cassie started to walk away, Amber reached out and grabbed her arm. "Wait a minute, Cass. About what Kari said…"

"Don't worry about it, Amber. So what if I'm going to graduate from college a virgin?"

"I wanted you to know that I think that's pretty wonderful actually. My first time wasn't so great. If I had it all to do over again, I would have waited for someone more special. You know, that one guy that you just can't get out of your mind day or night," Amber told her.

Cassie smiled at her. Unfortunately, she knew about that guy all too well… and he was a fifty year old ghost haunting her bedroom. "I know what you mean, Amber. Thanks."

Amber smiled at Cassie and they started down the path after Kari. They found her sitting on a log not too far down the trail. Cassie went over and sat down next to her.

"Kari, if you really want an introduction to the guys I'm staying with, that's fine. I don't have a problem with that," Cassie told her.

"I should have known that you wouldn't want at least one of them for yourself. What's with you anyway?"

"Nothing is with me. They are all really nice looking guys. I'm just not up for a one week fling," Cassie replied.

"I think it would do wonders for you. At the very least, you should try flirting with one of them. You haven't dated anyone in so long you're probably rusty," Kari said nastily.

"Gee, thanks Kari."

"So … you said there were three of them. Tell us about them," Kari said.

"Well, you saw Cole. He's the one who had lunch with me. He has a brother that looks like he's probably his twin, except Michael has blue eyes. Then there's Gabriel. I think he's a little older."

"And out of the three of them, you like?"

"I don't know. I don't really know any of them that well yet. They all seemed nice enough. Cole was pretty great during lunch. He goes to Blue Ridge State too, but he's about to graduate."

"Figures you would want Cole," Kari pouted.

"Kari, I didn't say I wanted him. I just said that he seems really nice," Cassie told her, hoping to avoid another fight. So far her vacation was more stressful than her usual day at home.

"Then you don't care if I go for it? With Cole?"

Cassie shook her head. "It's not really up to me, Kari. If he wants you, then by all means you can have him."

Kari got up from the log and started back to the cabins. "Aren't you and Amber coming?"

"Actually, I think I'm going to stay here a little longer."

"Whatever. Coming Amber?"

"Sure, Kari." Amber turned to Cassie. "I'll see you at dinner later."

"I'm just going to walk a little more," Cassie said with a smile.

Amber and Kari headed back down the trail. Cassie got up from the log and kept walking deeper into the woods. She was starting to feel unbalanced. Arguing with Kari could be exhausting. Normally being around her friends made her happy, but Kari was getting meaner and meaner these days. Cassie didn't understand what was going on, but she hoped it didn't last the entire trip.

Cole was sitting on the porch of the cabin when Kari and Amber walked by. He wasn't certain, but he would have sworn that Kari winked at him when she walked past. What was that about? He had a feeling he hadn't seen the last of her. By now he was used to women coming on to him, but he hadn't been on a date in a while. Cassie was the first woman who had even sparked his interest this year.

He looked up the trail, but he didn't see Cassie. Surely her friends hadn't left her out there alone. He waited a few minutes to see if she would follow. When there was no sign of her after fifteen minutes, Cole started down the cabin steps and decided to go check on her. It would be getting dark soon.

He walked for almost an hour before he found her. She was sitting on a rock by a spring with her knees drawn up to her chest. Her hair was down and it was blowing in the breeze. Her cheek rested on her knees and she had her eyes closed. As he got closer, he could tell that she had been crying. He felt an unexpected urge to comfort her. The feeling surprised Cole. He hadn't wanted to comfort a woman in a long time... not since his girlfriend, April, had left.

Chapter Two

Cassie wished more than anything that Matt were here with her. What danger had he foreseen? Did it have anything to do with Kari's idea that Cassie should flirt with Cole, or was it something else entirely? She knew of Matt's ability to sense danger. It had actually saved her more than once over the past few years. She really missed him. He always knew exactly what to say to make her feel better.

Cassie had walked a little further when she heard a noise to her right. She looked over and saw a girl coming towards her. Right away Cassie knew that the girl was a ghost. They seemed to have a particular aura or something, not to mention that the air always felt a little cooler around them.

"Hi," Cassie said as the girl approached.

"Hi, I'm Sarah."

"It's nice to meet you Sarah. I'm Cassie."

"I saw your friends leave. They were your friends, right?" the ghost asked.

"Yes."

"Just wondering. That one girl seemed a little mean."

"She normally isn't like that," Cassie said, wondering why she was defending Kari.

Sarah contemplated her for a minute. "I know where there's a stream nearby. Want to walk there? It's really pretty."

"Sure. Lead the way." Cassie followed Sarah further along the path. About half a mile down the trail, she looked to her left and saw a beautiful stream with a large rock beside it. She walked down to the stream and climbed up on the rock, pulling her knees up to her chest and wrapping her arms around them. It was late afternoon and the sun was already starting to sink behind the mountains. The air had gotten quite a bit cooler than when she had started her hike.

"What did you want to talk about?" Cassie asked.

"Nothing in particular. It just gets lonely sometimes. There aren't too many people like you who can see me and hear me."

Cassie reached over and grabbed the girl's hand. "Don't forget that I feel you too."

Sarah looked shocked. "I haven't been able to touch another person since I died. How did you do that?"

"I'm not really sure. It's just something I've always been able to do. I haven't talked to anyone in my family about it so as far as I know I'm the only one who has the gift. Y'all are just as real to me as my friends are."

Sarah looked thoughtful. "It must be strange, having ghosts walk up to you all the time. How do you deal with something like that? Isn't it hard keeping it a secret?"

"It was at first. I'm used to it now. It's a little embarrassing if I'm in the mall or someplace crowded though. Then people think I'm talking to myself. It's definitely hard keeping it a secret. Sometimes I would like nothing more than to have someone to share this with. I have two friends who know about my gift, but it would be nice if I could share it with my family or have a boyfriend who would understand." Cassie looked at Sarah. "Actually, my best friend is a ghost. His name is Matt. Right before you walked up to me, I was thinking how much I wish he were here."

Sarah grinned, "You don't think your family would understand? You had to have received this gift from somewhere."

"I've often wondered about that. I guess I'm just scared that if I tell my parents I see ghosts they will have me locked away." Cassie sighed. "May I ask you something personal?"

"Sure."

"How long ago did you die?"

"Three years ago. It was fall when I came here with some friends. We went hiking and it started to rain. We had veered off the path and crossed the stream further up the trail. When I tried to cross back over, I slipped on one of the rocks and hit my head. The next thing I knew, no one could hear me or see me."

"I'm sorry," Cassie said with compassion. She could only imagine what that must have been like.

"Don't be. It wasn't your fault. It was just an accident." Sarah smiled at her. "Being stuck here isn't too bad. It's just lonely. I stayed behind to watch over my boyfriend, but when he left the lake I wasn't able to go with him."

"That must have been very sad," Cassie replied.

"It was. The worst part is being alone all of the time."

Cassie laid a sympathetic hand on Sarah's shoulder. "You're not alone now. If I could find a way to release you from this place, I would. Matt and I researched that very topic over the past few weeks, but we haven't been able to find anything yet."

Sarah smiled at her. She turned and started to walk back into the woods. "I will leave you to your hike. Thank you for stopping and talking to me for a few minutes."

Cassie thought that Sarah' story was a very sad one. It didn't seem fair that she was stuck here. She wished that she had her Wicca books with her or her laptop. She might have been able to find a spell that would release Sarah's spirit. Of course, if she released Sarah from her prison on earth, she would have to do the same for Matt. Cassie wasn't sure she was ready for that step. She cared about Matt far too much to lose him. She knew it was selfish of her, but she couldn't help how she felt. She would be lost without him.

Cassie looked over at Sarah. "You're welcome. I'm staying here for a week so maybe we can talk again before I leave."

"I'd like that," Sarah said with a smile. She turned and disappeared into the woods.

Cassie decided she liked hearing the spring trickle by and decided to stay a little longer. As she sat by the water, she started thinking about Kari. Unlike Cassie, Kari had seriously dated several guys this year and two the year before. Even though Kari hung out with Amber and Cassie, she was far more popular than either of them. Cassie laid her head down on her knees and closed her eyes.

After a few minutes, she let the tears come. She didn't understand why Kari couldn't accept her the way she was. So what if she didn't date anyone seriously? Kari knew that Cassie wasn't like most people. She wished her friend could be more supportive. What was the big deal with sleeping with a bunch of guys anyway? Wasn't it better to wait for someone special? Someone like Matt?

Thinking of Matt just made her cry harder. Why did the most wonderful man she knew have to be a ghost? Cassie knew a large part of why she didn't date had to do with Matt. Even if Cassie knew they couldn't be together, she still compared every guy she ever met to Matt. Every date she went on, she wished that it was Matt sitting across from her or holding her hand. It wasn't fair to the men that asked her out, but she couldn't seem to help it.

Cassie sat on the rock for the longest time and eventually cried herself to sleep. An hour passed before Cole found her sitting on that same rock. He watched her for a few minutes... not sure if he should disturb her or not. Why had she been crying? Did it have anything to do with her friends leaving her out here?

"Cassie? Wake-up, Cass." Cole gently nudged her.

Cassie lifted her head and saw Cole standing by her. She looked around and noticed it was nearly dark outside. She tried to stand and nearly fell. Her legs had fallen asleep from sitting in a cramped position for so long. Cole deftly caught her around the waist and helped her stand up. Being this close to him, she could smell his woodsy scent. She wanted to wrap her arms around him and bury her face in his shirt. For the first time in her life, she wanted to take solace in someone's embrace other than Matt's. Instead, she took a step back and wiped the tears from her eyes.

Looking up at him she asked, "How did you find me?"

"I saw your friends come out of the woods without you. I waited a few minutes and when you didn't come back down the trail I thought I would come and get you. It's an hour walk back to the cabin and dinner will be served in less than two hours," Cole replied.

"Thanks for coming out here."

"Are you ready to walk back? Or do you need more time," he asked.

Cassie looked at Cole, noting the concerned look on his face. The thought that such a cute guy might like her was enough to put a smile back on Cassie's face. Maybe this time, she wouldn't think of Matt all the time. It would be nice to go out with a guy and be happy just to be with him.

"No, I'm all right. We can head back," she said.

As they drew closer to the cabin, Cole reached over and took Cassie's hand. Cassie looked at him in surprise, but then she smiled and threaded her fingers through his. They walked in silence back to the cabin. She had never felt this comfortable with anyone before. It was like she had known Cole her whole life.

"I think I'm going to go inside and freshen up a little," Cassie said as they came to the end of the trail. She knew her face was probably streaked from her tears and she had some fallen leaves stuck in her hair. In other words, she was a wreck.

"Okay. I'm going to sit out here for a minute. Want me to wait on you for dinner?"

"I'd like that," Cassie said with a shy smile before going into the cabin.

She grabbed her bag of toiletries and a clean change of clothes and headed to the bathroom. She took a hot shower, washing her hair with her favorite lavender shampoo and using her favorite lavender soap. When she was done, she got out and towel dried her long hair and put on her pink sweater and jeans. She quickly moisturized her face and put on a little mascara and lipstick. Her cheeks were pink enough from the hot water of her shower that blush wasn't necessary tonight.

Cassie put her makeup back in the little bag and put the bag in the mirrored cabinet above the sink. Even though her hair was still quite wet, it fell in long dark waves down her back. She put her dirty clothes in her room and put on her brown Dr. Martens. When she stepped out onto the porch, Cole turned to face her.

"Wow. You look great," he said as his eyes devoured every inch of her. He couldn't help but wonder what she was wearing under the pink sweater.

Cassie blushed. "Thanks. Are you ready to see if dinner's ready?"

Cole nodded. They started walking toward the lodge. Again, he reached over and took her hand. With their fingers laced together, they walked up the steps to the lodge and went inside. Most of the people staying at Whispering Lake were already filling their plates. They saw Kari and Amber across the room. Kari saw their joined hands and glared at her. Cassie should have expected that since Kari had mentioned she wanted Cole for herself.

"Would you like to sit at the same table we had during lunch?" Cole asked her.

"That would be great," Cassie replied.

"Let's go." Cole led her over to the buffet and handed her a plate before grabbing one for himself.

Cassie and Cole finished filling their plates and went to find their table by the window. Just as Cassie sat down, she felt something brush past her leg. She looked down and saw an adorable little dog. She knew she shouldn't acknowledge it though, at least not in front of Cole. The dog was a ghost. Cassie nonchalantly reached down as if she were going to pick something up and quickly patted the pup on the head. She noticed Cole was watching her.

"Dropped my napkin," she said with a grin. He smiled back and they started eating.

From across the room, Kari had noticed Cassie's move. She knew exactly what had happened. Cassie had attracted a ghost just as she always did. At that moment, Kari knew exactly how she could separate Cassie and Cole. After all, had she not told Cassie that she wanted Cole? Besides, Cassie wouldn't have the first clue what to do with a guy like that. All Kari had to do was let Cole know that he was interested in a freak who talked to ghosts. Everything else would fall into place after that. Who would want to date someone like Cassie anyway?

Kari got up and walked over to their table. After all, it wasn't like Cassie was going to seriously date him anyway. Kari might as well be able to have some fun during the trip and she planned on having fun with Cole.

"Hi Cassie. Seen Casper lately?" Kari asked snidely.

Cassie could see Cole watching her, waiting for her response. "I don't know what you're talking about Kari."

How could Kari do this to her? Cassie hoped she would drop it and walk away. No such luck!

"You know what I mean. Been talking to any ghosts lately? You know, like the one you were just petting under the table," Kari continued relentlessly.

Cassie gasped. She shot her eyes over to Cole to judge his reaction. He was just looking between her and Kari.

"Are you trying to tell me that Cassie can talk to ghosts?" Cole asked.

31

His calm tone wasn't the reaction Kari had hoped for. He was taking this news entirely too well. He was supposed to freak out and want to be as far from Cassie as possible.

"Yes, she can talk to dead people and animals. It looked to me like she was petting a ghost dog or cat under the table," Kari responded, sure that he would get up at any moment and walk away from Cassie.

Cole looked at Cassie. He could tell she was really uncomfortable with what Kari was saying. Could she really talk to and touch spirits? "Is that true, Cassie? You can see ghosts?"

"Yes, it's true," she whispered.

She started to get up from the table, but Cole reached over and took her hand. She looked into his eyes and saw that he wasn't repulsed or freaked over her news. If anything, he looked intrigued. Could she have finally found someone who would understand and accept her as is?

"Please sit back down. I'd like for you to finish having dinner with me. If you want to, that is," he told her with a smile.

Cole looked at Kari, "Anything else you'd like to share for her? I'm sure she's capable of telling me these things when she's ready."

Kari looked mad enough to spit nails. She spun away from their table and stormed back over to sit by Amber again. Amber looked at Cassie apologetically.

Looking back at Cole, Cassie said, "You certainly took that differently than I had thought you would. Aren't you freaked out?"

Cole shrugged. "Honestly, I think it's kind of cool. I always knew that things like ghosts existed. I've never seen one, but sometimes I've thought I could feel one. It kind of makes me wonder what else might be out there."

He smiled at her. "Who knows, maybe vampires and werewolves are real too."

Cassie was amazed. Cole was not only gorgeous, kind and seemed to like her, but he was also willing to accept her as she was... freakish powers and all. "I don't know what to say. I figured by now you would have been running as fast you could to get away from me. That's what most guys do anyway."

Cole grinned at her. "It will take a lot more than that to run me off."

He couldn't believe guys would run from Cassie. So what if she could talk to ghosts? It just made her different. Everyone was different in their own way. It was a small part of who she was. Any man should feel honored to have such a beautiful and caring woman in his life.

Cassie smiled in return and finished eating her dinner. Once they were done and had returned their plates to the kitchen, they left the lodge. When they stepped outside, Cole turned towards Cassie.

"I had a nice time tonight," he told her.

"Me, too." Cassie smiled at him. "Maybe we could do it again sometime? If you're interested, that is."

"Oh, I'm definitely interested." Cole smiled at her.

He thought she looked even more beautiful in the moonlight. She was a good foot shorter than he was, but she reminded him of a petite pixie. She had delicate features and a full mouth that he wanted to kiss. He wondered what she'd say if he leaned down and kissed her at that moment. Deciding not to tempt fate, he steered his thoughts in another direction.

"Would you like to walk around the lake? Or head back to the cabin? I think I saw a DVD player and some movies in the living room," Cole said.

"How about a short walk first?" Cassie couldn't think of anything more romantic than a moonlit walk by the lake.

Cassie had only dreamed of nights like this before. She felt comfortable around Cole, but she also felt a little guilty. She wasn't sure why, but it almost felt like she was cheating on Matt when she was with Cole. Would she ever get over him and allow herself to have a real life? Here she was with a gorgeous guy that accepted her unique ability and she was thinking of Matt again. There was something seriously wrong with her!

They held hands and walked in the moonlight, looking out over the lake. It was quiet despite the fact that all 30 cabins were full. It seemed like everyone had decided to stay at the lodge for whatever activity had been planned for the evening, while the rest were quietly heading to their cabins.

Cassie was starting to shiver. The night was getting cooler by the minute. "Cole, would you mind if we headed back to the cabin now? It's starting to get a little cold."

"Sure." He put his arm around her shoulders and started walking towards the cabin. "Do you think you'll feel up to a movie? Or do you want to head to your room? I'm sure you had a long day."

His thoughtfulness touched her. "I think I can handle a movie," she said with a smile.

Chapter Three

As they walked up the steps to the cabin, Cole removed his arm from around Cassie's shoulders. Secretly, he was hoping his brothers were still gone for the evening. He unlocked the door and motioned for her to go in first.

Cassie flipped the light on as she walked through the door. Sitting in the middle of the floor was the same little dog she had seen during dinner. She quickly glanced over her shoulder at Cole.

"What is it Cassie?"

"Um. Well, do you remember Kari saying something about me petting a ghost animal at dinner?" she asked.

"Yes. Is that what you really did when you leaned down under the table?"

"Yes. It was a cute little dog." She paused and chewed on her lip nervously. "It also happens to be sitting in the middle of our floor. I wanted to pick it up and talk to it, but I was worried it might freak you out if I did that," Cassie told him.

Cole smiled at her so she would know she had nothing to fear. "It's okay, Cassie. You can go ahead and talk to it or do whatever you feel you need to. Nothing you say or do is going to bother me."

Cassie walked over to the little dog and petted its head. "Hi there, sweetie. Aren't you a cutie?"

The little brown dog, an Italian Greyhound, licked her hand. It was about 15 inches tall, had long skinny legs, a long skinny tail, cute ears that flopped at the corners, and large brown eyes. Cassie walked over to the couch and sat down. The little dog immediately jumped into her lap and curled up.

As Cassie petted the little spook, Cole went over to the shelf of DVDs to let Cassie know what was available for them to watch. "Do you want horror, mystery, romance, or comedy?" he asked.

Cassie quickly chose the one that would get her the closest to Cole. Maybe Kari had the right idea when she said Cassie should flirt with one of the brothers. Who knows, maybe something good would come of this trip. They *did* live in the same town so who said their relationship would end when they left the lake? If things went really well, maybe she would end up with a steady guy in her life. A steady *living* guy!

"How about something scary? It seems fitting with a ghost in our cabin," she replied.

Cole was only too happy to select a scary movie. If he were lucky, maybe Cassie would be scared enough to slide closer to his end of the couch. Being around Cassie almost made him feel like he was in high school again, in a good way.

"I think I found just the one." He quickly put Rose Red in the DVD player.

Cassie smiled at him. She loved ghost stories. Granted, they were very seldom anything like real ghosts, but she enjoyed a good scare every now and then. The little dog had settled into her lap and was now sleeping, or whatever ghosts did during their down time. Cassie gently picked it up and placed it next to her on the couch. It didn't even seem to notice it wasn't being held anymore.

Cole sat on the opposite end of the couch from Cassie. As he reached over to take her hand, she slid closer to him. By the time the previews were over and the movie had started, she had pressed herself against his side. He put his arm around her and she rested her head on his chest. Whenever something scary or unexpected would happen, Cassie would close her eyes and bury her face against his shirt.

During a particularly suspense-filled moment, Cassie looked up at Cole and found him watching her. He lowered his head and gently kissed her on the mouth. It was a short kiss, but it made Cassie want more. She sat up and leaned closer to Cole. Hesitantly, she kissed him back.

Putting his hand on the back of her neck, Cole pulled her closer. When the tip of his tongue flicked across her lips, she gasped. Cole took advantage of the moment and deepened the kiss.

Cassie had never been kissed like this before. Normally she didn't let anyone get this close. Just as she thought she never wanted him to stop, he pulled away.

"I'm sorry. I shouldn't have done that," Cassie said as she tried to scoot away.

"Don't be sorry. I'm certainly not."

"Then why did you stop kissing me?" Cassie asked in confusion.

"My brothers could come back any minute. I had a feeling you would prefer for our kisses to be kept private," Cole responded.

Cassie wasn't sure how to respond at first. "Wait, you said kisses. We've only had one."

"Maybe I'm hoping there will be more to follow," Cole said with a grin.

It had taken everything Cole had in him to stop kissing her. He wanted her more than he had ever wanted a woman before. Being with her would be different from anything else he had experienced. It was the most alive he'd felt since April had moved away. He hadn't allowed himself to get close to anyone since then. He hadn't *wanted* to get close to anyone. Women were always throwing themselves at him and his brothers, but he just hadn't been interested in the past year. He knew that April wasn't his soul mate, but they had been together for a while and he sometimes missed her.

By the end of the movie, Cassie had dozed off. At some point, she had stretched out on the couch and was lying across his lap. Careful not to disturb her, he pulled his legs onto the couch and stretched out beside her. He put his arm around her so she wouldn't fall off, or so he told himself. He would have grabbed any excuse to hold her close.

Cole wasn't sure if being this close to her was heaven or hell. He felt something cold settle behind his legs and knew the little ghost dog was getting comfortable, too. He knew that Michael and Gabriel would be back soon and he should get Cassie to bed, but he was enjoying the feel of her against him too much to move right at that moment. Eventually, he fell asleep.

Outside, Kari was peeking in the window of the cabin. Her temper flared when she realized they were lying on the couch together. Kari decided to take action. It was time for magick to lend a hand. She had told Cassie that afternoon she planned on seducing Cole and now her friend was moving into her territory. If Cassie had finally decided to have some fun, she should have chosen one of the other brothers.

Kari walked deep into the woods. She normally didn't use magick for something like this, but she felt that desperate times called for desperate measures. Cole was supposed to be hers! Once she felt she was safe from prying eyes, she cast her circle, called the corners, and began chanting her spell.

God and Goddess here my plea.
Lend your strength and power to me.
I weave this spell for luck and love.
I draw down your power from above.
Take Cole from Cassie before the next night.
Make her wish he were out of her sight.
Bend his will to me.
So mote it be.

Kari closed the circle and thanked the God and Goddess. When she was finished, she went back to her cabin. She wasn't sure how exactly the spell would work, but she has a feeling that within twenty-four to forty-eight hours Cole would be away from Cassie. Once she had Cassie isolated, she was certain things would return to normal.

Chapter Four

In the morning, Cassie woke up to something warm behind her. She opened her eyes and saw the living room TV. At the same time, she realized that an arm was wrapped around her waist. She glanced over her shoulder and saw Cole stretched out behind her, sound asleep.

Cassie sighed, rolled over and snuggled into him. This was technically the first time she had ever slept in the same room with a guy. Well, unless you counted Matt. No, she wouldn't think of Matt!

She smiled and breathed Cole in. He smelled of woods, cinnamon and something slightly musky. This had to be one of the happiest mornings of her life. She felt safe, happy and cared about. Even though she had just met Cole yesterday, she could easily see herself falling for him. He seemed like a great guy.

"Good morning," Cole rasped. "I was afraid to move you last night. When the movie went off, I noticed you had fallen asleep."

"It's okay. I have to admit that waking up with you was definitely better than waking up in a strange place all alone." As Cassie sat up, the little dog came over to her. She bent down and patted it on the head. She would have to come up with a name for the little guy if he continued to hang around.

Cole smiled sleepily at her. "I guess we had better get ready and go grab some breakfast. I'm surprised my brothers didn't wake us up when they came in last night."

Cassie was a little embarrassed at the thought of Gabriel and Michael finding her asleep on the couch with Cole. She got up and went to her bedroom to gather her clothes. While she was figuring out what to wear, she heard the shower running and knew Cole was getting ready.

On the off chance Kari was still set on making her miserable, Cassie decided to choose her outfit carefully. She wanted something that would not only make Cole notice her, but something that would hold his attention all day. She had never tried to dress sexy before. She had clothes she knew *could* be sexy, but she hadn't tried to put together an outfit before for that express purpose. She'd never really had a reason to.

Cassie dug through her drawers until she found a form fitting v-neck emerald top and her snug fitting Gap jeans. She had a pair of black shoes identical to the brown ones from the night before. She loved her Dr. Martens because they were so comfortable. They were great if you wanted to look casual-nice, but also wanted to be prepared for the great outdoors. When she was finished putting her outfit together, she heard the shower turn off and headed toward the bathroom.

Cole was on his way out and Cassie hoped she wasn't drooling. He had on his jeans and nothing else. He definitely worked out! She had to try really hard not to stare at his muscular chest and six-pack abs. Looking up at his face, she noticed his hair was still wet and had been brushed back.

Cole had noticed Cassie the moment he stepped out of the bathroom. "I should have let you have the shower first."

"It's okay. It took me a minute to figure out what I wanted to wear," she replied with a smile.

"It's all yours milady," he said with a slight bow. Cole went to his room to finish getting dressed while Cassie took her shower. He would *not* think about the fact that she was naked on the other side of his bedroom wall! He quickly chose a dark blue long-sleeve shirt and threw on his boots. He heard the shower turn on and knew he had to escape his room. While Cassie showered and got dressed, Cole thought it would be best if he waited outside. Besides, the cold air would be good right about now.

Cassie didn't want to take a long time, knowing that Cole was waiting for her, but she couldn't resist smelling his soap. No wonder he smelled woodsy! It smelled like it was made with eucalyptus, cedar, and one other scent she couldn't quite identify. Closing her eyes, she let the scent take over her senses.

Opening her eyes, she reluctantly sat the soap back down and started to wash her hair. When she was done with her shower, she towel dried her hair and quickly ran a brush through it. Once she was dressed, she put on a little make-up. Cole seemed to like her just as she was, but it didn't hurt to try and look special for him. She grinned at her reflection pleased with the overall effect.

When Cassie came out of the bathroom, she couldn't find Cole in the cabin. She opened the front door and found him sitting on the porch. "I didn't take too long did I?"

"No, I just needed some fresh air," he said with a smile.

He wasn't about to tell her that the thought of her in the shower had about driven him crazy, not to mention that his pants had become exceedingly tight. Seeing her in that snug top didn't help matters any. He remembered all too well the way she had felt lying against him all night. It was all he could do not to drag her off to his bedroom and say to hell with breakfast!

"Let's go see what's for breakfast today," Cole said, holding his hand out to help her down the steps.

"Are your brother's not coming?" Cassie asked as she took his hand.

"They were already gone this morning when we got up. I'm sure we'll see them while we're at the lodge," he replied.

Cassie came down the steps and they made their way over to the lodge. When they entered, they saw that breakfast was not the buffet style they had become used to for lunch and dinner the previous day. Instead, everyone was seated at tables and ordering from menus. What had become 'their' table was still vacant. They headed toward it and sat down. A few minutes later, Gabriel came in and made his way over to them.

"Morning, Cole, Cassie," Gabriel said with a nod to both of them.

"Morning, Gabriel. Where did you and Michael run off to so early this morning?" Cole asked.

"I don't know where Michael went, but I took a short walk around the lake." Gabriel looked at each of them. "Would you two mind if I joined you?"

"Not at all," Cassie replied. At least, she hoped that Cole didn't mind.

Gabriel sat down. When he had found the cabin empty after his walk, he figured that Cassie and Cole would be together. They seemed to be getting along really well. "Have y'all ordered yet?"

"No, we just got here." Before Cole could look at his menu again, he saw Kari and Amber walked in. One look at Kari's face told Cole that she wasn't happy to see him and Cassie sitting together.

"Oh, shit. Incoming!" Cole knew he should be more sensitive since she was friends with Cassie, but he knew that Kari was bad news.

The women made their way over to the table. Kari was dressed in a tight mini dress and heels. Cole briefly wondered who in the hell wore heels during the day at a lake? Amber was dressed more appropriately in a fluffy blue sweater and jeans. They were complete opposites.

"I see you two are still *close*." Kari figured that if Cassie's little secret hadn't put a wedge between them she would have to try a new tactic. "I wonder what your boyfriend would think of this."

"Kari, you know I don't have a boyfriend," Cassie said, a bit embarrassed because she had *never* truly had a boyfriend.

"Then who is Matt?" Kari asked smugly.

"Matt?" Cassie was stunned. How did Kari know about Matt?

Kari looked like the cat who ate the canary. "You said his name in your sleep on the way here. You only dozed off for a minute, but I could tell that he must be someone special."

Cassie felt a little relieved. At least Kari didn't know who Matt really was. "He's just a friend."

"Wish I had more friends like that," Kari relied cattily.

"What are you talking about Kari?" Cassie was getting irritated with her so-called friend.

"From what I could tell, it sounded like a fairly hot dream... what with the *way* you were saying his name and all," Kari said, attempting to sound innocent.

Cassie blushed. She didn't remember having an erotic dream about Matt, but it wouldn't have been the first time. "Matt is just a friend. I don't have a boyfriend, which you already know."

Kari shrugged her shoulder. "Whatever you say, Cassie."

She sauntered off across the room.

"Aren't you coming Amber?" Kari called over her shoulder. She didn't even stop to wait for Amber, obviously assuming that she would follow her like always.

Amber glanced uncertainly at Kari's retreating back before looking back at Cassie. "I'm really sorry for the way she's acting. It's horrible being near her while she's like this."

Being an empath had its pitfalls, one of which was feeling your friend's jealousy and hatred toward your other friend. She was torn as to whether or not she should follow Kari.

"Why don't you sit with us?" Cassie said, sensing Amber's dilemma.

Amber looked at Cole and Gabriel. "Are you sure you wouldn't mind?"

The brothers both insisted that she sit with them. Amber walked around Cole's chair and sat across from Gabriel. She tried not to drool. He was definitely one yummy looking guy. She had thought Cole looked hot, but his brother was even better looking.

"I'm Amber," she said with a shy glance at Gabriel.

"Gabriel," he replied.

"It's nice to meet you," she said with a smile.

"Same here." Gabriel smiled at Amber. She wasn't as skinny as her friends, but she had a really pretty face that lit up when she smiled and beautiful green eyes that shined like emeralds.

Amber looked at Cole. "We didn't get a chance to officially meet yesterday."

"It's nice to meet you Amber. I'm Cole."

Amber smiled at him. She could see why Cassie liked him so much. Amber glanced at Gabriel from under her eyelashes and wondered if he had ever considered dating a slightly plump red-head. He definitely fell into the 'hot' category.

The waitress came over to take their order. The guys insisted the women order first. Cassie ordered pancakes with cinnamon apples on top. Amber ordered eggs, toast and bacon. Gabriel told the waitress he would have the same. When it came time for Cole to order, he seemed to order almost everything on the menu.

"What? I'm a growing boy," Cole said with a grin. The group just laughed.

They talked about their different interests and hobbies while they ate their breakfast. Amber was too shy to discuss herself too much, so she tried to get Cassie to talk about some of her talents. Amber remembered that karaoke was on the activity list later that night. She knew that Cassie had to sing.

"Cassie, during dinner tonight they're going to have karaoke. Won't that be fun? You could serenade us while we eat." Amber grinned at her friend.

"Forget it Amber. I'm *not* singing," Cassie told her with a glare.

"But Cass, you have to! Kari said she was going to sing tonight. It's your chance to put her back in her place. I can't believe she's been such a bitch to you since we've been here. You know you sing way better than she does," Amber told her vehemently.

Cole looked at Cassie, "Can you really sing?"

"Well, I tend to sing in the shower and around my friends, but that's it," Cassie replied.

Cole tried valiantly not to think of her singing in the shower. He glanced at Gabriel and caught his brother's knowing look. Trying not to blush at being caught thinking of Cassie in the shower, Cole said, "I think you should go for it. Besides, I'd love to hear you sing."

"I'll think about it," Cassie said.

Amber knew what would put Cassie in a good mood... shopping! "Cass, would you like to head into town for a bit today and do some shopping?"

"That sounds great." Cassie smiled at her friend. She looked at Cole and Gabriel, "Would you like to join us? If we can find Michael, he's welcome to come, too."

Cole looked at Gabriel for a confirmation before answering. "We'd love to."

Gabriel watched Cassie and his brother all through breakfast. There were definitely sparks flying between them; they couldn't look at each other without smiling. It was nice to see Cole showing an interest in someone again. Over the past year, Cole had dated a few college girls here and there, but he hadn't seemed to be really interested in any of them.

As Cassie reached for her ticket, Cole put his hand over hers. "I've got this one."

"No you don't little brother," Gabriel said as he grabbed not only Cassie's ticket, but also Amber's and Cole's. Gabriel walked up to the register and paid for their meals.

"That was awfully nice of him," Amber said. She was beginning to like Gabriel more and more. Maybe he could be her knight in shining armor. She almost giggled at the thought.

The women excused themselves to the restroom before they went to look for Michael. The guys decided to wait outside while the ladies went and fluffed and primped, or whatever it was women did when they flocked to the bathroom in pairs.

In the bathroom, Cassie fixed her lipstick and brushed her hair. She wanted to look perfect for Cole. She had seen the look on his face when she'd come outside in her outfit earlier. It had made her want to throw her arms around him and kiss him senseless. She had never felt so desirable before.

"You can't get any more beautiful, Cass. With that gorgeous hair and that beautiful face, you already look like you fell from heaven. Don't go and give the guy a heart attack by trying to make yourself look even better," Amber told her with a grin.

Cassie giggled at her friend. "You're being silly Amber, but thank you for the compliment."

Amber looked at her friend in the mirror and smiled. She was trying to tame her wild red hair, but didn't seem to be having much luck. She sighed in defeat. It was useless.

"Want some help?" Cassie offered.

Amber glanced at Cassie, "Sure. I think it's a lost cause, but have at it."

Cassie brushed Amber's hair until it was nice and smooth. Then she twisted it into a knot at the back of her head and put a pretty butterfly clip in it. When she was done, she turned Amber around to face her. Cassie rummaged through her purse a moment and pulled out some blush and lipstick. She applied a light layer of blush to Amber's cheeks and put some sheer pink lipstick on her lips. She turned Amber back around to face the mirror. "There, now take a look."

Amber stared at herself in disbelief. Just those few small changes made her feel like a different person. "Wow, thanks Cass!"

Cassie smiled at her friend. She had noticed Amber covertly looking at Gabriel throughout breakfast. For her friend's sake, she hoped Gabriel took notice of the slight transformation. Amber was beautiful regardless of how her hair was fixed and she deserved a guy to take notice. Unfortunately, guys tended to notice the outer package before getting to know what's inside.

They washed their hands and headed out of the restroom. On the way to the parking lot, they bumped into Michael.

"Hi, Michael, we were just about to go look for you." Cassie smiled at him.

"Well, looks like you found me." Michael gave her a wolfish grin.

"Amber and I were going into town to do some shopping. Your brothers are going too and we thought you might want to join us."

Amber slid past Cassie. "I'll just go outside and wait with the guys while the two of you decide who's going with us."

Michael watched as Amber walked out the door. "So, an outing with all five of us, huh? That could be fun. Or ..."

"Or?"

"Or, we could let the three of them go to town and you and I could head back to the cabin."

Cassie wasn't sure she liked Michael's tone. "Excuse me?"

"Looked to me like Cole passed out last night before he got to the good stuff. I figured that you and me could head back to the cabin and play while everyone else went to town." Michael had a cocky grin on his face, as if he were sure her answer would be yes.

Cassie gasped in outrage. "I think I've heard enough. I don't know how you got that impression of me, but I don't sleep around."

"No? Too bad. We could have had a lot of fun today." Michael reached over and ran a finger from her collar bone down to her cleavage.

Cassie shook her head and took a step back. "I have to go."

Cassie tried to walk past Michael, but he reached out and grabbed her arm. "I think you need to know what you're missing before you make any hasty decisions."

Without warning he pushed her against the wall and lowered his lips to hers in a bruising kiss. It was nothing like the gentle kiss she and Cole had shared last night. Michael was starting to scare her.

She tried to twist out of his grip, but he was too strong for her. He moved forward and pinned her body to the wall with his, making it impossible for her to move, much less escape.

Michael lifted his head and looked down at Cassie. "Isn't this much more fun?"

"Michael, please stop. You're hurting me," Cassie said. While she was typically brave, she had never been in this type of situation before and her insides were quaking in fear. She hoped she portrayed a calm exterior, but she was fairly certain her fear was showing in her eyes.

Michael just grinned and kissed her again. He knew she would come around. She just needed a little persuading. After all, Michael had yet to meet a woman who didn't want him.

Cassie struggled as much as she could, but she was no match for him. Just when she was really starting to get scared, she felt the weight of his body ripped from hers. Opening her eyes, she saw Cole holding Michael by the scruff of his neck.

"I believe I heard her say she wasn't interested." Cole looked at Cassie. She didn't appear hurt, just scared. Her swollen, bruised lips made Cole want to tear his brother apart.

"Are you okay Cassie? Did he hurt you?" Cole asked her quietly.

Cassie was shaking. "I'm okay."

Cole pushed Michael away from him and held his hand out to Cassie. She hesitantly walked toward him and placed her hand in his. Cole gently tugged her around behind him so that he was between her and Michael.

He looked at his brother in disgust. "What is wrong with you, Michael? Didn't you learn anything from Dad?"

Michael grinned at him. "You know she liked it. All women want me."

Cole shook his head at him. "No, Michael. All women *don't* want you. You just think they do. Cassie was clearly trying to get away from you."

Michael just shrugged his shoulders. "Not like there aren't plenty more where she came from. Y'all have fun in town. I'm going to go find a real woman. That one's apparently defective." Without another word, he turned and walked away.

Cole turned to face Cassie. He gently brushed the hair back from her face. "Are you sure you're okay?"

Cassie nodded and wrapped her arms around him. She hid her face in his shirt so he wouldn't see her tears. Michael hadn't been far off when he had called her defective. It wasn't the first time a guy had referred to her that way and she doubted it would be the last.

If Cole hadn't come along when he did, she could only imagine what might have happened. Michael could have carted her out the back door and no one would have been the wiser. The hall to the bathroom was very isolated and the lodge was noisy enough that no one would have heard her if she had cried out for help.

Cole gently rubbed her back and held her. He could only imagine what she was feeling. He placed a kiss on the top of her head and held her away from his body. Immediately he saw the tears streaking her face. He wiped them away one by one. "You're safe now Cassie. I promise that I won't let anything happen to you."

Cassie sniffled, hating the fact that he had seen her crying. "Thank you. We should probably get back to the others before they come looking for us."

Cole took her hand and led her outside. Amber took one look at Cassie's face and knew that something was wrong. She came running over to her friend, worry and fear etched on her face.

"Cassie, what's wrong?" Amber asked.

Cassie just shook her head. She knew that if she talked about it right then she would start crying again. She looked to Cole for help.

Cole pulled Amber aside. "Michael had her up against a wall and was kissing her. I don't think he was rough enough to hurt her, but I don't think he planned on stopping either. Cassie was struggling to break free when I found her."

Amber was in shock. She couldn't believe Michael would have done something like that. She looked toward the lodge to see if Michael had followed Cassie out. If she had thought for a moment Michael would have hurt her friend, she wouldn't have come outside and left Cassie alone with him.

Gabriel, having heard what Cole said, decided to intervene. "Let me go talk to Michael. He's never forced himself on anyone before in his life. There has to be something going on with him."

Cole sat on the steps of the lodge and pulled Cassie down onto his lap. He wrapped his arms around her and just held her. She was still shaking from the encounter.

Cole didn't know what to make of his brother's behavior. They had grown up in an abusive home with an alcoholic father. If nothing else, being in that environment had taught them to respect women and never harm them. Night after night, the brothers had watched their father beat their mother... until they were old enough to defend her anyway. Two years ago, their father had finally drunk himself to death. It had been the best thing that could have ever happened to his family. The brother's had inherited the garage and stayed with their mother to help support her.

"I hope Gabriel gives Michael what he deserves," Cole said. He was still holding Cassie; she hadn't said a word since they had come outside.

Cassie still had tears in her eyes, but she felt better now that she was being held by Cole. Just being near him made her feel better... He was being very gentle with her;

almost as if he were afraid she would break. "Don't let your brother do anything to Michael."

Cole looked at Cassie. "He won't do permanent damage if that's what you're worried about, but he'll make sure Michael knows he screwed up."

He personally hoped his brother was beating the shit out of Michael. Any guy who forced himself on a girl needed to be taught a lesson. Violence against women was one thing the three brothers couldn't, and wouldn't, tolerate. It was odd that Michael was breaking that code.

Michael definitely had a reputation for sleeping around, but he had never forced himself on anyone, he never had to for that matter. There always seemed to be plenty of women who fell for his good looks before realizing he was only looking for a good time and not anything permanent. Cole had a feeling that when Michael finally fell for a woman, he would fall hard.

Amber looked back toward the lodge. "Maybe I should go and check on them... just to be safe."

Hurrying around the back of the building, Amber saw Gabriel and Michael. Gabriel had pushed Michael up against the wall and had apparently punched him a few times, as Michael's mouth had a small trickle of blood in one corner. Gabriel was whispering something in Michael's ear. Michael nodded his head once and Gabriel let him go.

Gabriel turned and looked at Amber. "Is Cassie okay?"

Amber nodded. "I think she's fine. A little shaken, but I think she'll be okay."

"Good. Let's get back to them," Gabriel said, walking towards Amber.

The two walked back around to the front of the lodge. Cassie was still sitting in Cole's lap. She had stopped crying and didn't seem to be shaking anymore.

Cole brushed Cassie's hair back from her face. She was still a little pale, but seemed to be pulling herself together again.

Cassie looked up as Amber and Gabriel walked over. "Is everything all right?"

"I don't think you'll have to worry about him bothering you again. I told him that the next time he came anywhere near you I'd beat the shit out of him." Gabriel looked at Cole. "Just to be safe, we should make sure Cassie isn't alone in the cabin with him. He said he'd stay away from her, but he doesn't appear to be himself right now. I'm not sure we can trust him."

Cole nodded his agreement. He would definitely be keeping a close eye on Cassie. Hopefully Michael would come to his senses before the week was out, but there was no point in taking any chances.

Cassie climbed to her feet and the two couples walked to the parking lot. They decided to take Amber's SUV so there would be plenty of room. Cole and Cassie sat in the back, while Gabriel sat up front with Amber.

Amber started the car and headed down the road towards the town of Whispering Lake. Unknown to them, Kari was watching them from the porch of the lodge.

This was just too much for Kari. How had the mousy little Cassie wrapped Cole around her finger so tightly? She should have been more specific with her spell. It had gotten the wrong brother away from Cassie. She knew she had said Cole's name, but it had somehow backfired.

Kari had made sure she wore her hottest, shortest dress today. Guys had always told her she had a great body and great legs. It would figure that the one guy she wanted didn't even notice.

She turned and walked back to her cabin. She would have to try her spell again if it didn't work on Cole, but she would wait until tomorrow night. By then she should know for sure if the spell would get Cole away from Cassie.

Cole held Cassie close to his side. He wished he had been able to defend her better against Michael. Instead, it had been Gabriel who had gone to her defense and taken care of Michael. Cassie seemed to really like him. He hoped his brother hadn't screwed up his chance with her.

Cassie rested her head on Cole's shoulder and closed her eyes. She was still scared over what had happened with Michael. Sharing a cabin with him was going to be difficult. She knew that Gabriel and Cole were going to make sure she wasn't alone with Michael, but what about at night when everyone was sleeping? She would have to check her door for a lock when they got back.

Had Matt's vision, for lack of a better word, been a warning about Michael? She wished that he were here to talk to. She missed him terribly. While being in Cole's arms was comforting, it was Matt she really wanted to be with right then. He was her best friend and always made her feel better when things were bad.

Snuggling closer to Cole, she hoped to drive Matt from her thoughts. Once more she had to remind herself that Matt was a ghost, and she couldn't have a relationship with a ghost... no matter how gorgeous he was. Cassie closed her eyes and tried to relax.

Amber and Gabriel were talking quietly. Cole pulled out his iPod and listened to music the rest of the way to town. His day was definitely going differently than he had originally planned. He wasn't going to complain since he had Cassie by his side, but he had hoped to spend some quality time with her alone. After kissing her last night, he knew there was definitely something there, something he wanted to explore further.

The moment Cole had laid eyes on Cassie, he knew she was special. He didn't believe in love at first sight, but something had definitely happened at that moment. He hoped that she would allow him to explore those feelings with her for the rest of the week, and possibly longer.

There was one obstacle though; Cassie had shared her secret with him, but he hadn't shared his with her. There was no way for him to do that without breaking his brothers' trust. Cole had hoped that when he mentioned vampires and werewolves Cassie would tell him they existed, because Cole already knew they existed. He and his brothers were all werewolves. It was a secret that only their mother knew.

He had heard stories about vampires since he was little. He should have known that ghosts existed, too. It made him wonder if anything else out of fairy tales and nursery rhymes were real, like witches, fairies, goblins, and other things that go bump in the night.

Werewolves didn't look the way the movies projected them. Cole and his brothers changed into actual wolves. They were about a foot taller and a bit broader than most wolves, but aside from that they were the same. It was also a myth that they could only change at the full moon. While Cole and Michael couldn't change as freely as Gabriel, they could still change at any time of night regardless of the moon phases. Gabriel, being the eldest and the strongest, could change any time, even during daylight.

Chapter Five

When they arrived in Whispering Lake, Amber parked on Main Street. Cole put his iPod away and helped Cassie out of the car. Gabriel was already out of the car and Amber was walking around the front of the Explorer. She locked the car and set the alarm.

Cassie looked up and down Main Street. She loved towns like this. "Where should we go first?"

Cole took her hand in his. "Any place you want is fine with me. Anyone else have a preference?"

Cole noticed that Gabriel was watching Amber intently. It looked like his brother was interested in her. Gabriel could definitely do worse than the little red-head. She seemed to be really nice and had kept a level head at the lodge when Michael had attacked Cassie. Plus, she seemed to know about Cassie's ability and was cool with it. That bode well for Gabriel if things became serious. Although, there was a vast difference in seeing ghosts and believing in werewolves.

Amber walked over to Cassie. "I don't really care. I definitely want to check out the clothing shop and that soda fountain though."

"Soda fountain it is. I could really use a drink right now." Cassie was also hoping they might have old fashioned sundaes or banana splits. Ice cream was her weakness. Well, that and chocolate cake, but what woman didn't love chocolate cake.

The group walked over to Miller's Five-N-Dime. When they entered the shop, they felt like they had been swept back to the fifties. The floor was black and white checked tile; the white counter at the little deli was white and trimmed in silver. It had red leather bar stools, also trimmed in silver. A jukebox stood in the corner playing Buddy Holly's *Peggy Sue*.

They chose seats close to the jukebox and gave the man behind the counter their drink order. Cassie's first thought was that Matt would love this place. They probably had tons of places like this when he was alive.

When Cassie asked for a menu, Amber just knew that Cassie was going to order some horribly delicious looking dessert. Amber had been trying to lose some weight so she was doing her best to avoid sugar on this trip. As Cassie ordered her triple chocolate fudge sundae, Amber gave in and ordered two scoops of vanilla ice cream.

When Cassie's sundae was delivered, the older gentleman behind the counter smiled at her. "It's nice to see a young person today that isn't afraid of eating; too many of you young girls are always dieting and watching your weight."

"Thank you," Cassie said with a smile and dug into her treat.

Cole and Gabriel eyed her giant sundae. Cassie noticed their attention. "What? Never seen a girl eat before?"

Cole just shook his head. "How can you eat all of that and still be so skinny?"

"I'm not really all that skinny; just well proportioned." Cassie didn't want to draw attention to the fact that she could eat anything she wanted and never gain a pound. She knew Amber had been trying really hard to lose weight. While her friend wasn't as thin as she was, Amber wasn't what Cassie would consider fat either. She was just curvy.

The boys talked while the girls finished their ice cream. When they were done, they left the shop in search of other goodies. The girls quickly honed in on the vintage clothing shop and begged to stop. The brothers mutually agreed to wait outside while the girls shopped for clothes. There wasn't a worse torture for a guy than shopping for clothes with a woman, except perhaps shoe shopping with a woman.

In the store, Cassie and Amber dug through the racks of clothes looking for buried treasure. Cassie found a beautiful sapphire blue shirt with flared sleeves. She moved toward the back of the store to check out the dress rack. If she was going to attempt to sing tonight, which she hadn't completely decided on yet, she wanted to look extra nice. As she neared the end of the rack, she had almost given up hope of finding anything. Then, on the very last hanger she found what she was looking for. It was a stretchy cotton dress in a deep ruby red. It had a v-neck with short tiered sleeves and a knee length skirt that would flare out if she twirled in it. Luck was on her side because it was just her size. Cassie grabbed the dress and went to find Amber.

Amber was looking through the shirts when Cassie came over. "Find anything?"

She knew Cassie had probably found a ton of stuff. As small as she was, she always found nice clothes in stores like this one.

"I found a great dress for tonight and a pretty blue shirt. What about you?" Cassie asked.

"Nothing that is really calling my name," Amber said with a sigh.

Cassie remembered seeing a green dress that would look stunning on Amber. "Come with me. I think I saw something you'll like."

Amber followed Cassie to the back of the store. When Cassie pulled the green dress off the rack, Amber knew she had to have it. It was her size and the color would make her eyes look really green. Surely Gabriel wouldn't be able to resist a green eyed red head in a sexy green dress. She smiled as she took the dress to the register to check out.

They left the shop each carrying a bag. Both of them were smiling so the guys knew they must have found something they really liked. Cole was hoping that whatever Cassie had bought looked half as good as what she was already wearing. He was having a hard time keeping his hands to himself.

"Where to next?" he asked.

Cassie looked at Amber. "Do you have any place special you want to stop?"

"No. I already got what I wanted," Amber said.

Cassie thought a moment. "Okay. How about we forage for snacks then? The kitchen at the cabin is bare."

"Food it is." Cole took her hand and the group moved further down the sidewalk. There was sure to be a small grocery store or convenience store along the way.

"A woman after my own heart! She thinks of food before all else." Gabriel smiled at her. "And here I thought only guys thought with their stomachs."

Cassie laughed. "No. I pretty much eat all the time."

Cole looked to the left and saw a small convenience store across the street.

"Hey guys. Look over there," he said, pointing to the store.

They walked across the street. As they entered the shop, a bell jingled over the door. Cassie made a bee-line for the chip and cracker aisle. Cole grabbed a small basket and followed her. Cassie threw Doritos, Fritos, and Ritz crackers into the basket. "Should we get some cookies, too, or some sodas?"

"Whatever you want Cass. We should definitely get a few 2-litres though," Cole suggested.

Cassie headed to the drink aisle. "Do you or your brothers have a preference?"

"Anything but Pepsi is fine," he answered.

Cassie bent over to pick up a coke, two cherry cokes and a 7-up. "Variety is the spice of life."

Cole gulped. She may be talking sodas, but after watching her bend over in those tight jeans he most definitely had other things on his mind. Thankfully he was carrying their basket; it would buy him some time to get himself under control before Cassie noticed the rather large bulge in his pants. If she kept wearing tight jeans, he was going to have to seriously think of buying some larger pants.

Once Cassie was finished with her shopping, they met the others at the register. Gabriel was carrying a basket as well. Cole assumed it belonged to Amber since the redhead wasn't carrying anything. Sure enough, when it was Amber's turn to check out, Gabriel put her basket on the counter for her. Cole could see that something was going to happen between those two before the trip was over. If both of them played their cards right, they might end up with steady girlfriends by the time they returned to Ashton Grove.

They left the store with their snacks and headed back to the SUV. After putting their bags in the back of the vehicle, they climbed into their seats. Once again, Gabriel was up front with Amber, while Cole and Cassie sat in the back.

Cole reached over and took Cassie's hand. She smiled at him and slid over closer to him.

Gabriel looked over at Amber and smiled. "It seems like we're all buckled in and set to go. We're ready when you are madam chauffer."

Amber smiled at him. She shifted in her seat to look at Cassie over her shoulder. Her friend seemed really happy despite what had happened earlier. Facing forward again, she started the car and eased out of her parking space.

Gabriel was doing his best not to notice Amber's body. She was a curvy little thing. The sweater she was wearing looked so soft it practically begged to be touched. He looked out the window and decided to focus on the scenery instead.

Amber couldn't have been happier. Gabriel was paying attention to her and seemed to be enjoying her company.

She was hoping he would ask her to sit with him at dinner tonight. Oh no! Dinner! She had forgotten to convince Cassie to sing!

"Cass?" Amber asked.

Cassie looked her way. "What is it, Amber?"

"You *are* singing tonight, right?" Amber asked, looking at her in the rearview mirror.

Cassie groaned. "Give it up Amber. I'm still deciding."

"But you have to sing Cass! Please," Amber begged.

"Oh, all right. I'll sing tonight. But just one song," Cassie finally relented.

"Yesss!!!" Amber smiled victoriously.

Cassie shook her head at her friend. Later she would be wondering how she had gotten roped into singing in front of complete strangers. For now, she would just enjoy the quiet ride back to the lake.

Cole reached over and took Cassie's hand. He brought it to his mouth and gently kissed the back of it. He felt Cassie's indrawn breath.

"I can't wait to hear you sing. I bet you sound like an angel," Cole told her with a smile. She certainly looked like an angel, and he already knew she felt like one when she was in his arms.

Cassie was tingling all the way to her toes. Maybe she wouldn't mind singing so much after all, not if Cole kept looking at her like that anyway. She felt like she could climb mountains with him by her side. Cassie would have given anything at that moment to lean over and kiss him, but she didn't dare while Amber and Gabriel were so close. It was bad enough that Gabriel knew she and Cole had fallen asleep together on the couch. Her first night at the lake and she was already working on a bad reputation, she thought with a grin.

Okay, so in today's society a bad reputation required a hell of a lot more than kissing and having sex with your boyfriend. Maybe Cassie had been around Matt too long, but she still felt she should be saving her virginity for someone special. She wasn't sure if that someone was Cole or not. First she would have to stop thinking about Matt all the time.

As Amber pulled into the parking lot by the lodge, everyone unfastened their seat belts. When Amber had parked and turned off the car, they got out and went around to the back to get their things. Cassie grabbed her sack of clothes and Cole grabbed all of their snacks. He immediately started off in the direction of the cabin.

"Cass," Amber called.

She looked back at Amber.

"Do you want to meet outside of the lodge around 5:30 tonight? I was thinking we could all sit together."

"Sure, Amber." Cassie smiled. She looked at Gabriel. "You'll join us too won't you?"

Gabriel and Amber agreed they would meet outside the lodge later that night. Gabriel grabbed Amber's bags and helped carry them to her cabin.

Cassie looked for Cole. She spotted him half way down the path to their cabin. She hurried to catch up to him.

"Was it okay for me to ask the others to join us for dinner?" she asked.

Cole looked at her. "That's fine. I just wanted to get these drinks in the fridge so they'll be cold tonight."

"Oh. Okay." Cassie followed Cole into the cabin.

They put the snacks and drinks away and Cassie took her sack to her room. When she came back out, Cole was standing by the living room window with his arms crossed. Cassie walked over to him and wrapped her arms around his waist. Cole looked down at her and wrapped his arms around her.

"Cole, are you sure you're all right?"

"I'm fine Cassie," he told her quietly.

Honestly, he didn't know what was wrong with him. When Cassie had agreed to have dinner with Amber and

Gabriel, he had felt a sudden flare of anger and jealousy. Cole had never felt like that before and he wasn't sure where the emotions had come from.

Cassie looked at him doubtfully. She brought one of her hands up to his face and cupped his cheek in her hand. She stood on her tiptoes, trying to kiss him, but she was too short.

Cole realized what she was doing and picked her up. She smiled at him and gently kissed his mouth. He carried her into his room and laid her on the bed without breaking their kiss. He deepened the kiss.

It felt wonderful to have Cassie's soft body under his. Cole knew he could easily lose control, but she was so intoxicating that he couldn't help himself. One small kiss was enough to bring him to his knees and have him begging for more. No one had ever made him feel like this before. It was both terrifying and exciting. Supposedly a werewolf would recognize the woman destined to be his mate. He wondered if that's what he had felt when he first laid eyes on Cassie.

Cassie broke the kiss and looked into Cole's eyes. She had never felt like this with anyone before. The guys she had dated had never even wanted to kiss her goodnight. Everything she was experiencing with Cole was new and exciting.

"Cole, there's something I think you should know," she said softly. It was time to come clean with him.

"Shh." Cole gently laid his finger over her lips. "You don't have to say anything and you don't have to do anything you don't want to."

"That's just it. I do want to, even though I know I shouldn't. I mean, we just met and it really isn't like me to sleep with someone within a day or two of meeting them." She refrained from telling him that she hadn't ever slept with *anyone* and was a twenty-one year old virgin. She doubted that he would believe her anyway. She was something of a rare breed.

Cole sat up. It was bad enough that he was close to losing control, but if Cassie decided to give in he wasn't sure he could tell her no. This was something she obviously wasn't ready for, and he didn't want to push her. If she decided she wanted to sleep with him, he wasn't about to say no to her. However, he didn't want her to feel pressured into doing something she wasn't sure she really wanted.

"I think we need to head back to the living room," Cole said as he stood up.

Cassie stood, looking hurt and disappointed. Cole leaned down and kissed her again. He ran his hands through her long hair and down her back.

"Trust me Cassie. I'm not stopping because I want to. I'm stopping because it's the right thing to do… and it's killing me," he told her with an agonized look.

Cassie smiled at him and reached up to kiss him again. Cole backed up until his legs hit the bed. He sat down, bringing Cassie with him. He leaned back on the bed and Cassie sprawled on top of him.

Rolling over so that Cassie was lying under him, his tongue gently stroked hers as he kissed her. His hand moved slowly from her hip to her stomach. His fingers slid under the hem of her shirt and he lightly brushed his finger tips across her stomach. Cassie moaned into his mouth, wanting more. Cole slid his hand up to cup her breast through the satin bra she was wearing. Cassie gasped and arched into him. She had never felt anything like this before in her life.

Cole and Cassie were so wrapped up in each other that they didn't hear the front door open. Michael called for Cole and Cassie. When they didn't respond, he headed toward Cassie's room. Before he got there, he noticed noises were coming from Cole's room. He opened the door, banging it into the wall. Both Cassie and Cole jumped.

"Michael? What the hell are you doing?" Cole demanded.

"I called for the two of you, but you were obviously too occupied to hear it," Michael replied.

Cole looked a little embarrassed and really mad. "Did you stop to think that maybe if someone doesn't answer that means they're busy?"

"Obviously." Michael looked over at Cassie. Her lips were swollen from being kissed and her hair was slightly tousled. He had no doubt that his brother would have done a lot more if they hadn't been interrupted. Michael was slightly pissed that when he offered her a good time she had denied him, and yet here she was in his brother's room. Apparently he was just the wrong brother.

Cassie was blushing furiously. "If you'll both excuse me, I think I'll go for a walk." She hurried out of the room and out the front door. Part of her wanted to thank Michael for stopping her from making a mistake, but the other part wanted to know what it would have been like if Cole hadn't stopped. No one had ever kissed her like that before; her lips still throbbed from his kisses.

Cassie walked down the steps and started down the hiking trail. Walking would help clear her mind and give her time to get her hormones under control again. She couldn't believe that she had almost had sex with someone who was pretty much still a stranger to her. What was wrong with her?

After walking for fifteen minutes, Cassie realized she had forgotten both her key and her watch. Hopefully one of the brothers would be in when she returned. Although, she hoped it wouldn't be Michael.

She would have to make this a short walk if she wanted to be ready in time for dinner. Looking at the sun, she guessed it was around three o'clock already. Cassie walked a little further and noticed a fallen tree to her right. She left the trail and sat on the tree.

How had her life become so complicated so quickly? She finally had a guy that liked her and she had experienced her first real kiss, but in the process she had lost her friend. She was also concerned about her obvious lack of control around Cole. She had never felt this way before, well not about anyone living that is.

Cassie was so preoccupied she didn't notice Sarah approaching.

"Hi," Sarah told her.

Cassie looked up and saw Sarah, the ghost she had spoken to the day before. "Hi Sarah."

"I thought I sensed your presence. I wanted to see if you wanted to talk." Sarah looked at Cassie with a slight frown. "You look a little upset. Is everything all right?"

"Yes. No. I don't know. Things are complicated right now," Cassie said with a sigh.

"Ah. It must involve a guy then." Sarah smiled at her. "Things always get complicated when a guy is involved. Does it have anything to do with the hottie that was walking with you yesterday?"

"Yeah. I like him a lot, but I'm a little confused. On the one hand, when he's kissing me, I feel like I never want him to stop, but when his brother walked in a few minutes ago I felt a little relieved. Part of me wants to know what it's like to be with a guy, but the other part knows I should wait for the right guy. Does that sound weird? Any weirder than a twenty-one year old virgin?"

"Not at all. If I were you though, I would really make sure that I was ready before taking that leap. Once you've jumped, you can't go back. You should make sure that you're first time is with someone really special... Someone you want to be with for the rest of your life. I wish that I had waited for Rob, my boyfriend. He was a really great guy," Sarah said wistfully.

Cassie nodded. What Sarah said made sense. "Thanks Sarah. I appreciate you listening to me."

Sarah smiled at her. "I'm glad that I was able to help. I'll leave you to your thoughts. Try to come see me again before you leave to go home. It may be a while before I find someone else I'm able to talk to."

"I will." Cassie watched her walk back into the woods. She was glad Sarah had shown up. It was nice to have someone to talk to about this kind of stuff. She could talk to Amber, but she was worried about what her friend would think of her. She'd already lost Kari over Cole. She didn't want to lose Amber, too.

Cassie got up and dusted off her jeans. She had better head back to the cabin if she wanted to be ready by 5:30. The walk back only took twenty minutes. When she arrived at the cabin, she could still hear raised voices inside. It made her miserable to think that Cole and Michael were fighting because of her. She gathered her courage and opened the door. There was only one way to stop this.

Chapter Six

Michael and Cole had started arguing the second Cassie had left the cabin. Cole figured that part of it was just Michael being mad and jealous. Cole knew he and Cassie shouldn't have taken things so far this soon, but it really ticked him off that his brother was sticking his nose where it didn't belong. After all, if he and Cassie wanted to have sex, who was Michael to say they couldn't? They were both consenting adults.

The brothers were still arguing when they heard the cabin door open. They stopped and looked up to see Cassie coming inside. Her cheeks were pink from the autumn air and her hair was windblown. In other words, she was beautiful.

"Hey guys." Cassie walked over to them. "Michael, can I talk to you for a minute?"

"Sure." He followed Cassie into his bedroom.

Behind the closed door, Michael tried to pull Cassie into his arms. Cassie held back.

"That isn't why I asked to speak to you Michael."

"Then what did you want to talk about? You could start with why Cole had his hand up your shirt, but one kiss from me had you running away," Michael said.

"That isn't fair! You didn't ask to kiss me, you just took what you wanted," Cassie replied fiercely.

"And if I had asked?"

"I probably would have said no. It's not that you aren't attractive, but it takes more than just looks. Cole has a completely different temperament than you do. Quite frankly, you're a little too rough for me," she told him.

"You know, you might like it a little rough if you just gave me a chance. I'm not really all that different from Cole. We are twins after all," he told her.

"I'm really sorry Michael. I'm just not interested in you that way."

"Then I guess our conversation is over."

Cassie turned to go, but Michael stopped her and turned her to face him. When she looked up at him, he bent down to kiss her. He knew that if he could just get her to relax and kiss him back she would enjoy it. It should have been him in that bed with Cassie.

Cassie broke the kiss. "Michael, you have to stop. I told you that I'm not interested. Please respect my decision."

"You know you want me Cassie."

Cassie looked at him. "Not in that way. And honestly, I'm glad that you interrupted me and Cole when you did. I'm not into one night stands, or even one week flings. Things just got carried away." Cassie turned and left the room.

When Cole heard the bedroom door open, he turned to face Cassie. Her lips were swollen so he knew that she and Michael had been kissing. She didn't seem upset so he wasn't sure if it had been freely given or if Michael had coerced her again.

Cassie walked over to Cole and took his hand. She led him to her room and closed the door. "I talked to Michael and hopefully he understands that I'm just not interested in him."

"Is that why it looks like the two of you were kissing in his room?" Cole immediately regretted his tone.

Cassie blushed and looked down at the floor. She looked back up at Cole. "If he hadn't shown up when he did, I may have done something I would have regretted."

"You would have regretted being with me?" Cole asked.

He looked hurt and it pained Cassie that she was the one who had hurt him. "It isn't that."

She took a deep breath. She hadn't planned on telling the guys she was a virgin, but she didn't see any other way around this. "The fact is I'm still a virgin."

Cole looked shocked. "You're a what?"

Cassie blushed. "You heard me. I'm still a virgin."

"Why didn't you tell me? I never would have let things get as far as they did." Suddenly things started to make a lot of sense.

"I started to, but you stopped me from saying anything. You said that I didn't have to do anything I didn't want to do. That was the problem... I *did* want to be with you. It was wrong of me not to tell you that I hadn't been with anyone else though," Cassie explained.

"Do you have any idea how much I could have hurt you by not knowing? It isn't exactly pain free the first time. Not for a woman."

"Yes, I know." Cassie looked at the floor in embarrassment. She knew it had been wrong of her to withhold information from him, but she had just been so caught up in the moment that she hadn't been thinking clearly.

"Do you still want to spend time with me?" he asked quietly.

Cassie looked up at him. "Of course I do. That is, if you still want to be around *me*."

Cole smiled down at her. "I would be crazy not to want to spend time with you. You may have kept something really important from me, but under the circumstances I can't really blame you. Besides, I'm just as much to blame. I never asked and was just as caught up in the moment as you were."

Cassie smiled at him. "Thank you for being so understanding. Most guys would have run in terror from me by now."

"I'm not most guys." Cole looked like he wanted to say more.

"What is it?"

"I know you said you talked with Michael, but I'd feel better if I had a little talk with him, too," he told her.

"Is that really necessary? I don't want to cause problems between you and your brothers."

"Don't worry about it. My brothers and I have fought many times over the years. In the end, we're still brothers and will always stand by one another when needed," Cole reassured her.

Cassie nodded her head. If he wanted to talk to Michael, she couldn't really stop him anyway. "If you think it will help, then I guess I'm okay with that."

Cole kissed her on the cheek before leaving her bedroom. He closed the door behind him and went to Michael's room. Thankfully his brother was still there.

"Michael, can I speak to you a sec?"

"What? You don't think your girlfriend made her point?" Michael asked, rolling his eyes.

"She isn't my girlfriend. I know she already spoke to you, but I wanted to make sure that things were okay between us."

"Why wouldn't they be? It's not like we've ever let a woman get between us before," Michael replied.

"True, but then I've never seen you act like this before. You have me a little worried," Cole said.

"Don't worry, Cole. I'm not going to force myself on your girlfriend. Regardless of what you call her, that's what she might as well be... at least for the duration of this trip. We've never poached on each other's territory before and I won't start now. She's safe from me for the remainder of the week," Michael told him.

"Thanks for that. I think I'm going to take a walk. Want to join me?"

Michael shook his head. "No, thanks. I'm going to head over to the lake for a bit."

Both brothers left the cabin together. Gabriel was still nowhere in sight. Cole figured things must be going well with Amber. Gabriel had hardly been able to keep his eyes off the redhead today. Cole briefly wondered if his brother would run into the same problem that he had with Cassie. It was too bad that Michael wasn't interested in Kari. He felt it was a pretty safe bet that Kari wasn't a virgin. She seemed like the type that slept around, which made her right up Michael's alley.

Cole walked through the woods for about fifteen minutes before turning around. He knew that Michael had promised to leave Cassie alone, but he still didn't trust him. It would be best if Cassie weren't alone in the cabin. Cole hated to think that way of his flesh and blood, but Michael hadn't given him much choice. His behavior today had been unforgivable. The only sure way to keep Michael away from Cassie was for Cole to declare her as his mate... but he still wasn't one hundred percent sure that's who she was.

When Cole returned to the cabin, he heard the shower running and knew Cassie was getting ready for dinner. He groaned and smacked his head against the wall. If she insisted on taking daily showers, he wasn't sure he could keep his hands to himself. Now that he knew she was a virgin, he was determined not to take advantage of her. He just wasn't sure that his self control was strong enough to maintain his distance.

Cole went into the bedroom and quickly changed his clothes. He went back out to the living room to wait on Cassie. He was sitting on the couch when Cassie came out of the bathroom. She apparently hadn't been expecting him, or anyone else for that matter, because she was wrapped in nothing but a towel with her long hair dripping down her back.

If Cole thought imagining her in the shower was bad, actually seeing her practically naked was much worse. Their little episode in the bedroom already had his overactive imagination running wild, but seeing her fresh from the shower and unclothed was more than he had bargained for.

"Oh! I'm sorry Cole. I didn't know you would get back so fast. Just give me about fifteen minutes and I'll be ready to head to dinner." Cassie ran to her room and closed the door.

She was so embarrassed! Cole probably thought she looked like a drowned rat. Since Michael and Cole had left together, she hadn't thought to grab her clothes when she went to shower; she had thought it would take Cole longer to return. Gabriel had been gone so long she didn't think he would return until after dinner. She hoped that he was spending time with Amber. Her friend really seemed to like him.

Cassie quickly pulled her new red dress out of the closet. She sighed. It really was a beautiful dress. Cassie decided that instead of wearing it for Cole as she had originally planned, she would wear it for herself. She still liked Cole, but knew she needed to slow things down. This dress was definitely *not* the way to slow anything down, but it was just too beautiful to sit on a hanger.

She toweled her hair dry and got dressed. She grabbed her dress shoes off of the floor and slipped them on her feet. They were black three inch heels and always made her feel sexy. Cassie opened her bedroom door to find Cole sitting on the couch. "Just give me a few more minutes and I'll be ready." She dashed through the living room and into the bathroom.

Once she had closed the door, she dried her hair with the hair dryer. While her curling iron was heating, she put on her make-up. Cassie sectioned off her hair and used the curling iron to make large spiral curls. After she had finished, she turned off the curling iron and ran her fingers through her hair.

Looking in the mirror, she was pleased with her reflection. The red dress gave her cheeks color and the iridescent eye shadow she had chosen made her eyes look bright and alive. She finished the look off with cherry lip gloss. She almost didn't recognize the sexy woman in the mirror.

Cole looked up as Cassie entered the living room. From the brief glimpse he'd had of her as she ran through the living room moments before, he already knew the red dress fit her like a glove. Seeing the finished product of her labor was another story... she was breathtaking!

Cole cleared his throat, "You look lovely."

Cassie smiled at him. "Thank you. Just let me get my coat and I'll be ready."

She grabbed her coat from her room, slipped it on, and rejoined Cole in the living room. Cole opened the front door and they stepped out onto the porch. As the cold air hit Cassie's bare legs, she shivered.

"Are you going to be warm enough in that?" he asked with concern.

"I'll be fine once we get to the lodge," she reassured him.

After seeing the look on his face when she stepped out of the bathroom, there was no way a little cold air was going to make her change clothes! Knowing that Cole found her attractive was reason enough to be a little chilly tonight.

Cole motioned for her to go ahead of him. As Cassie walked down the porch steps, Cole admired the sway of her hips. The heels she had on were definitely working some magic. If he couldn't remember to keep his eyes above waist level, his pants were going to get tight again. Then again, that dress was so low cut he had best just try to maintain eye contact with her. He already knew how perfect her breasts were. Seeing them partially exposed in that dress was going to be the death of him.

They walked together in silence until they neared the lodge. Before they reached the steps, Cole put his hand on her arm. She turned to face him.

He gave her a serious look. "Cassie, you know that Michael will be here tonight. I'm going to talk to Gabriel so we can make sure that Michael stays on his best behavior. If you would prefer that he not sit at our table, I'll make sure he stays away."

Cassie looked up at Cole. Even in her three inch heels, she still had to tip her head all the way back to look into his eyes. "I know that we both talked to him this afternoon, but it would be nice if he didn't spoil the evening. Would it be horrible of me to ask that he not sit with us tonight?"

Cole smiled at her. "No, it doesn't make you horrible. I'll talk to Gabriel. Hopefully he selected a table that only seats four so it won't be an issue anyway."

As they started up the steps to the lodge, Cassie stopped Cole by placing her hand on his arm. "Cole?"

Cole turned to look at her.

"I just wanted to say thank you for being so understanding earlier. I know I must have freaked you out when I told you that I hadn't been with anyone else. I appreciate the way you handled it."

Cole blushed and was thankful the lighting outside of the lodge was horrible. "You're welcome Cassie. Let's go inside so you can get warm."

Cassie nodded and continued up the steps. Cole opened the door for her and they stepped inside. It only took them a moment to spot Amber and Gabriel. Looking around the room, Cassie spotted Kari sitting with a group of guys. Michael was sitting alone at a table not far from them.

Cassie and Cole walked over to Gabriel and Amber. The only two seats available were next to each other. Cole pulled her chair out for her and she sat down. Gabriel watched them with interest. He noticed Cassie looking over his shoulder at something and glanced over to where

Michael was sitting. Cole walked around the table to whisper in Gabriel's ear.

When he was finished explaining the afternoon's events to Gabriel, Cole came back around the table and sat next to Cassie. There were menus on the table again so apparently there would not be a buffet tonight. Cassie picked up her menu to decide what she wanted to order. She was trying hard to ignore the questioning look on Amber's face. She would tell her friend soon enough what happened, but that would have to wait. Thankfully Gabriel didn't say anything when Cole was done speaking to him.

The waitress came by and took their orders. After she left, Cassie motioned for Amber to follow her to the restroom. When the girls entered the restroom, Cassie locked the door.

Amber turned to face her. "Are you going to tell me what's going on now? You should have seen your face when you saw Michael was sitting on the other side of the room. I know he scared you earlier, but Gabriel said that Michael was going to leave you alone now."

"I had a talk with Michael earlier. He kissed me again and tried to convince me to go to bed with him. I told him that he was too rough and I wasn't interested. His response was that I'd probably like it that way," Cassie explained quickly.

Amber's eyes just about bugged out of her head. "Are you serious? Where was Cole when this was happening? I thought they weren't leaving you alone in the cabin because of Michael?"

"He was in the other room."

"Why didn't he do anything?" Amber demanded.

"Well, I went to Michael's room to talk to him, and being the idiot I am, I closed the door. Cole wasn't aware of what was going on. I wanted to talk to Michael for a minute and give him the benefit of the doubt. Cole swears that Michael isn't usually like that," Cassie replied.

Amber was staring at Cassie intently. Cassie could tell she had a million questions, but her friend was being quiet so she could finish the story. "I also wanted to thank Michael."

Amber was incredulous. "For what?"

"He kind of interrupted me and Cole. When we got back earlier we started kissing. Somehow or other we ended up in his bedroom... on the bed. When Michael came in, things had progressed enough that Cole was caught with his hand up my shirt," she finished with a slight blush.

"Wow. I don't know what to say Cass," Amber said, stunned.

Amber was a little surprised since she knew Cassie had never slept with anyone. She was also happy her friend was apparently really interested in Cole. If Michael would back off, maybe something good would happen between Cassie and Cole. It was about time a guy realized what a gem she was.

Cassie shrugged. "I just wanted you to know what happened. We should get back out to the guys."

Cassie unlocked the door and the girls headed back to their table. Cassie could see Kari leaning over Cole, practically shoving her chest in his face. Kari was wearing a tight black dress that was extremely short and a pair of spiked heels. In Cassie's opinion, she looked like a cheap hooker. When Cassie and Amber got to the table, Gabriel and Cole stood up and pulled the ladies' chairs out for them.

Kari was mad as a hornet that Cole was ignoring her. "Cole, did you know I'm going to sing tonight during dinner? They're having karaoke and I was the first to sign up." Kari smiled at Cole and batted her eyes.

Cole looked at Kari. Did she really think she looked attractive in that outfit? He thought it made her look cheap. Her jealousy wasn't attractive either. "I'm sure you'll do fine. Cassie will be singing, too."

Kari threw a malicious look at Cassie. She knew that Cassie was a much better singer and had hoped that her 'friend' wouldn't have the guts to get up and sing in front of everyone.

Kari took in Cassie's tousled spirals and red dress. She looked like she'd just gotten out of bed and thrown her dress on. It made Kari wonder if she really had been in someone's bed. Maybe Cassie wasn't as mousy as she had thought her to be. If that were the case, Kari knew she had some real competition for Cole's attention. Her spell had partially worked and gotten Michael out of the picture, but Kari hadn't counted on Cole sticking by Cassie like glue.

"Cassie doesn't like to sing in front of crowds, do you Cass? I hope you don't get stage fright and fall flat on your face." Kari said snidely before turning and walking back to her table.

Cole looked at Cassie. "You're going to do just fine. Don't listen to her; she's just jealous."

Cassie looked surprised. "Jealous? Of what?"

Amber shook her head at her friend and looked at Cole. Didn't Cassie understand that not only Cole saw her as beautiful, but everyone did? Cassie was probably the prettiest woman she knew, but she was also clueless.

Cole was looking down at her. "Of you."

"She has no reason to be jealous of me," Cassie replied.

Just then, the lights dimmed and the lodge manager took the stage. "Tonight we have something special planned for you. You will be serenaded by our guests for the next two hours. Hopefully they can sing." The lodge manager grinned. "Our first singer is Kari Matthews."

The audience clapped as Kari took the stage. Her performance was pretty good. She was a very dramatic person and had stage presence. Her vocals weren't as great as Cassie's, but Cassie knew that her stage fright would keep her from doing as well. When Kari's song was over, another girl took the stage. Cassie was at the bottom of the list so she had plenty of time before she had to sing. Maybe the butterflies in her stomach would quiet down by then.

As Kari walked past them to go back to her table, she looked at Cole from under her eyelashes. She knew that she had performed well and hoped that Cole had noticed. Later, when Cassie performed, he would see that he had picked the wrong woman. Cassie didn't have a tenth of Kari's confidence. She still couldn't figure out why Cole would want chubby little innocent like Cassie when he could have a real woman like her.

Their food arrived by the end of the second performance. As they ate, they talked about the different things they had done that day. Amber had gone boating with Gabriel and had later gone fishing. After boating with Amber, Gabriel had hung out by the lake and relaxed.

Cole and Cassie recapped what had happened that afternoon with Michael. They didn't go into the other details so that Cassie wouldn't be embarrassed. The group decided to take a hike the next day and planned to take a picnic lunch with them. Cassie thought of her place near the stream, where Sarah had taken her. She remembered Sarah saying they had found a great spot off the path, but Cassie knew they wouldn't be crossing the stream. Maybe they could find a nice place further down the trail.

Toward the end of dinner, it was Cassie's turn to the take the stage. She had chosen to sing *Blue* by Angie Hart. As she took the stage, the lights dimmed and they put a spotlight on her. At first, she wasn't sure she would be able to sing... she was terrified! Closing her eyes, she started singing when the song began.

As Cassie sang, her voice gained in strength. Opening her eyes, she sought out Cole. Knowing that he was enjoying her performance gave her a confidence boost. She felt the music flow through her and let it take her over. At the end of the performance, she received a standing ovation. Cole was grinning at her and she would have sworn he was clapping the loudest.

After walking off the stage she rejoined her friends at their table. It was funny how she was already thinking of Gabriel as one of her friends even though she had only known him a few days. She thought of Cole as her friend, too, but her feelings for him were different. Cassie tried not to think of Matt. She still missed him terribly, but being with Cole was good for her. She needed a healthy relationship, even if it was just a short one.

When she arrived back at her table, Cole pulled her chair out for her. When she was seated, he bent down to kiss her cheek.

"You were wonderful," he whispered in her ear.

She smiled at him. "Thank you."

From across the room, Kari witnessed the exchange with narrowed eyes. She was going to get her revenge on Cassie one way or another. She wondered if she could get Michael to help her break the two apart. She wasn't sure what had happened between the two of them, but it must have been something.

She glanced his way and noticed he was staring at Cassie. Judging from his expression and clenched fists, she figured he had witnessed the kiss, too. She would definitely be talking to Michael later. And if that didn't work, she would have to work another spell. Next time she would be more specific.

Cassie was going to pay. She had not only stolen the guy Kari wanted, but she had upstaged her tonight. With

Cassie's new dress and her new over-all look, Kari knew that she had to act fast if she wanted Cole. She had always been the most beautiful of the three girls. Now that Cassie was wearing more makeup and taking time to curl her long hair, there was no denying that she was gorgeous. Everyone else would know it too.

Kari got up and left the lodge. She would go back to her cabin and come up with a plan to get Cassie away from Cole. Kari wanted him and she *always* got what she wanted.

Cassie and her friends watched Kari leave. They were relieved when she didn't stop by their table. Maybe Kari would finally leave her alone. Looking across the room, Cassie noticed that Michael was staring at her and she instinctively leaned closer to Cole. She knew that Michael was mad that she had rejected him, but it wasn't her fault that she wasn't attracted to him.

Why couldn't Kari have wanted Michael? They would have been perfect for each other. It would have been the perfect solution. Kari would have left Cole alone and Michael would have left Cassie alone. Maybe it wasn't too late to get the two of them together.

Cole felt Cassie lean into him and looked down at her. He followed her gaze across the room and saw Michael looking their way. He could tell from where he was sitting that Michael was beyond pissed. He knew they would have to be careful. While Michael wouldn't hit a woman, he had inherited their father's temper and would find another way to get back at them.

Cole put his arm around Cassie's shoulders, not only to make her feel safer but also to stake his claim on her for Michael's benefit. Werewolves were just as territorial as wolves were. While he hadn't claimed Cassie as his mate, he knew that his brother would back off and respect the mark that Cole had placed on her.

Gabriel and Amber asked if they were ready to leave. The four got up and left the lodge together. The temperature had dropped even more since they had arrived an hour ago. Cassie was now freezing in her thin dress and heels. "I hate to run guys, but I need to get back to the cabin and put on something warmer. Maybe even a few layers of something warmer!"

Amber laughed at her friend. "You didn't buy the dress for warmth and you know it."

Cassie smiled back her. "No, I didn't. I'm definitely ready to change though."

"Does everyone want to meet back here at nine tomorrow for breakfast?" Amber figured that she would have breakfast with Gabriel whether her friend and Cole could make it or not. They had been spending quite a bit of time together and Amber couldn't have been happier.

Cassie looked at Cole. "Sounds good to me, what about you?"

"Works for me, too. We'll see y'all in the morning." Cole took Cassie's hand and led her down the lodge steps and they started down the path to their cabin.

Chapter Seven

Gabriel offered Amber his arm and escorted her back to her cabin. "I'm guessing that Cassie gave you the full version of what happened when you two took off to the restroom tonight."

"Yes, she did. She's feeling confused at the moment. She's still a little scared of Michael, but she's glad that he interrupted her and Cole tonight," Amber told him.

Gabriel looked over at her. "Interrupted her and Cole?"

"I shouldn't have said anything. I thought that's what Cole was telling you at dinner when he whispered something in your ear," Amber said, immediately regretting that she had opened her big mouth.

Gabriel swore under his breath. "No wonder Michael is pissed. He wanted to have sex with Cassie and she turned him down. Even though I know Cole well enough to know he wasn't intending on that happening so fast, Michael wouldn't have been able to differentiate between what he was wanting and what's happening with Cassie and Cole. Michael tends to think he's God's gift to women."

Amber could understand both sides. She was worried about her friend though. All of this was pretty new for her. Her unusual gift made it hard for her to have a relationship with someone. She knew that Kari had told Cole about Cassie's ability. Apparently he accepted her as she was.

Amber was a little hesitant to tell Gabriel about her gift. Only her two friends knew about it. She could only hope that he would be as accepting as his brother was of Cassie. At least hers was easier to hide than Cassie's.

"Here you are. Safe and sound at your door." Gabriel smiled at her. "Want me to stop by in the morning and walk with you to the lodge? Say around 8:45?"

"That sounds great. Thanks Gabriel. You've been wonderful today," she told him with a smile.

Gabriel leaned down and brushed a quick kiss on her cheek. Usually guys were grabby when they dropped her off, not that she had been on loads of dates. It was nice to have a guy that seemed to respect her.

"If you don't have someplace to be right now, would you like to come in and watch a movie with me?" Amber asked hesitantly.

Gabriel smiled at her. "I'd love to."

Gabriel followed Amber inside her cabin. It was a smaller version of the one he and his brothers were sharing with Cassie. He assumed the second bedroom was Kari's. Hopefully she wouldn't return anytime soon.

On the other side of the lake, Michael was watching Cassie and Cole. He couldn't understand why she had chosen Cole over him. They were almost identical. It didn't make any sense to him. And why did Cole have to choose now to get over his last girlfriend? This week was not turning out the way he had expected.

When Cassie and Cole arrived at the cabin, Cole opened the door for her. She quickly dashed inside, shaking from the cold. "That's the last time I wear a short dress with no stockings in October!"

Cole laughed at her. "Go get warmed up. I'll see if there is anything good to watch."

As Cassie went to change, Cole perused the DVD selection. He noticed that Rose Red was still in the DVD player. Cassie hadn't had a chance to finish it. When she came out of her room, he would ask her if she wanted to finish the movie or select another one.

There was a knock at the cabin door just as Cassie came out of her room. She was dressed in a snug fitting lavender shirt with Tigger on it and flannel pajama pants with Pooh and Tigger all over them. Cole could tell she wasn't wearing a bra and quickly lifted his gaze to hers.

"Who's at the door?" Cassie came to stand beside him.

"I was about to go answer it. Did you want to wait in your room since you're dressed for bed already?" Cole asked, looking pointedly at her pajamas.

"No, I'm fine. I'm just going to sit down." Cassie plopped down on the couch as Cole went to answer the door.

Cole opened the door and found himself eye to eye with Michael. "What do you want?"

"I forgot my key. Let me in." Michael paused, "I need to talk to Cassie a minute."

"I think you've said enough tonight," Cole told his brother.

"Would you at least ask her if she'll talk to me?" Michael demanded. His brother was making this more difficult than he had thought.

Cole turned to ask Cassie if she wanted to see Michael and found her standing behind him. He could tell by the look on her face that she was torn. If she wanted to speak to him, Cole would honor her wishes.

Making her decision, Cassie said, "Let him in."

Cole stepped back to let Michael enter the cabin. "I'll be in my room so you two can talk, but I'm leaving my door open."

Cole headed to his room and closed his door just enough to give them some privacy, but he left it open enough so he could hear Cassie if she needed him. He loved his brother, but he wasn't about to trust him around Cassie. Normally Michael would have respected Cole's mark on Cassie, but he was acting out of the ordinary. Anything was possible at this point.

In the living room, Cassie walked over to the couch and sat down. Michael sat down beside her. She drew her knees up to her chest and wrapped her arms around her legs. She wasn't sure what Michael wanted, but she thought she should at least hear him out.

"Cassie, I don't even know how to start."

"What do you want from me Michael? Haven't you done and said enough already?" Cassie asked.

Michael sighed. He couldn't blame her for feeling that way. "I don't want anything Cassie. I just wanted to tell you that I'm sorry."

Cassie looked at him incredulously. "You're sorry. That's all you have to say?"

"All I can say is that I'm sorry I hurt you. I admit that I would still love nothing more than to have you in my bed, but you obviously don't feel that way about me. I just wanted to let you know that I won't bother you again. I respect your decision to be with Cole," he told her.

Cassie looked at Michael and reached over to take his hand. "I believe that you didn't mean to hurt me Michael and I forgive you. I'm just not sure if I can trust you." Cassie took a breath. "Besides, I want more from a relationship than just sex. That isn't enough for me and that's all you were wanting."

"I understand. I'll show myself out," he replied, standing to leave.

"But your room is here..." Cassie faltered.

"I'll be back later. I think I need to take a walk," Michael told her as he headed for the door.

When the door closed behind Michael, Cole came back out of his room. "Are you all right?"

Cassie nodded. "I'll be fine."

Cole sat beside her and pulled her into his arms. He just sat there holding her for a few minutes. "Did Michael say anything to upset you?"

"No. He apologized for what happened earlier, but I don't know that I can trust him," Cassie replied.

"I'm right here, Cassie. I promise I won't leave your side unless you ask me to. Do you feel up to a movie?" Cole asked.

"Sure." Cassie smiled at him. "Why don't you pick something out for us?"

"Do you want something funny, dramatic or scary? Or do you want a horror movie or action movie?"

"I actually like scary movies. Besides, it gives me an excuse to sit close to you." Cassie looked up at him. "That is, if you don't mind holding me."

"I don't mind." Cole smiled at her.

He would prefer to hold her because she really wanted to be with him, but he wouldn't be picky. If she needed to be held to feel comforted, then that is what he would do. Besides, they weren't even half way through the week yet. There was plenty of time to be with Cassie.

"Since I fell asleep during Rose Red last night, do you care if we put it back on?" Cassie asked him.

"That's fine. It's still in the DVD player," Cole told her.

He sat down and got the movie started. Cassie slid over next to him and rested her head on his shoulder. Grabbing the throw off the back of the couch, he draped it across her legs. Putting his arm around her shoulders, he pulled her closer. "Warm enough?"

"Yes, thank you." She was touched at his thoughtfulness. He was such a sweet guy.

They settled in to watch the movie. Cassie hid her face against Cole's shirt during the scary parts. By the end of the movie, she had fallen asleep. Cole very gently picked her up and carried her to her room. He tucked her into bed and softly closed the door.

Cole wasn't sure what to make of this whole situation with Michael and Cassie. He hoped that his brother really had come to his senses. It wasn't like Michael to act this way and that worried Cole the most. What was going on with his brother?

Even though it was late, Cole wasn't tired. He went to his room and changed into a pair of flannel pajama pants. The cabin was warm enough that he didn't bother with a shirt. He selected another movie and started the DVD player again. Part way through the movie, Cole fell asleep on the couch.

In the morning, Cassie awoke in her bed. Since the last thing she remembered was watching a movie with Cole, she knew he had to have carried her to bed. She smiled at the thought. He really was a good guy.

Cassie quietly padded across her bedroom and opened the door. As she stepped into the living room, she noticed Cole asleep on the couch. He was still sitting up and had fallen asleep with his head tipped back. Looking around the cabin, she noticed that Gabriel and Michael were already gone... assuming they had come back last night at all.

Cassie crept over to him. As she watched him sleep, she realized that he and Michael really did look almost identical. Their eyes were a different color and their noses were also slightly different. They both worked out a lot and were gorgeous to look at. Looking at his naked chest reminded her of yesterday and what it had felt like to have Cole's hands on her body. Just thinking about it made her want a repeat performance.

Cassie gently sat on the couch beside him, careful not to wake him. She contemplated whether or not she should throw a blanket over him. He had to be freezing without a shirt on. As she leaned across Cole to grab the blanket, his arms went around her and pulled her close to him. She ended up sitting in his lap with his face buried in her neck.

"Cole? Are you awake?" Cassie asked softly.

Cassie couldn't move. Cole had managed to trap her arms when he had pulled her into his lap.

Cole was still asleep, but he felt much warmer. As he slowly swam out of his dreams and back into consciousness, he realized there was a very delectable woman in his lap. Without opening his eyes, he began to kiss her neck. He trailed kisses along her jaw to her mouth.

Cassie was surprised when Cole started kissing her, but she couldn't pull away... she wasn't entirely sure she wanted to pull away. Before she could say anything, Cole wrapped one hand behind her head and tugged her closer to him. When he kissed her, Cassie let out a little moan. When her mouth opened, he flicked his tongue inside teasing her a little.

Cole wasn't a hundred percent awake yet and took Cassie's soft noises to mean he should keep going. He shifted his body so that he could lay her down without breaking the kiss. He urged her closer to him.

Cassie knew she should get him to completely wake up and stop kissing her, but she couldn't seem to help herself. Cole's kisses had the ability to take away her common sense; they were both demanding and gentle at the same time. It was more like he was coaxing her to do what he wanted. She wrapped her arms around him and snuggled as close to him as she could get. She would make him stop in a minute, but for now she was just going to enjoy the moment.

Cole ran his hand down the side of the lush little body pressed to his. When his hand got to her hip, he pulled her more snuggly against him. Somewhere in the back of Cole's mind, his brain was screaming for him to wake up. On some level he knew he should listen, but it was far more interesting to ignore that little voice. He opened his eyes to see who had crawled into his bed. The moment he saw Cassie and realized they were on the couch, he stopped.

Cassie opened her eyes and looked at him. "What's wrong Cole?"

Cole sat up and scooted to the other end of the couch. He ran his hands over his face and groaned. "Cassie, what are you doing out here? I distinctly remember putting you in your bed last night."

Cassie was a little puzzled over Cole's reaction. "I woke up and found you on the couch. When I reached across you for the blanket, you put your arms around me. Before I could say anything you started kissing me."

Cole looked at her. "You didn't think to stop me? Especially after what happened yesterday?"

Cassie looked embarrassed. She couldn't understand why Cole was so upset. Guys were just too confusing. One minute he wanted her and the next he didn't. To be fair, Cassie had to remind herself that she was going through the same thing. Except it wasn't that she didn't want Cole, she just felt guilty about wanting him. While she didn't have a boyfriend, she still felt she was cheating on someone. Not just someone, if she were honest with herself, she would acknowledge that it was Matt she was thinking of.

Cassie got up and started walking to her room. As she passed Cole, he reached out and took her hand in his.

"Cassie, wait. I didn't mean that to sound the way it did."

Cassie started to sit next to him on the couch, but her impish side won out and she ended up sitting in his lap instead. "Then how did you mean for it to sound?"

Cole could tell that Cassie wasn't going to make this easy for him. He didn't want her to feel rejected, but he wanted to be sure that she knew what she wanted and what she was asking for.

Waking up to find himself kissing Cassie had been a little scary, but it had also been wonderful. It had been a while since he'd wanted to wake up next to someone. He could definitely get used to more mornings like this one, assuming that he didn't screw things up before they reached that stage.

"I promised you that I wouldn't take advantage of you when you told me you were a virgin. It hasn't even been twenty four hours and I'm already breaking that promise," Cole told her.

Cassie put her finger over his lips. "You can't break the promise if I let you kiss me. You were asleep and didn't realize what you were doing. The moment you opened your eyes and saw me you stopped. You're every bit the gentleman and kept your word."

"I may have stopped, but I didn't want to," he replied honestly.

"Then why did you? You might have been sleeping, but I was wide awake. I kissed you back because I wanted to," Cassie told him.

Cole looked at her and brushed her hair back from her face. "I'm mostly worried that you don't know for sure what you want. I don't mean that in a bad way. I just know that all of this is new for you. We've only known each other for three days. That's a really short time for someone as inexperienced as you."

Cassie leaned into him. "I know you're right. I know I'm not ready for that step yet, but when you kissed me I couldn't help but kiss you back. Guess I'm just a typical wishy-washy female."

Cole wrapped his arms around her. "Cassie, you're not wishy-washy. You're just experiencing new things."

"I'm glad to hear you say that." Cassie looked into his eyes.

Leaning forward she brushed her lips across his. She wasn't getting quite the response she was hoping for, so she looped her arms around his neck and pressed herself close to him. Cole put his arms around Cassie and held her close.

Before either of them could really think about what they were doing, Cole had her lying on the couch again. Cassie wrapped her leg around one of Cole's to hold his body close to hers. As he kissed her, Cassie's body instinctively arched into his. Even though all of this was new for Cassie, her body seemed to have a mind of its own and knew exactly what to do.

Unfortunately, that's exactly how Michael found them when he entered the cabin a few minutes later.

Chapter Eight

Michael knew that he should leave, but he couldn't seem to make his feet move. He cleared his throat to make his presence known. It had the desired effect. Cassie and Cole broke apart and sat straight up on the couch.

Cassie looked over the back of the couch and saw Michael near the front door. "Michael, I thought you had already left for the morning. What are you doing back so soon?"

"Obviously interrupting the two of you."

Cassie got up and walked over to him. Putting her hand on his arm she said, "Michael, please don't do this."

"Do what? I'm just standing here, witnessing my brother do the exact same thing that I wanted to do. The difference is that when it was me kissing you it was a mistake, but now that it's Cole you can't seem to get enough," he replied angrily.

"Please Michael. It isn't like that. Cole wasn't trying to get into my pants. We were just kissing," Cassie told him.

"Looked like it was quickly turning into more from where I was standing," Michael mumbled, glaring at his brother.

"Don't do this. It isn't fair of you to act this way. I told you before that I wasn't interested in you like that. Nothing is going to change that. You seemed to accept my decision last night," Cassie said.

Michael raised his hand to slap her, but stopped at the last minute. What was he doing? This wasn't him! "Oh God, Cass! I'm sorry! I don't know what came over me."

Michael held his hand out to her in supplication. He had never tried to strike a woman before. The last thing he wanted to do was hurt Cassie. Until he had caught her and Cole on the couch, he had thought that all of this was behind him. Last night, he had been at peace with her decision and had been happy for his brother. Why were things so different all of a sudden? He didn't understand his own emotions anymore.

Cassie backed away and ended up backing right into Cole. She didn't know when he had come around the couch, but she was glad he had. Cole put his arms around her.

"I think it's time for you to leave Michael." Cole looked at him with contempt.

Michael looked at his brother. "I'm going. I'll stay away from her for the rest of the trip."

He turned and opened the door. Before he left, he turned to tell his brother one more thing. Cole had to know that this wasn't like him. There was some unseen force guiding his actions.

"I don't know what's happening to me Cole, but you know this isn't me. I would never have hit Cassie," Michael told his brother, imploring Cole to believe him.

Cole just watched him leave. He had always thought that Michael wouldn't hurt a woman, but after today he was wondering if he had been wrong. Michael had a lot of anger in him. Cole would be keeping a very close eye on Cassie until the week was up. He wasn't taking any chances with her safety.

Cassie turned to look up at him. "What's wrong with him? He seems different than he was when I first got here."

"It's the same Michael. He just didn't show this side of himself to you. He's used every girl he ever dated. Don't let his act fool you. To Michael, you're just here for his enjoyment," Cole told her harshly.

He wasn't angry with Cassie, but he didn't want her harboring any delusions over who his brother was. If she felt safe around Michael, she would let down her guard.

Cole wasn't sure what was going on with his brother, but he knew that he didn't trust him at the moment.

Cassie hugged Cole tightly. She was glad that he had been here with her. She knew now that she definitely didn't want to be left alone with Michael. He may have apologized, but apparently he wasn't going to leave her alone.

Cole picked Cassie up and carried her to her room. He kissed her before he sat her down. "Why don't you get ready to go? Its 8:00 and we're supposed to meet Gabriel and Amber in half an hour."

Cassie snagged Cole's hand as he turned to leave. "I'm glad you're here with me."

"Me too." Cole smiled at her. He brushed a kiss over her fingers and went to his own bedroom.

Cassie looked through her stuff. They were going on a picnic today so she knew she was going to wear jeans, but she couldn't decide on a top. Toward the bottom of the drawer she found a lavender angora v-neck sweater. On the off chance that things with Cole progressed beyond kissing again today, she also selected her lavender silk bra and panties. Once she had gathered all of her stuff, she went to the bathroom to take a shower.

As Cole selected his own clothes, he heard the shower start. Picturing her naked in the shower was torture. His imagination had been bad enough before, but now that he knew what those curves felt like pressed against him and had seen her dripping wet in a towel it was even worse. He decided to lie down on the bed while he waited on Cassie to finish. He was going to jump in the shower really fast once she was done... a very cold shower. He would have to quickly throw his clothes on so they wouldn't be late for breakfast.

Since time was short this morning, Cassie decided to just towel dry her hair. She put on a little blush and lipstick before getting dressed. She quickly pulled on her clothes and headed to the living room to put on her socks and shoes.

Cole heard the bathroom door open and went to take a shower. He found Cassie sitting on the couch in yet another form fitting sweater. Her wardrobe was definitely going to keep him on his toes. Her tops left little to the imagination. He closed the bathroom door and took the fastest, coldest shower in history. He threw on a black shirt, jeans and his socks and shoes. When he stepped out of the bathroom, Cassie glanced up from where she was sitting.

"Ready to go? Gabriel and Amber will probably come find us if we don't leave soon." Cassie said, standing and walking over to him.

"I'm ready if you are," he told her with a smile.

They left the cabin and headed down the path toward the lodge. Cassie reached over and took Cole's hand. By some miracle, they beat Amber and Gabriel. Cole sat on the steps of the lodge and Cassie sat beside him. Leaning over, he kissed her softly on the lips. The kiss was brief, but it was enough to make both of them want more.

Cole looked up and saw his brother and Amber heading their way. Judging Gabriel's expression, Cole realized that he had witnessed the kiss. He knew that Gabriel was going to give him grief once they were alone.

"Good morning," Amber said as she helped Cassie up from the steps.

The two girls walked ahead of them into the lodge. One look at Gabriel and Cole knew his brother wanted to talk before they followed the girls in.

"What is it Gabriel?" Cole asked with impatience.

"I saw Michael this morning. He said that he was at the cabin last night," Gabriel replied.

"Yes, he talked to Cassie. We also saw him this morning after everyone had left. I don't know what's wrong with him, but he almost hit her," Cole said with a shake of his head. Michael's behavior still baffled him.

"Hit her? Michael?" Gabriel asked in disbelief.

Hitting a woman is the one thing that none of the brothers would have ever done. For Michael to have even acted like he would hit Cassie, meant that something really strange was going on. Gabriel knew he would have to get to the bottom of it before something bad happened. He just wasn't sure where to start.

"I know. I think Cassie's scared," Cole said.

"She looked really scared a minute ago," Gabriel said with a smirk, trying to lighten the mood.

"Shut up." Cole grinned at his brother affectionately.

"Let's get inside before they come looking for us."

Gabriel and Cole entered the lodge and found Amber and Cassie waiting for them in the lobby. The girls looked like they had been deep in conversation when the guys came in, but they stopped talking when Gabriel and Cole came up to them.

Cole reached over and took Cassie's hand. "Let's go see what they have for us today."

Amber and Gabriel followed behind them. The lodge had set up a buffet for breakfast this morning. The foursome fixed their plates and chose a table away from everyone else. They hadn't been seated long before Kari came in. She started to pass by their table, but Cole reached out and stopped her.

She turned to Cole with a smile on her face. "Good morning, Cole."

She thought that finally things were turning around for her. Maybe a second spell wouldn't be necessary after all.

"Morning, Kari," he replied.

"Did you want something?" Kari asked in a syrupy sweet voice.

"I actually wanted to ask you why you seem to have such a problem with Cassie. For the past few days you have gone out of your way to be a real bitch to her. It's had me a little puzzled seeing as how you're supposed to be her friend," Cole told her, deciding to be straight forward about it.

Kari wasn't sure how to respond. Maybe if she told him the truth she would get further with him. "She took something that I wanted. She knew I wanted it, but that didn't seem to bother her. Would a true friend do that?"

Cole had a feeling he knew where this was going. "What did she take?"

"You. She took you, Cole," Kari said in a husky voice.

Cole sighed. "Kari, it wouldn't have mattered if Cassie and I hadn't even crossed paths on this trip. I still wouldn't be spending time with you. It isn't that you're not pretty, because you are... it's just that you're not my type."

"Let me guess. Your type is Cassie," Kari said with a sneer.

"Yes, it is," he told her.

Kari just stared at him. She had thought that if Cassie were removed from the equation that Cole would be hers. Apparently that wasn't the case. If Cole was telling her the truth, she didn't have a chance with him regardless. She sighed. It was time to come clean. Maybe she could salvage her friendship with Cassie and Amber at the very least. After all, there were other guys.

"Cass, there's something I think I should tell you," Kari said as she looked at Cassie.

"What is it Kari," Cassie asked, almost afraid to hear what would come next.

Kari glanced uncertainly at Cole before continuing. "I know about what happened with Michael and you should know that it wasn't completely his fault. I may have helped a little."

"Helped?" Cassie has a sinking feeling she knew what Kari had done.

"I sort of... well, you know. I sort of cast a spell on him." Kari continued in a rush, "I wanted to separate you and Cole, but it didn't work the way it should have. It didn't seem fair that you were getting all of the attention and all three of them were ignoring me. I'm really sorry! I've been a complete and total bitch to you."

Cole looked at Kari like she was nuts. "You cast a spell on my brother? You really expect us to believe that?"

Cassie looked at Cole. She had known that spell-casting wouldn't go over well with him, but she had hoped he would be understanding. After all, he hadn't flinched when she told him about her ability to see ghosts. Why should this be so different?

"Yes, Cole. Kari can cast spells. She's a witch," Cassie told him matter-of-factly.

Cole looked at Cassie incredulously. Witches existed? As in spell-casting, broom riding witches? Part of him wanted to believe in such things, but having never met one before he wasn't sure what to say. "You believe that?"

"Yes, I do," she replied quietly.

Cassie was having a hard time looking at Cole. If he couldn't understand Kari casting spells, how was he going to react when he found out that she cast them too? Not for the first time, Cassie wished that Matt were here with her. He would know exactly what to say to make her feel better. Then again, if Matt had been here with her, she wouldn't be in this predicament.

Kari looked at her friend. "I really am sorry Cass. I don't know specifically what happened between you. I just know that I asked the God and Goddess to separate you. I wasn't very specific so I kind of let the magick guide itself. I know it was wrong, but I was feeling pretty desperate."

Cole didn't know what to make of all of this. He looked at his brother to gage his reaction. Gabriel seemed calm and accepting.

"Do you believe in this hocus pocus stuff? I mean, witches? What's next? A troll?" Cole asked sarcastically. Witches!

"I believe that a lot of things are possible, as you should know." Gabriel gave him a meaningful look.

Gabriel wondered how could his brother be a werewolf and think that no other mythical creatures or people existed? Was he really that narrow minded? Or was the spell Kari had cast spilling over onto Cole now? It had already worked on Michael, was it going to hit all three of them?

"I've also known some Wiccans who cast spells. Usually for good and not to cause harm though," Gabriel said with a pointed look at Kari.

"Wiccans? What kind of a nut calls themselves a Wiccan?" Cole asked in disbelief.

Cassie looked at Cole with tortured eyes. "I do."

She got up from the table and ran from the lodge. Cassie didn't stop running until she reached her cabin. After closing the front door, she ran to her room and threw herself on her bed. Today was the worst day ever! It seemed that all men really *were* jackasses.

Back at the lodge, Cole looked after Cassie with a dumbfounded expression on his face. He looked at his brother again.

"You're an idiot Cole! How could you not accept that witches could exist? Is magick really so hard to believe in?" he asked Cole in anger.

Gabriel shook his head at his brother. "You have got to be the dumbest, most narrow minded guy on the planet! Go after her and apologize before it's too late."

Cole got up without another word and went after Cassie. She had already made it to the cabin and was in her room crying by the time he caught up with her. Cole started to knock on her door, but decided to just see if it was unlocked. He wasn't sure if she would let him in if she knew he was there. He quietly opened the door and stepped inside.

"Cass, can I come in?" he asked her quietly.

Cassie sniffled. "It looks to me like you already *are* in."

"I'm sorry for what I said at the lodge. If I had known that you practiced Wicca too, I wouldn't have made such a dumb comment. I've just never known anyone who was into that stuff before. It took me by surprise and I reacted badly," he told her apologetically.

Cassie looked at him. Her face was streaked with tears and her lips were trembling. "What's wrong with being a Wiccan and casting spells?"

"Nothing. I guess I just really don't know much about it. It just seemed really silly to me when Kari thought she had caused the trouble between you and Michael because of a spell. Things like that only happen in movies. Then again, I had never met anyone before you who could talk to ghosts. Guess I need to be a little more open-minded," he told her with a sheepish look.

"They can happen in real life too, Cole. Kari isn't the only one who casts spells. I usually only do spells for clarity, protection or to relieve stress, but I cast them just the same. While Kari tampered with dark magick, which is vastly different from what I do, if it was the thought of spell-casting that put you off, then I need you to understand that Kari and I are no different in that respect," Cassie told him.

Cassie looked down at her hands. Most people didn't understand Wicca and were quick to condemn anyone who practiced magick, but Cassie had hoped that Cole would be different. Things had been going so well between them. She had thought she might have finally found the right guy.

Cole sat beside her on the bed and covered her hands with his. "I meant it Cassie. I really am sorry for what I said and how I reacted."

Cassie looked up at him. He seemed sincere. She hesitantly scooted closer to him. When she was close enough that her body was touching his, Cole put his arms around her. He may not understand Wicca or why Cassie wanted to be part of it, but it was part of her so he would try to be accepting.

"It's something that is obviously important to you. I may not understand it, but I'm not going to make fun of something that means so much to you. I promise that I'll try to keep an open mind. I'm even willing to do some reading on the subject so I will be more informed. Maybe you can even explain it to me sometime, assuming you want to see me once we get back home," Cole said.

"I think I would like that," Cassie replied with a small smile.

"You would?" he asked, his eyes full of hope.

"Yes, I would," she replied.

Cassie smiled at Cole. "That is if you don't mind going out with a Wiccan who can talk to ghosts."

Cole smiled back at her and hugged her tight. "Want to go finish breakfast? I'm sure that Gabriel and Amber are still there waiting on us."

"Sure," she said, placing her hand in his.

The two got up and headed back to the lodge. Just as Cole had predicted, Gabriel and Amber were still sitting at their table. Cassie's and Cole's plates were still waiting on them. Pulling out her chair, Cole waited for Cassie to sit before resuming his own seat.

"We figured the two of you would come back. Are you all right Cassie?" Gabriel knew his brother had to have made things right with her. Thankfully, Cole was able to admit when he was wrong about something.

"I'm fine, thank you. What happened with Kari after I left?" Cassie looked at Amber. She knew that her friend would be able to tell her whether or not Kari's apology had been real.

"She apologized again and left. I think she really felt bad about what happened and how she's been acting. Maybe this was a wake-up call for her," Amber said.

"I'll have to talk to her later. Right now let's think of more pleasant things... like our picnic," Cassie said with a smile.

Amber smiled at her friend. She knew that Cassie was having a rough week, but she was trying to make the best out the situation. Even though they knew Kari's spell had been behind Michael's behavior, it was likely that he was not only acting on the spell but also on his typical behavior. She hoped that Michael would stay away from Cassie. Amber and Gabriel had talked about Michael for a few minutes after Cassie and Cole had left. Gabriel told her about the kind of women Michael normally dated... women like Kari.

"I thought we could come here and grab some sandwiches and stuff then we could take a hike through the woods to find a good spot. I found a nice stream our first day here. It wasn't a great spot for a picnic, but I think if we walked a little further we might find something," Cassie told them.

"Sounds good Cass. What do you think guys?" Amber asked Cole and Gabriel.

Gabriel looked at Amber. "Whatever y'all want to do is fine with me."

Cole hadn't taken his eyes off Cassie since they had come back to the lodge. "Anything Cassie wants is okay by me."

Cassie smiled. "It's settled then. Want to meet here in about an hour and a half?"

Everyone agreed on the time and meeting place. Gabriel and Amber left the lodge together. Cassie was happy for her friend. Gabriel seemed like a really great guy. If nothing else came of the trip, maybe Amber would at least have found her someone special. Cassie still wasn't sure how things would end for her and Cole.

Cole helped Cassie up from her chair and they walked back to their cabin. On the way there, they were both surprised to see Kari and Michael talking by the lake. Cassie hoped that Kari knew what she was doing. Michael probably wouldn't react well when he found out he had been under a spell. Then again, maybe Kari was hitting on him. They seemed to be birds of a feather.

When they arrived at the cabin, Cole held the door open for Cassie. Closing the door, he followed her into the living room. Cassie had fallen asleep twice during Rose Red so he put it back on for her. He figured if they didn't finish it now, she would probably want to watch it again later that night. As he was setting up the movie, Cassie went to sit on the couch.

"Cole, can we talk a minute?"

"We can talk anytime you want to, about anything you want," he said as he sat beside her.

"This has been a really weird week for all of us, but for me especially. When I first started this trip, I didn't have a boyfriend and hadn't done much in the kissing department. I know that Kari cast a spell to keep all of you from liking me, but I was wondering if it was really the spell making Michael act like that... or does he normally just want sex from the women he's with?" Cassie asked.

"Cassie, you didn't do anything wrong with Michael. He acted the way he did because he's an ass. Spell or no spell, he hasn't been known to care about anyone other than himself. The spell didn't make him do anything he wouldn't have normally done – except try to hit you.

That's something that none of us would ever do. I don't want you to feel like you might have accidentally led him on or anything. That's just the way he is," he assured her.

"Thanks, Cole. I guess I was feeling a little guilty over the whole thing. Maybe Kari can reverse the spell and things will return to normal," Cassie replied.

"You did the right thing when you asked Michael to stay away from you. Don't beat yourself up over it," Cole responded.

"I just feel bad about the whole thing."

"Come here." Cole tugged her closer to him. "I don't want you to spend another moment worrying about Michael."

Cassie smiled at him. She could really see herself spending time with Cole on a long-term basis. Before that could happen though, she had to come clean with him. He needed to know about Matt. While Cassie and Matt had never dated, for obvious reasons, she still felt it was important to tell Cole about him.

Looking into his eyes, she said, "We haven't really discussed it much, but I wanted you to know that I would rather be with just one special guy than date several guys. Before you decide if you want to be that guy, I should probably tell you..."

Cole placed a finger over her lips to keep her from saying more. "I can't think of anything that would make me happier than to be that guy. You don't have to tell me anything else."

Cole leaned down and kissed her. "Let's finish this movie before we have to meet Amber and Gabriel for our hike."

Cassie snuggled up next to Cole and they watched the remainder of the movie in silence. By the time the movie ended, it was time to meet Gabriel and Amber. Cole helped Cassie up off the couch and pulled her into his arms.

"Have I told you how glad I am that fate has thrown us together this week?" Cole asked.

"No, but I'm glad to hear you're happy." Cassie smiled at him. "I'm happy, too."

Cassie went up on her tiptoes to kiss Cole, but of course she was too short. Cole leaned down and kissed her briefly on the lips. He knew that anything more would lead them down a path they weren't ready for.

Pulling back, he smiled down at her. "Let's go meet Gabriel and Amber."

Cassie smiled and took his hand. They walked to the lodge in silence. Amber and Gabriel were already waiting on them when they arrived.

Amber held up a wicker basket, "I already asked for a basket for our picnic. All we have to do is order our food."

"Sounds great," Cassie told her.

They walked into the lodge and headed for the dining area. It was still extremely early for lunch, but they figured they would have to walk for at least an hour before they found a nice picnic spot. After ordering their sandwiches, side items and drinks, they left the lodge and headed for the trail into the woods.

Gabriel carried the picnic basket and walked beside Amber. Cassie and Cole trailed behind them, walking hand in hand. It was a beautiful day outside. The sun was shining and the air was crisp. As they walked through the woods, the birds were singing and they could hear rabbits hopping through the fallen leaves and the deer grazing on what little grass they could find.

As they walked along the trail, they talked about their lives back in Ashton Grove. Cole and Gabriel told them about their garage, which they shared with Michael. All three brothers were mechanics, but Cole was the only one who was in college. He only had another semester to finish his degree in Biology. He was hoping to get into medical school, but had already had a few offers from some bio-med companies in the area. It would be nice to have a steady full-time job and get his student loans paid off before going back to school again.

Gabriel and Michael worked as mechanics full-time. The brothers had inherited the garage from their father. It was the only nice thing their dad had ever done for them. It allowed them to support themselves and their mother. Working in the garage wasn't glamorous, but it was honest work. Truth be told, Gabriel really enjoyed it. He'd been offered a scholarship to Georgia Tech for Engineering, but had turned them down. He was great at math and science, but knew it wasn't the right life for him. He would have made a lot more money, but he wouldn't have been happy.

Amber talked a little about her degree. She was in college with Cassie and was about a year away from graduating with a bachelor's degree in History and a minor in English. She was planning on applying to a Master of Arts in Teaching program with secondary licensure. While teachers didn't make a lot of money, she knew that she wanted to teach teenagers. Her History and English teachers had made a huge difference in her life. Becoming a teacher seemed like a terrific way to not only pay them back, but to make a difference in the lives of other people.

Cassie had two or three semesters left to finish her bachelor's degree in Psychology. She knew that it was useless unless she went to graduate school for her master's degree and later a doctoral degree, but it would be a huge relief to finish the first four years. She had already talked to a few area clinics about interning over the summer. The acceptance, or rejection, letters should be arriving any day now.

After walking for over an hour, they saw the perfect spot for a picnic. To the left of the trail there was a clearing near the river. Gabriel sat the picnic basket on the ground and Amber pulled a thin blanket out of it. She spread the blanket on the ground and motioned for everyone to sit down.

Cole sat beside Cassie. He had enjoyed talking to her during their walk and felt that he knew her a little bit better. She was an amazing woman and he looked forward to getting to know her even better. He hoped that she felt the same about him.

Amber passed around the paper plates and napkins. She sat out the sandwiches and side items and handed everyone a drink. They each fixed a plate and started to eat. Cole started a conversation about movies to break the silence.

When they were finished, they packed their trash into the picnic basket and started back down the trail. It would be after one when they returned to the cabin. Cassie wasn't sure what she would do to kill time between now and dinner. She was enjoying her stay at the lake, but she just wasn't much of a lake kind of girl. Fishing didn't really hold any interest for her. She enjoyed boating, but typically became bored in less than an hour. If she had been smart, she would have bought some novels while they were in town.

Since they were full, it took them a little longer to walk back. Amber and Gabriel offered to take the picnic basket back to the lodge. Afterwards, they were going to take one of the boats out on the lake for a while. Cole figured that was his brother's subtle way of saying he wouldn't be back at the cabin for a while.

Cassie and Cole went to their cabin. Once inside, Cassie wasn't really sure what to do. She felt restless, which wasn't like her. It almost felt like there was something she should be doing, or something she should know about. Typically, she tried to listen to these feelings when she had them, but at the moment she was having a hard time concentrating on anything other than Cole.

"Is there anything you'd like to do this afternoon?" he asked her.

"I'm not really sure. Boating and fishing aren't really my thing and there isn't much else to do other than hike," she looked around the cabin as if searching for something.

Cole looked down at her, "Is everything okay Cassie?"

"Hmm?" She looked up at him. "Oh, everything's fine. I just have this weird feeling. I'm probably just tired. Would you mind if I took a short nap?" she asked.

Cole smiled at her. "Not at all. Why don't you rest and I'll go find Michael. Maybe if I spend some brotherly time with him, things will get back to normal around here."

Cassie smiled her thanks. "I'll see you in a little while then."

Cole left the cabin so Cassie could take a nap in peace. It didn't take him long to find Michael. His brother had been spending a large amount of time by the lake since they had arrived a few days earlier. Maybe it had a calming effect on him or something. Cole decided it was time to have a brotherly chat and headed Michael's way.

Back at the cabin, Cassie crawled into her bed and pulled the covers over her legs. She wasn't sure why she suddenly felt so tired. Her body felt heavy and useless. As her eyes drifted shut, the strange dreams began.

Cassie was in the woods, running faster than she ever had before. Something was wrong. Someone she loved was in danger. Around her, she heard the noises of animals scurrying through the dead, fallen leaves that covered the ground. Her senses were hyper alert. In the distance she heard a wolf howl and her heart nearly froze in fear.

Coming to a clearing, she saw Matt on the ground. A large red wolf, larger than any she'd seen before, had him by the throat. One snap of its huge jaws and Matt would be dead. Somehow Cassie knew that he was alive in her dream, no longer a ghost, but a flesh and blood man.

The wolf paused and looked at her. Its blue eyes going wide in shock. Before her very eyes, the wolf shifted into Michael. He immediately began apologizing to her... telling her that he had only done it for Cole. He believed that she was Cole's soul mate and he would do anything to make sure they stayed together.

Her dream shifted. She was no longer in the woods, but standing by the lake. The moon was full and despite the cold night air she was wearing nothing more than a long, thin white satin nightgown with crimson red bows on the shoulders. It had a plunging neckline unlike anything she had worn before.

Looking up at the moon, she felt its power. She had never felt so close to the God and Goddess before. The allure of it was intoxicating. Cassie slowly walked out into the water, except she wasn't walking into it... she was walking *on* it. Never before had she experienced magick this strong.

Holding her arms in the air, she called down the power of the moon. On the shore behind her, three wolves gathered. Cassie looked over her shoulder at them. Turning, she faced the wolves and pointed at the black and silver one. The gray eyes told her that it was Cole. She commanded the wolf to come to her. The wolf hesitantly stepped toward her. The moment he realized that he too could walk on top of the water, he quickly made his way over to her.

Cassie whispered in his ear for him to shift to his human form. In a flash of blinding light, Cole stood before her. Drawing his head down to hers, she kissed him passionately. They made love under the moon, on top of the water from the lake.

Her dreams shifted once more. She was standing beside a fresh grave. Looking at the headstone, she read the name... Matthew Spencer. The date of his death was just a week away. How can a ghost die a second time? Cassie was feeling confused and lost, until she felt a hand slide into hers. Glancing to her right, she saw Cole standing beside her.

"It was the only way," he told her. "If he had lived, we couldn't have been together. And you're *mine*... my mate, my life, my everything."

Cassie looked up into his eyes and saw the depth of his feelings for her. She gently ran her fingers over his cheek. She had lost Matt, but she had gained so much more. Part of her felt hollow and forever changed, but she also felt power unlike any she had ever known. She knew that had she not joined herself with Cole, a powerful werewolf, that the God and Goddess would not have blessed her with her new gifts. She now had the ability to see the future and to read people's thoughts if they intended her or her family harm. She could also levitate, but that only seemed to work when she and Cole were making love.

Cassie rubbed the small bump where her flat stomach had once been. She was expecting their first child in a few months. The child of a witch and a werewolf was destined for great things. If the child was a daughter, she would be even more powerful than her mother. If it was a boy, he would one day be leader of their pack as the firstborn boy.

Cole returned to the cabin an hour later. He checked on Cassie and saw that she was still sleeping. Apparently their walk had taken a lot out of her. Not wanting to disturb her, he left the cabin again. This time he spent some time alone by the lake.

He'd had a nice talk with Michael. Things seemed to be okay between them. He no longer had to worry that Michael would hurt Cassie. Whatever had caused his brother's unusual behavior seemed to be over. If Kari was to be believed, her spell had seemingly run its course. While he still had trouble believing in spells and magick, he couldn't deny that something had made his brother act oddly.

Cole stayed by the lake until dark. As he opened the cabin door, he was surprised to find Gabriel and Michael standing outside of Cassie's bedroom door. He noted the concerned look on their faces and instantly feared that something had happened to her.

"What is it? Is something wrong with Cassie?" he asked them anxiously.

Gabriel shook his head, "I'm not really sure. We heard her cry out in her sleep, as if someone were hurting her. When we tried to wake her up, she became very still and very quiet... but she wouldn't open her eyes."

Cole pushed his way between them and headed into Cassie's room. The first thing he noticed was how pale she looked. Something had to be wrong! He knelt beside the bed and took her hand in his.

"Cassie? Cassie honey, it's time to wake up," he told her gently.

There was no response. He could tell that she was breathing, but it was almost like she was in a deep trance. What had caused this? Why wouldn't she wake up? He gently nudged her, but she didn't move. Getting up, he headed back out of her room.

Closing the door behind him, he faced his brothers. "I've never seen anything like this before. Maybe we should get her friends."

Michael nodded and went to fetch Amber and Kari. They needed to find out if this was normal for Cassie or if they should be concerned. It only took a few minutes for him to find the girls and rush them back to the cabin.

Amber immediately went to Cassie's room and opened the door. The sight before her scared her. Cassie was deathly pale and barely breathing. She looked behind her at Kari.

"Please tell me you haven't been doing more spells," Amber said.

Kari looked affronted. "Of course not! I even rescinded the other one."

Amber sighed. "I've never seen anything like this. What do you think?"

Kari looked over Amber's shoulder. Moving into the room, she placed a hand on Cassie's forehead. Cassie was clammy to the touch. She was in a very deep sleep, but it wasn't an ordinary sleep. It was filled with powerful dreams. The very air of the room felt heavy with magick. Kari hadn't realized that Cassie was this powerful. She wasn't even sure that Cassie realized it for that matter.

Turning to face her audience, Kari said, "She's fine. Her dreams are filled with visions of the future, or rather what her future could be. She probably won't wake until morning."

Cole looked between Kari and Cassie. "But she'll be okay?"

Kari smiled at him. "She'll be fine."

Kari and Amber managed to talk the guys into going to dinner with them. It had taken a lot to convince Cole to leave Cassie's side, but he had eventually relented. The five of them had a nice time and the brothers returned to the cabin an hour later. Feeling emotionally drained, Cole checked on Cassie one more time before heading to bed. She was still in a deep sleep. When she woke in the morning, he would tell her about their plans to meet Amber and Gabriel for breakfast.

While dinner had been pretty nice, it would have been better if Kari had kept her hands to herself. Every chance she had, she had touched him. Cole had thought that he had made himself clear earlier. Obviously, Kari didn't understand that he wasn't interested... or she was just stubborn. He had hoped she and Michael would hit it off. Even Michael was turned off by the blonde and that was saying something.

Chapter Nine

Morning dawned bright and clear. Cassie stretched in her bed and slowly opened her eyes. Her dreams had been strange all night, but she felt extremely rested. Climbing out of bed, she headed for the living room.

Cole was on the couch watching a movie. "Hey sleeping beauty! I was starting to wonder if you were ever going to wake up."

Cassie blushed. "I'm sorry I slept through dinner. I must have been more tired than I thought."

He gave her a concerned look, "How do you feel this morning?"

"Much better!" Cassie smiled at him. "I'm just going to freshen up."

She scurried into the bathroom to brush her hair and her teeth. Morning breath was a definite turn off! Her dreams flashed through her mind a few pieces at a time. It was odd that Matt had been alive in her dreams. The fact that she had ended up with Cole in her dreams was definitely a sign.

When she was finished, she went back into the living room and joined Cole on the couch. Sitting beside him, she rested her head on his shoulder. He put his arm around her shoulders and pulled her closer. Looking into his eyes, she smiled at him. She gently ran her finger tips over his cheek and along his jaw.

Cole picked her up and carried her to her bedroom. He sat on the bed with Cassie in his lap. Part of him knew that this would lead to trouble, but he was just so happy that she was okay that he didn't much care. Bending his head to hers, he kissed her softly on the lips.

Cassie enjoyed his soft, sensual kisses, but she wanted more. Cole flicked his tongue against her lips. She tentatively touched her tongue to his. Cole leaned back on the bed and rolled over so that Cassie was lying under him.

Cassie moaned into his mouth and tried to pull him closer. She couldn't seem to get enough of him and he couldn't get enough of her. She wanted to be as close to him as possible.

Cassie slid her hands under Cole's shirt and up to his chest. She loved the fill of his firm smooth skin. She could feel his chest muscles ripple under her fingers and she felt his heartbeat. Cole stopped kissing her long enough to remove his shirt. Once his shirt was off, he pulled her back into his arms and kissed her again. He lifted his head and looked down at her.

"Cassie, maybe we should stop. I don't want you to regret anything later," he told her softly.

"I know we should, but I don't want you to stop. I want to feel your skin against mine. I want you to kiss me until I'm out of breath," she replied.

Cassie's face was flushed, her lips were swollen from his kisses and her eyes were glazed with passion. Cole wasn't sure he could say no to her, and he wasn't sure he wanted to.

"Please kiss me Cole," she begged.

Cole bent his head to hers and did as she had requested. She was so soft and warm, and she tasted so very sweet. Cole had never wanted anyone more than he wanted Cassie. His desire for her wasn't just physical like Michael's had been. He craved her body and soul.

He lifted the hem of her sweater and rubbed his hand across her soft belly. Her skin felt like silk. His finger tips drifted higher and brushed against the underside of her breast. Cassie gasped and arched against him. Even if Cassie wasn't one-hundred percent sure of what she was doing, her body knew exactly what it wanted.

Cole pushed her sweater further up to expose her breasts. He looked at the lavender satin and gently ran his thumb across the material. He lowered his head to her breast and nipped her through the satin material. Cassie moaned deep in her throat. She had never felt anything like this before. Cole trailed kisses up the swell of her breast. He kissed the hollow of her neck. Lifting his head, he looked into her eyes before reclaiming her mouth.

Back home in Ashton Grove, Matt was in Cassie's bedroom. He missed her terribly and wished he could be with her. He had borrowed Cassie's computer to run another search on spells or amulets that would allow him to travel to Whispering Lake. Matt wasn't entirely sure what was going on at the lake, but he felt that Cassie needed him.

He was about to give up the search when he finally saw something of interest. It was a ring that supposedly had the power to allow a ghost to travel from one place to another. The trick was that the ghost had to have a loved one in the location they wanted to travel to. Matt had never told Cassie about his feelings. He knew that there was no hope for them as he had been dead for a long time and her young life was just beginning.

The ring was gold, with a band made of dragons. The dragons' mouths were holding a large ruby in the center of the ring. Something about it looked oddly familiar. Suddenly, Matt remembered why it was so familiar. Cassie's father had a ring that looked just like it in his study in the desk drawer. Matt hurried downstairs and entered the study. Cassie's father was at the desk. When Matt entered the room, Cassie's dad looked up from his desk. Matt could have sworn that Mr. Morgan was looking right at him.

Mr. Morgan looked back down at the ledger on his desk and Matt walked around to stand by his side. How was he going to get the ring out of the desk while Mr. Morgan was here? Before he could contemplate it further, Mr. Morgan opened the drawer in question and pulled out the ring.

"Looking for this?" he asked Matt.

Matt looked at him in surprise. "You know I'm here?"

Mr. Morgan smiled. "Yes, Matt. I know you're there. My wife and daughter don't know about my ability and I would like to keep it that way. After all, Cassie's isolation led her to you."

Matt wasn't sure what to say in response to that. He had always suspected that Cassie had inherited her gift from one of her parents, but neither had ever let on that they knew of his existence. What kind of dad allowed a strange guy to hang out in his daughter's room? Even if the guy in question *was* a ghost and the daughter was a full grown woman, it still didn't seem right.

"Why are you helping me?"

"Because I think you care about my daughter a great deal... This ring has more power than you realize. It will not only transport you to my daughter, but it also has the power to bring you to life again."

Matt became very excited at the prospect of being human again. Mr. Morgan looked him in the eye before continuing. "However, the change will be temporary."

"How temporary?"

"It will last for three days. That is, unless you can convince the woman you love to love you in return. Assuming that I'm correct in believing that you love my daughter, you must get her to confess her love for you within three days. Otherwise, you will return to being a ghost forever."

Matt swallowed hard. "I understand." He reached over and took the ring from Mr. Morgan. "Thank you for trusting me with your daughter."

Mr. Morgan smiled at Matt. "Son, you come from an era that even pre-dates mine. Men were different back then.

You are more likely to treat her right than any of the guys she'll meet in this day and age. Besides, I have a few other gifts my daughter doesn't have. Let's just say that I have a feeling things are going to turn out for the best."

Matt smiled back at him. "I promise to treat her like the princess she is, sir. If she loves me, I will spend the rest of my life showing her how much she means to me."

Matt slipped on the ring and thought of Cassie. When he next opened his eyes, he was in Cassie's bedroom at the cabin at Whispering Lake. The sight before him was a complete shock!

"Cassie! What are you doing?" Matt demanded.

Cole and Cassie both jumped up. As Cassie stood, she pulled her sweater down, embarrassment flooding her face.

"Who are you?" Cole demanded of the intruder.

"Matt?" Cassie whispered in surprised. Not only was she surprised that Matt was here in her room, but he was apparently human again since Cole could see him too.

Cole turned to look down at Cassie. "Matt? The same Matt that Kari mentioned? Why is he here in our cabin?"

Matt looked between Cole and Cassie. "Your cabin? As in, you're sharing one?"

This was going to be a lot harder than he had thought. He didn't realize that Cassie was seeing anyone. She had never mentioned anyone during their talks. He knew that he should be happy for her, but all he felt was anger and jealousy.

"Matt, it isn't the way it sounds. We're sharing a cabin, but we each have our own rooms. The reservation desk made the arrangements," Cassie explained, not entirely sure why she felt so guilty all of a sudden.

"Those separate bedrooms don't seem to be doing much good." Matt folded his arms over his chest. He knew that he had no right to feel jealous or disappointed, but that's exactly how he felt.

Cassie blushed and looked down at the floor. She had wanted Matt to be here with her more than anything, but she never wanted him to catch her in bed with a guy. Things may not have progressed very far, but she still felt like she had been caught in a compromising situation. Matt's opinion of her meant a lot. She hoped that he didn't think any less of her.

Gabriel had entered the cabin unnoticed and was standing behind Matt. "Ahem!"

All three of them jumped up and turned to find Gabriel in the bedroom doorway.

"Amber was getting worried about Cassie so I offered to come find you. I'm glad I left her at the lodge," he said with a questioning look at Matt.

Matt turned back toward Cassie. "Can we talk a minute? In private?"

Cassie looked at Cole and Gabriel. She knew they both had questions about Matt. Cole was probably wondering what her relationship with Matt was. Right now, she wasn't entirely sure of that answer herself. When Matt had shown up, she felt like she had been caught cheating on him, which made her really confused since the two of them had only ever been friends. It isn't like you can become romantically involved with a ghost.

"Would the two of you mind heading on without me? I need to talk to Matt for a minute," she said quietly.

Cole looked at Cassie with indecision written on his face. "If that's what you want. We'll meet you at the lodge when you're done."

Cole picked up his shirt and drew it over his head. The brothers turned and walked out of her room. A moment later, she heard the front door open and close and knew they were gone.

Cassie turned to face Matt. "How did you get here? And more importantly, how did you become human again?"

Matt went and sat on her bed. "I found something online about a special ring. When I saw the picture of it, I recognized it." He held his hand up so she could see the dragon ring.

Cassie walked over and took Matt's hand in hers. She looked at the ring and recognized it immediately. "This is my father's ring! It belonged to his father, who inherited it from his grandfather."

"I found it in your dad's desk drawer. When I slipped it on, I thought of you. The next thing I knew, I was standing in this room and saw you with ..." Matt stopped and looked down.

"You saw me with Cole," Cassie whispered.

"Yes," he said, continuing to look at the floor.

Cassie reached up and brushed Matt's hair back from his face. "I'm sorry you saw that. I don't know what came over me."

Matt looked up at her. With a gentle tug on her hand, she was sitting in his lap. "I know that I don't have any right to tell you who to kiss or how to act, but I have to admit that I didn't like seeing you with that guy. I didn't like seeing his hands on you, or yours on him."

Cassie was embarrassed. Before this trip, she hadn't really kissed anyone. Now she had made out with Cole on two separate occasions.

"Are you ashamed of me? For acting that way?" she asked.

Matt looked at her. "Cassie, I could never be ashamed of you. I was hurt and jealous, but I know that I don't have a right to feel those things. Until a few moments ago, I was nothing more than a ghost, and hopefully a friend, in your life. You deserve someone alive, someone you can love who can love you in return. I can't deny you any of those things if you think you can find it with that guy."

Cassie looked at Matt in surprise. "I had no idea you felt that way about me. I figured you probably thought of me as a pesky little sister."

Matt smiled down at her. "Cassie, you're beautiful and caring. You've been a wonderful friend to me. I would have given anything to be alive and be able to hold you like I am now. I can honestly say that any thoughts I've ever had of you were not brotherly."

"You hold me all the time when I'm upset. We sit together every day in my room. For that matter, we've slept in my bed together many times," Cassie pointed out.

"Yes, but I've done all of those things as a ghost and as your friend. Now I'm holding you not as a ghost, but as a man. A man who would very much like to do more than just hold you," he told her honestly.

Cassie could feel another blush creeping up her cheeks. She had always thought that Matt was a great guy and that he was very handsome. However, she had always known that nothing could ever happen between them because he was a ghost. Now that he was flesh and blood, things were different.

"I don't know what to say Matt. I have to admit that on more than one occasion I wished you were alive. I guess I'm a bit shocked at the moment," she said.

"Cassie, I have no right to ask this, but I'm going to anyway. Do you have feelings for the guy you were with when I arrived? Because if you do, then I'll walk out the door and leave you alone," Matt told her.

"I don't know. I thought that I did, but then you showed up. You know that I haven't been on very many dates, much less been in a serious relationship." Cassie sighed. "Honestly, I haven't been able to commit to anyone because they weren't you. Not to mention that it's kind of hard to explain to your boyfriend that you see ghosts."

"So you do have feelings for me?" Matt asked, his eyes full of hope.

"Yes. Very much," she replied softly.

"And what I walked in on?" he asked, uncertain that he really wanted to know her answer.

Cassie blushed. "Cole knew about my ability and accepted me as I am. I even told him I was a virgin and he promised to take things slowly. He's been really nice and hasn't just been trying to have sex with me."

"Looked to me like Cole was doing a pretty good job of getting you into bed," Matt replied with a raised eyebrow.

Cassie blushed so hard her whole face turned red. "It wasn't his fault. I actually instigated it."

Matt put his hand on her cheek. "Do you care for him? Or were you just curious what it would be like?"

Cassie looked at Matt. "I guess it was a little of both. He was really nice to me so I started to have feelings for him, but another part of me just wanted to know what it would be like to be with someone in that way. I've never felt anything like that before and got carried away. Since I knew I couldn't have you, I thought I'd see how things went with Cole. I knew I couldn't go forever without having someone to share my life with." Cassie looked back down at her lap. "You must think I'm a tramp, or whatever they called loose women back in your time."

Matt lifted Cassie's face so he could look her in the eye. "Cassie, I could never think of you that way. You were curious. If he knew that you were inexperienced, then he should have been more responsible."

"Is it impossible for you to think that I might be so desirable to another guy that he might lose control?" Cassie asked waspishly. Why couldn't he picture someone wanting to be with her like that?

"No, Cassie. It isn't unthinkable for a guy to find you that attractive, but he still should have had more control. In his place, I can't say that I would have fared much better, but I would have definitely tried to preserve your innocence. At the very least, if I couldn't keep my hands off of you, I would have asked you to marry me," he responded.

Cassie smiled at him. "You really are from a different era. Innocence isn't prized like it used to be."

"Just because it isn't prized doesn't mean it shouldn't be," Matt said.

Cassie threw her arms around Matt and hugged him. "I'm so glad you're here."

Matt smiled and hugged her back. "Me, too. Now, what are we going to tell your friends about me?"

"I don't suppose that you poofed yourself to Whispering Lake with a car in tow did you? It might make things easier as far as explaining *how* you got here."

Matt laughed at her. "Probably not."

"Then I guess we'll say that a friend dropped you off," Cassie said, trying to piece together a story.

"And what do we tell them about how we know each other? Aren't they going to be curious as to why they haven't seen me before?" Matt paused. "I imagine that Cole will especially have questions."

"We can say that you've been living between Ashton Grove and Whispering Lake. You knew that I was coming here with my friends and wanted to surprise me," she said.

"That could work. What if they ask about our relationship to each other? Do you want me to be a distant cousin or something?" Matt asked.

Cassie looked at him and thought for a moment. Now that Matt was by her side again, the past few days became clearer. She was so embarrassed over her behavior and how easily she had fallen into bed with Cole. She had already told Cole that she didn't have a boyfriend and as far as her friends knew she didn't have one.

"I don't think it would be appropriate to say you were a cousin." Cassie certainly didn't have cousin-like thoughts about Matt.

"And why is that?" he asked, his curiosity peaked.

"Because it might look odd if I were to do this in front of them..." Cassie bent her head and gently kissed Matt on the lips. It was a short kiss, but it lasted long enough for her to realize the difference in kissing Cole and kissing someone she loved.

Cassie sat up in shock. Loved? When had she decided that she loved Matt? She had always cared about him and thought of him as her very best friend, but since he was a ghost she had never thought of him romantically. Sure, she had daydreamed about what things might be like if he were alive, but that's all. She had never imagined that it could really happen. Well, okay, if she were *really* honest, she would admit to having fantasized about making love to him.

"I'm sorry. I shouldn't have done that." Cassie started to get up from Matt's lap, but he put his arms around her and held her in place.

"I'm glad you did," he told her quietly.

"You are?" Cassie asked hesitantly.

"Yes, Cassie. I'm very glad. I've often wondered what it would be like to kiss you," Matt replied.

Cassie could not have been more surprised. "You have?"

Matt smiled down at her. "Yes, Cassandra."

Cassie looked at him a moment. She quickly made her decision about what to tell her friends. "Would you mind if I told them you were my boyfriend?"

"Your older boyfriend from out of town whom they know nothing about? Won't that seem a little odd to Amber and Kari? Especially since you don't have a picture of me in your room," he asked practically. Not that he wasn't thrilled with the idea, but he wanted their story to be believable.

"Probably, but I'm sure I can think of a way to explain it." Cassie realized he hadn't said no to the possibility of being her boyfriend. Well, pretending to be her boyfriend. "Wait, does that mean you wouldn't mind me telling them that?"

"No, Cassandra. I don't mind if you tell them that I'm your boyfriend. Just remember that you may have some extra explaining to do with Cole," he gently reminded her.

"Especially since I told him that I didn't have a boyfriend," she said with a grimace.

Matt thought a moment. "We can always say that we argued before your trip. I felt bad about it and came here to make up with you."

"There is one other problem," she told him.

Looking down at her he asked, "What's that?"

"Well, two actually. The first is that there aren't any other cabins at the lake that are available. The second is that you could change back into a ghost at any moment," she said.

"I have at least three days to be human. As to the other, if we've been dating for at least the past year, we could tell them that I will be staying with you," Matt responded, answering her problem with an easy solution.

"In my room?" she squeaked.

"Wouldn't be the first time we've shared a bed," Matt said, seeming to have an answer for everything.

"True. Granted, you were a ghost last time," Cassie reminded him.

"Yes, but you could touch me even then," he said with a grin.

Cassie nodded. It seemed logical. "Okay. Let's head over to the lodge. I'm sure they'll have a ton of questions, but I'm sure we can muddle through it."

Cassie started to get up, but Matt held her in place. He slowly lowered his head to hers and claimed her lips in a gentle kiss. Taking her chin between his fingers, he deepened the kiss. Neither he nor Cassie were prepared for the tidal wave of emotions that hit them.

Matt lifted his head and looked into Cassie's eyes. He brushed her hair from her face and lightly trailed his fingers down her cheek. Before they got carried away, he stood and helped her to her feet. They left her bedroom and headed out of the cabin. On the way to the lodge, Matt took her hand in his. Cassie looked up at him in surprise.

"I figured we should get into character."

"Right. Good thinking," she replied, a little breathless from the close contact.

Cassie felt as if her whole body were on fire. She had always had feelings for Matt, but after kissing him things were different. She had to keep reminding herself that they were only acting as boyfriend and girlfriend and were not actually dating. It was going to be a hard thing to remember for the next three days. She wished more than anything that Matt could remain human for the rest of their lives, but apparently that wasn't to be.

Cassie tried not to think about her new sleeping arrangements. The prospect of sharing a bed with Matt was exciting and daunting. What if she decided she *was* ready for something more? She knew without a doubt that she wanted Matt to be the one who took her virginity. They had known each other for years and Cassie knew how gentle and caring Matt was. She also knew that it would be tough to convince him that he wasn't taking something from her because of his old fashioned beliefs. She would have to work hard to prove to him that he was only taking what was rightfully his. If she couldn't have forever with him, she wanted this to be the best three days of her life.

Before they entered the lodge, she needed to get her thoughts out of the bedroom. She glanced at Matt out of the corner of her eye. He seemed completely at ease with the situation. Holding hands with him felt natural, but it made her wonder what it would feel like to have his hands elsewhere.

Cassie could tell she was going to have work really hard at keeping her thoughts neutral. Was he having the same problem? Cassie snuck a look at Matt, but he was looking straight ahead. Apparently he wasn't having the same issue that she was.

Chapter Ten

When they arrived at the lodge, they didn't see Cole, Gabriel or Amber waiting out front. Assuming they had gone inside, Matt held the door open for Cassie. They entered the dining area together and spotted the small group at a table in the corner.

Cassie spoke first. "May we join you?"

Cole looked from her to Matt and back again. "Sure. We decided to eat here instead of going into town for breakfast."

"That's probably for the best." Cassie looked from Cole to Gabriel and finally at Amber.

"There's someone I'd like for all of you to meet. I was pretty surprised to see him today when he came to the cabin." She tipped her head back to look at Matt, who had walked up behind her and placed a hand on her shoulder. Matt squeezed her shoulder in encouragement.

"Everyone, this is Matt. Matthew Spencer." Cassie took a breath and dropped the final bomb on her friends, "Matt's my boyfriend."

Cole regarded her in astonishment. "I thought you said you didn't have a boyfriend?"

"I did. I mean, I did say that I didn't have one. And I didn't, or at least I thought I didn't," Cassie rambled. This was more difficult than she thought.

Cassie was really bungling this. She looked at Matt for help. He always seemed to know exactly what to say.

"What Cassie means to say is that we had an argument before she left for Whispering Lake. We both said stuff we didn't mean and said that we didn't want to be together anymore." He paused and looked down at Cassie for effect.

"I haven't been able to sleep very well since our last conversation. I only live an hour from here and thought I would come by and surprise Cassie. I wanted to apologize to her and hoped that we could mend our fences." Matt looked at everyone, finally letting his gaze rest on Cole. "Needless to say I was a little surprised when I found Cassie with someone else."

"Matt." Cassie reached up and put her hand on his in warning.

He was taking his role a little too far. If she didn't know better, she would have sworn he wasn't pretending. He was acting exactly like a jealous boyfriend.

Matt looked down at Cassie and back at Cole. "Sorry."

Cole stood to face Matt. "It's okay. I probably would have felt the same way if I were in your shoes."

Matt reached out and shook Cole's hand. "No hard feelings?"

"Sure, no hard feelings."

Amber couldn't contain her curiosity another moment. "Cassie, would you come help me with my hair? Maybe the guys could get to know one another better and place our orders. I already told Gabriel what I wanted for lunch, do you know what you want to eat?"

"Matt can pick something for me. You don't mind do you, honey?" Cassie asked, looking up at him with adoring eyes. She was going to enjoy the next three days regardless of what happened afterward.

"Not at all," Matt replied.

He sat down at the table and picked up a menu. After having spent so much time with her over the past several years, he knew her pretty well and felt pretty confident that he could choose something she would like. He had also enjoyed hearing her call him 'honey.'

The girls left and headed to the bathroom. When they were sure that no one else was in there, Amber locked the door and turned to face Cassie. "Okay, spill it."

Cassie looked at her innocently. "Spill what?"

"You know what! As far as I know, you've never had a serious boyfriend in your life! So who is this guy and where did he come from?" Amber asked, not quite sure what her friend was up to. Why was she throwing away her chance with Cole?

"We've actually been dating for quite a while. I just don't talk about him much and only get to see him a few times a year. He lives between here and Ashton Grove in a small town. Our dads are friends and introduced us a few years ago," Cassie explained.

"You've been dating someone and didn't tell me?" Amber asked shocked at Cassie's explanation.

"I'm really sorry. I just didn't want everyone to know. He's almost six years older than I am and I knew it would look bad to everyone else... especially since we've been dating for a long time. I knew that they wouldn't understand."

"Okay. So what he said was true about your argument and everything?" Amber looked at her skeptically.

"Yes. We talked on the phone the day before our trip. We ended up arguing and I told him that I didn't want to see him anymore. I hung up on him and wouldn't answer the phone when he called back." Cassie paused and looked down at the floor, as if ashamed of her actions. "I realize that was really juvenile, but I was upset and not thinking straight."

"How do you feel now that he's here?" Amber asked gently, starting to believe her friend's story.

"I don't know. I was really surprised at first, but now I guess I'm happy to see him. I was so embarrassed when he showed up at the cabin. Even though we had said we were through, I still felt like I had been caught cheating on him," Cassie said.

"Cheating on him? What exactly *were* you doing when he showed up?" she asked, extremely intrigued.

Cassie blushed. "Cole sort of had his shirt off and he'd pushed mine up over my bra. We were kissing and touching, and... did I mention we were on my bed?"

"Oh my!" Amber's eyes were huge. "No wonder he made that comment to Cole!"

"I know. I'm so ashamed of myself," Cassie whispered. "I know that it isn't a big deal these days, but it just isn't like me to act like that. I don't know what's come over me, but I can't seem to shut it off."

"Are y'all back together now?"

"We talked after Cole left the cabin. I think that things are okay with us now. At least, I hope they are." Cassie looked at Amber. "I think I love him."

"Are you serious?" Amber was surprised to say the least. Especially since Cassie had never mentioned Matt to her before. Something just didn't seem quite right.

"Yes," Cassie replied.

"Wow! So what does this mean for you and Cole? He seems to really like you."

Cassie sighed. "I know he does and I thought I felt the same way about him, but then I saw Matt and I felt ashamed. I hadn't seen Matt in a while and I guess I had forgotten how I really felt. When I saw him, it was almost like being hit by an emotional tidal wave." Cassie looked at Amber. "You should have seen his face when he came in my room. I have never seen him look like that before. He looked so hurt!"

Amber could feel Cassie's anguish. She hugged her friend. "I'm sure that everything will be fine Cass."

"We should probably head back out," Cassie said, heading for the door.

The girls unlocked the door and headed back out to the dining area. When they arrived at the table, the guys seemed to be getting along pretty well. At least, no one appeared harmed and they seemed to be having a civilized conversation.

"Miss us?" Cassie asked as they approached the table.

Matt stood when he saw Cassie. He pulled out her chair for her. "Always."

He smiled down at her. As he pushed her chair in, he bent down and placed a kiss on her cheek. Hopefully he wasn't over playing his hand. It wouldn't do to have everyone questioning their relationship. Well, questioning it more than they already were. Having a non-existent boyfriend pop up in the middle of your vacation was a hard one to explain.

Cassie could really get used to this. She was in absolute heaven. It didn't seem fair that she would only have Matt in her life for three days. She wished it could last longer.

"Thank you." She smiled up at him.

By the time the girls were seated again, their food arrived. When Cassie saw her plate, she knew she was in love. Matt had ordered her a thick turkey sandwich with melted cheddar and swiss and a side of fries. It was one of her favorites. Peeking under the top of the sandwich, she saw he'd asked for her favorite mustard too.

When the waiter had finished placing everyone's plates in front of them, he addressed Cassie. "When you're done miss, just let me know and I'll bring your dessert out."

"Thank you." She looked over at Matt questioningly. "Dessert?"

"They have homemade chocolate pie ala mode. I figured you would want a slice," he said with a grin.

She smiled at him. "It's perfect."

After seeing Cassie and Matt together, Cole realized that they were perfect for each other. They made a nice looking couple and seemed to know what each other liked. So far Matt had been a perfect gentleman around Cassie. Cole figured he must have been mistaken about Cassie being his mate. It was obvious that she was in love with Matt.

As they were eating, everyone talked about their plans for the rest of the day and the next. Gabriel suggested they go fishing that afternoon. Everyone was in agreement, except Matt. "I'm not trying to be antisocial or anything. I was just hoping to spend some quality time with Cassie this afternoon. I've been so busy with work that I haven't been able to spend as much time with her the past few months as I would have liked."

He looked at Cassie. "I plan on making that up to you, if you'll let me."

"I'd like that." Cassie smiled at him.

She looked at her friends, "Would y'all mind if we met up with you around dinner tonight?"

"Not at all. You two go have fun." Gabriel looked at Matt. "When do you have to leave?"

"I thought I'd stay for a few days. If that's okay with Cassie..." he asked, looking down at her.

"It's fine with me, but I wish you could stay for the rest of the trip," Cassie replied wistfully.

Cole looked at them. "If you need a room Matt, I'm sure that I could bunk with one of my brothers."

Matt looked at him with respect. "Thank you, but that won't be necessary. It won't be the first time that Cassie and I have slept in the same bed."

Cassie blushed. "He didn't mean that the way it sounded. He meant that we have literally slept in the same bed before, not that we had done anything else."

Matt quickly realized his error. "Sorry, I should have clarified that. I didn't mean to embarrass you Cassie."

"It's okay Matt." She reached over and took his hand in her own. "I know you didn't mean for it to sound that way."

Gabriel decided to interrupt the awkward moment. "Does six o'clock sound okay for dinner? We could all meet out front on the steps."

"That would be fine with us." Cassie was thankful for the save.

Cole and Amber both agreed on the time as well. They all got up and paid for their meals. Cassie would ask Matt later about the money he had in his wallet. She found it odd that a guy who had been dead for fifty years would have current money in his wallet. Amber, Gabriel and Cole left the lodge together and headed for the lake.

Matt took Cassie's hand and led her toward the woods. "I thought my little Druid might enjoy some time in nature."

"That sounds wonderful," she said with a smile.

As they walked past the cabin, Matt glanced over and saw a guy standing on the porch. "Is that a friend of yours?"

Cassie looked towards the cabin to see who he meant. When she saw Michael on the porch, she instinctively moved closer to Matt. "No, that isn't one of my friends. That's Cole's twin brother, Michael. He isn't very nice."

Deciding to be completely honest with him, she told Matt what had happened. "Actually, shortly after we got here, he sort of took advantage of me. He had me pushed up against a wall and was kissing me. Thankfully Cole showed up and pulled him off of me before he could do worse. If Cole hadn't been there, I don't know what would have happened."

Matt pulled her into his arms. "Would you like for me to get rid of him?"

Cassie wrapped her arms around Matt and snuggled into him. "No, let's just ignore him and go on our hike."

"Whatever you want." Matt kissed her forehead and took her by the hand. "Let's go."

They continued down the trail and into the woods. They hadn't been walking long when Matt stopped and turned toward Cassie. "Cassie, you know that if you don't want me to be here that I'll go, right?"

"Why wouldn't I want you to be here?" she asked in confusion.

"I just know that you haven't dated anyone more than once or twice for as long as I've known you. It seems like you have someone here who is really interested in you. If

I'm in your way, just tell me and I'll leave." It killed Matt to say that, but he meant it. If he thought Cassie would be happier without him around, he would leave.

"No, Matt. I don't want you to leave. Don't you understand?"

"Understand what?" he asked.

"That you're the guy I want to be with, you're the one I want to have interested in me." She looked into his eyes. "When you showed up in my room earlier and I realized you were human again, that was the happiest moment in my life. Your timing could have been a little better, but aside from that I was very happy to see you," she said wryly.

Matt smiled at her. "I'm glad to hear that." He lifted her hand and kissed the back of it. "Do you have any idea just how special you are?"

"Why, because I can talk to ghosts?"

"No, because you're you. There isn't another woman anywhere in the world like you Cassandra. Past or present," Matt gave her a smoky look. If he weren't a gentleman, he would drag her back to the cabin and show her just how desirable she was.

Cassie was starting to get that warm tingly feeling again. As usual, Matt knew just what to say. "I bet you used to say that to all of your women."

Matt's face turned serious. "There's never been anyone like you and there never will be. If you weren't so young and things were different, I would ask you to marry me. As it is, you haven't finished college yet, and technically I'm old enough to be your grandfather."

Cassie was so shocked you could have knocked her over with a feather. "Marry you?"

Matt blushed. "I said if things were different. Obviously I don't have the right to ask that question."

Cassie looked at him in wonder. "What if things *were* different? Who said you have to go in three days?"

"It's part of what I read Cassie," he replied evasively.

Cassie looked down at the ring on his finger. "I wish I had my laptop with me so I could find a way to keep you with me forever."

Matt looked at her intently. "What would you do to keep me here?"

"Anything." Cassie looked into his eyes.

Cassie decided it was time to tell him how she felt. Even if he were only human for a few days, she felt he had a right to know. "I need to tell you something…"

Before she could finish her sentence, they heard a rustling noise behind them. As they turned, they saw Michael coming up the path. Cassie took a step back and backed into Matt. He put his arms around her and kissed the top of her head.

"You sure do move fast Cassie, for someone who isn't interested in sex that is," Michael said as he walked toward them.

"I never said I wasn't interested in sex, Michael. I just said that I didn't sleep around," Cassie clarified. After all, when Matt was involved, she was definitely interested in sex.

"Then why did you hop from my brother to this guy so fast," he asked her.

Matt couldn't believe the way Michael was speaking to Cassie. If he had ever spoken to a lady that way, his father would have taken it out of his hide. "You should watch how you speak to her."

"And who are you to tell me how I should talk to Cassie?" Michael demanded.

"Her boyfriend," Matt replied with steel in his voice. Between Michael's attitude and what Cassie had told him, he would love nothing more than to punch him.

"Excuse me?" Michael figured he must have heard the guy wrong. After all, Cassie had told them she didn't have a boyfriend.

"You heard me. I'm her boyfriend," Matt repeated.

Michael looked like he didn't believe him. "If she had a boyfriend, then what was she doing making out with my brother?"

"It's a long story. The short version is that we argued before the trip and broke up. I came up here to make up with her. We're back together now and that's all that matters," Matt told him.

Michael looked at Cassie. "Is that true? You've been dating this guy?"

"Yes. Matt and I have been together for quite a while," Cassie said, not quite sure why she felt the need to justify her relationship with Matt.

Michael's jaw tightened. Something wasn't right, but he wasn't sure what it was. "So does Cole know about your good fortune? Has he met your boyfriend?"

"Yes, he has. We actually had breakfast this morning with Cole, Gabriel and Amber," Cassie responded. What was it going to take for Michael to leave? Why the interest in her love life?

Michael looked at the two of them. They seemed so at ease with each other that he had no choice but to believe their story. He wasn't sure if Cassie was telling the truth, but if Cole was okay with it then so was he. His werewolf senses weren't picking up on anything. Normally he could tell if someone was lying to him.

Figuring something was fishy, Michael decided to probe a little further. "So what am I interrupting? You two looked pretty cozy before I walked up."

Matt looked him in the eyes. "I don't think that's any of your business."

Michael ignored him. He continued questioning Cassie relentlessly, "How long have you two been together?"

"Three years," she responded promptly.

"Isn't he a little old for you to have been dating for three years? You would have been what? Nineteen?"

Michael paused and looked at Matt. "He looks quite a bit older than you. Just how much older is he anyway?"

"I'm twenty-seven. There is five and a half years between us, but I love her regardless of the age difference." Matt realized what he had said the moment the words left his mouth. He hadn't meant to say that he loved Cassie.

Cassie turned to face Matt. She looked up into his eyes and saw that he spoke the truth. He really did love her. "You love me?"

Matt trailed his fingers down her cheek. "I love you very much. I only wish I had told you sooner."

Cassie smiled at him, "I love you too."

There was a flash of red from the dragon ring on Matt's hand. Cassie looked at it in surprise. When she looked back at Matt, he was grinning from ear to ear. "You have no idea how happy I am to hear that."

"What was that?" Michael had seen the flash, but he couldn't tell where it had come from.

"Just the light reflecting off my ring." Matt showed him the dragon ring.

"Cool ring." Michael though something a little off about it, but he couldn't figure out what. He could have sworn he'd seen it somewhere before. Maybe it would come to him later.

"Thanks," Matt said, hoping Michael would leave.

"Michael, would you excuse us? I want to walk a little further before we have to turn back for dinner," Cassie said.

"Sure, I'll leave you two alone." Michael turned and headed back down the trail, deep in thought.

He knew he'd seen that ring before. Heading to the lodge, he decided to do some digging. Hopefully turning down a date from his waitress the other night wouldn't come back to bite him in the butt. If he wasn't able to use a computer at the lodge, he'd have to head into town and see if the local library had one.

Cassie looked up at Matt. "What did it mean when the ring flashed like that?"

"It means that I get to stay," Matt told her with a smile.

"You mean you'll be here longer than three days?" Cassie asked.

"It means that I get to stay human, Cassie. I get to stay with you," he told her gently. He hoped she would think this was good news.

"But, why? How do you know?" Cassie asked, slightly stunned.

Did she dare hope it was true? Nothing could make her happier, but it sounded too good to be true. What exactly would this mean for them? For Matt in particular? Not having been alive for a while, he didn't have a birth certificate or any other documents he would need to survive in today's world. Not to mention a place to live, a job ... it was a lot to think about.

"I wasn't entirely honest with you before. I didn't just find this ring in your dad's desk drawer." Matt took a breath, not really wanting to continue. "He gave it to me."

"Gave it to you? But how? He can't see you," Cassie said in confusion.

Matt gave her a tortured look. He didn't want to lie to Cassie, but he hated to break her father's trust as well. It was one of those damned if you and damned if you don't scenarios.

"He didn't want you to know. Somehow he knew that we would meet. For some reason, if you knew that your dad could see ghosts too, then we wouldn't have ended up together. I'm not sure I completely understand it myself.

He only explained it briefly." Matt paused a moment before continuing.

"I went down to your father's study after I found the internet article about the dragon ring. I walked around the desk and was contemplating how to get the ring while he was sitting there. I figured he would notice a drawer opening by itself. Next thing I knew, he opened the drawer and handed the ring to me." He stopped and looked at her face. She looked stunned and a little sad, but he knew he had to continue.

"He didn't want me to tell you about his ability. He mentioned something about not being able to tell you or we wouldn't have met. Your father seemed happy about the idea of us being together if that's any consolation."

"Why wouldn't he tell me he could see you? All this time I've felt like a freak," Cassie wondered, a little hurt by her father's actions.

"You're not a freak Cassie. Your special, but you could never be a freak," Matt responded vehemently. He hated when she talked about her gift that way.

Cassie looked up at Matt. "He really gave you the ring and said all of that? About us meeting?"

"Yes. He also told me about the ring's ability to make me human. I hadn't read that part in the article. The ring will transport a ghost to the location of someone he or she loves. It will also make the ghost human for three days. If the person he or she loves confesses their own love within three days, then the change is permanent." He paused to judge her reaction. She looked hurt and confused. "I wanted to tell you, but I was afraid that you would say you loved me just to keep me human. I'm sorry I lied to you Cassie. I promise that I will never lie to you again."

Cassie looked overwhelmed. "It's a bit much to take in. I don't know what to say."

"Do you still love me?" Matt asked, almost afraid of her answer.

Cassie put her hand against his cheek. "Of course I still love you. You have no idea how happy it makes me that we'll get to spend the rest of our lives together... that is, if you meant what you said about marrying me. Or were you just saying that because it couldn't happen while you were a ghost?"

"I don't have the right to ask for your hand in marriage Cassie. I don't have a ring, a job or a place to live for that matter. It wouldn't be right for me to ask you to share a life that doesn't exist at the moment. Besides, we may have known each other for a long time, but the idea of having a relationship outside of friendship is still new to both of us. I think we need to spend some time getting to know one another as a man and a woman, and not just friends," Matt responded practically. In all honesty, the thought of marrying Cassie was wonderful. He couldn't think of anything he would like more.

"I would love nothing better than to get to know you. I love you Matt. Not only as a friend, but as a woman loves a man. I think I always have," she said with a smile.

Matt leaned down and gently kissed her. "I don't deserve you Cassie."

Cassie smiled up at him. "Yes, you do. Let's go back to the cabin and figure out how we're getting you home in a few days. Our trip is half way over and I don't know if Amber and Kari will let you ride back with us or not."

They walked back to the cabin in silence. When they opened the door to the cabin, it was dead quiet. The brothers must still be out. Cassie wasn't going to complain. She was looking forward to spending some one on one time with Matt.

"Do you want to watch a movie or something? I'm afraid there isn't a lot to do at the cabin," Cassie said as she walked into the living room.

Matt didn't care what they did as long as he was able to spend time with Cassie. "A movie would be fine. Why don't you pick something out?"

Cassie moved over to the DVD shelf. She was in a rather romantic mood, so she chose *Sweet Home Alabama*. She had seen it with Matt before, but this time she felt they would watch it together with new eyes. If she was lucky, maybe it would set the mood for romance. Her two kisses with Matt today had been brief. She wanted to know what it would be like to *really* kiss him.

Cassie sat on the couch next to Matt. As the movie started, she got as close to him as she could. Matt looked down at her and smiled. If only he knew what she had planned for him! Cassie took his hand and focused on the movie.

Even though they both knew what happened in the movie, neither of them took their eyes off the TV. Cassie rested her head on Matt's shoulder and he put his arm around her shoulders. They stayed like that until the movie ended.

"I really love that movie." Cassie couldn't resist a happy ending. And now it was starting to look like she might get hers after all.

Matt looked down at Cassie. "I enjoyed it, too." He bent his head and kissed her on the mouth. Just as Cassie leaned into the kiss, Matt pulled back. "Easy Cassie. It isn't a race."

"I know. I just love kissing you," she told him.

Matt smiled at her. Before he could kiss her again, there was a knock at the door. Cassie figured it wasn't the brothers since it was their cabin, too. She got up to answer the door and received the second largest shock of the day.

"Dad! What are you doing here?" Cassie asked in surprise.

"I came to check on you and Matt. I wanted to see how things were going," he said, peering around her into the cabin.

"Everything's fine, Dad. We're fine." Cassie stepped back to allow her dad to enter the cabin.

Mr. Morgan stepped inside and smiled at them. "I'm glad to hear that things worked out."

"Daddy, why didn't you tell me that you could see ghosts?" Cassie asked.

"I had a dream when you were little. In the dream, you were a teenager and met a handsome young ghost. The two of you fell in love with each other. A few nights later, I had another dream. This time, I told you about my gift and when Matt came into your life the two of you didn't grow close and didn't fall in love. Since you had someone you could share your gift with, you just treated him as another ghost instead of your friend. I knew that if I told you I could see ghosts, you would never get close to Matt. Not like you would if you felt alone. It was the hardest decision I've ever made. It's been torture watching you hide who you really are from me," her father said.

Her dad regarded her with sad eyes. "It's been lonely for me, too. I've never told your mother about any of this."

"I'm glad you made that decision, Dad. It was the best thing you could have done for me. I'm in love with Matt, but we have another problem," Cassie told him.

"I'm sure it's something we can overcome," he said with a smile.

"Matt doesn't have a birth certificate, diploma, job, or house. How do we get him all of the legal documents he needs to survive in this day and age?" Cassie asked in a rush.

"I actually have a friend who can help with some of that and already have answers to the rest." Mr. Morgan looked at Matt. "Did you have a college degree and a job when you died?"

"Yes, sir. I had a degree in architecture and was one of the top designers in the southern part of Georgia. Although, I'm sure the field has changed a great deal since then. I probably wouldn't know the first thing about architecture today," Matt answered.

"Yes, I imagine it has changed. Let me worry about the details. I have a friend with special gifts like mine and Cassie's who happens to be an architect. I can set up training sessions with him if you'd like. He can show you anything that's different from when you were alive. You seem pretty handy with a computer so maybe you can pick up the software pretty quickly. I doubt the math has changed," Mr. Morgan replied.

"That would be wonderful Mr. Morgan, but I really hate to impose." Matt figured that Cassie's father had already done enough for him. It wasn't every day you got a second chance at life… especially when it was fifty years into the future.

"Nonsense." Mr. Morgan smiled at them. "Besides, I'm hoping you'll be part of the family before too long."

Cassie blushed. "Dad!"

"What honey? A father can't be happy that his only child has found such a wonderful young man? I'm surprised he hasn't already asked you to marry him," he said with a raised eyebrow in Matt's direction, as if to ask what was taking so long.

"We actually did discuss it sir, but as I explained to Cassie I don't have the right to ask her something like that without a job, a house or a ring," Matt explained. "I can't ask her to spend the rest of her life with me when I don't have any idea where it's going to take me."

Mr. Morgan pulled a ring out of his pocket. "You mean a ring like this?"

"I can't accept that, sir. It wouldn't be right to offer Cassie a ring that was paid for her by her father." Matt was touched by Mr. Morgan's generosity, but his pride wouldn't allow him to accept that much of a handout. It was bad enough that he would have to rely on someone else to teach him how to do his job again.

"It wasn't. It's a family heirloom that belonged to Cassie's great-grandma. I always planned on giving it to Cassie's boyfriend when he decided to propose. That just happens to be you, or at least I'm hoping it's going to be you," he said, handing the ring to Matt.

Matt reached over and took the ring from Mr. Morgan. "Thank you, sir. This means more to me than I can say, but I still can't ask her to marry me without first having a job and a house of my own."

"You'll have a job within a few months and you can have a house now if you want. I have a small house on Burberry Street in Ashton Grove that I was holding onto. It was my mother's house. I've done a lot of repairs on it so it should be ready to live in. It's even furnished. Well, mostly furnished," he replied.

"That's very generous of you, sir, but ..." Mr. Morgan stopped him before he could finish his sentence.

"No buts. Consider it an early wedding present." He looked at his daughter and back at Matt. "Besides, my little girl will eventually live there, too."

Cassie looked at her father in amazement. Within half an hour, he had solved all but one of their problems. "Thank you, Daddy."

"You're welcome, sweetheart. It's the least I can do. I know I can never take away the hurt you must have felt growing up, feeling like you were all alone with this strange ability. The least I can do is try to make your future a little easier," he told her with a sad smile.

"Mr. Morgan, I hate to ask you for anything else, but we have one more problem," Matt said.

Stan Morgan looked at his future son-in-law, or so he hoped, "What's that son?"

"Cassie's trip is over in a few days. The dragon ring brought me here, but I don't have a way back," Matt answered.

"Sure you do. I had a friend follow me up here. There's a 1964 red mustang in front of the lodge. I already had the papers put in your name." Mr. Morgan placed the keys in his hand. "I had bought her for Cassie when she was younger and fixed her up, but Cassie really had her heart set on that Jetta when she got her license. I didn't have the heart to say no to her. Although I must say that I never could understand what she saw in that car. Would *you* have turned down a vintage mustang?"

"No, sir. I don't expect I have would have." Matt shook Mr. Morgan's hand. "I don't know how I will ever repay you, sir, but I'll find a way."

"You already have by making my little girl happy. Now, I'm going to leave you two alone. I believe you have more important things to discuss than to sit here talking to an old man," he said with a smile.

He started to turn away and paused a moment. "Before I forget, I also had someone draw these up for you."

Mr. Morgan pulled an envelope out of his jacket pocket and handed it to Matt. He had friends with the FBI, CIA and other government branches. While he typically didn't ask for favors, these friends had gifts similar to his and Cassie's. He had explained the situation to them and had already come up with a birth certificate and social security card for Matt.

Cassie smiled at her dad and gave him a hug before he left. "I'll see you at the end of the week, Daddy."

"Enjoy your trip, Cassie." Her father smiled at her as he left the cabin.

"Your father is a really great guy," Matt said, opening the envelope.

"Yes, he is," Cassie said with a smile.

"Wow! You're father is not only great, but an amazing guy!"

Cassie tried to see what was in Matt's hand. "What is it?"

Matt smiled at her. "A birth certificate and social security card."

Cassie smiled. "Guess Daddy was a little ahead of us today."

Matt looked at the ring in his hand. "It seems that I have a ring, a car, a house and a possible job. I still think we should get to know one another a little better." Matt looked at her. "But I *will* propose to you before too long. I want to know that you're going to be mine for the rest of my life. My second one that is."

Cassie smiled. "I'm already yours. The ring will just be a formality."

Matt went to Cassie's room and placed the ring in her top dresser drawer. He didn't want to take a chance on the two-carat diamond ring getting lost. When Matt returned to the living room, he hugged her to him and inhaled her scent of lavender. That scent would always remind him of Cassie and of this trip.

"There's one other thing we need to talk about Cassie," he told her, his voice serious once more.

"What is it?" she asked.

"I know we've shared a bed before without anything happening, but I want to make it clear that I don't expect anything from you. I'm still planning on sleeping with you, but that is *all* that we will be doing. People may act differently now than they did when I was born, but I still believe in a woman being a virgin when she's married," he told her.

"I understand, Matt, and I respect you for that. I'm glad that nothing happened between me and Cole because I want you to be my first," Cassie replied with a shy smile and slight blush.

"Nothing would make me happier, just as long as you understand our first time together will be our wedding night. I mean it Cassie. I want our wedding night to be special," Matt said. He had a feeling that Cassie had other plans.

"I understand Matt. But I can honestly say that whether I was a virgin or not, our wedding night would still be special. It would still be the first night of our married lives," she replied.

"We still have three hours before we're meeting your friends. What would you like to do?" he asked.

"I'm a little tired. Would you mind if we just watched a movie and hung out here for a while?"

"That's perfectly fine with me. Why don't you select another movie while I go check out the car your dad left for me," he said.

"Okay. Hurry back," Cassie smiled at him.

He bent to kiss her cheek. "I will."

Matt left the cabin and Cassie walked over to the shelves of DVDs. She was tired enough that she would probably fall asleep no matter what movie they watched. She was about to give up on finding anything when she noticed an older movie starring James Dean called *Rebel Without A Cause*. Cassie figured that it would have come out around the time Matt had died. She put the DVD in the player and got it set up.

While she waited on Matt to return, she decided to freshen up a little. She went into the bathroom and brushed her teeth and her hair. She returned to the living room and was about to sit down when the front door opened. Matt came in carrying a duffle bag.

"Where did you get that?" Cassie asked him.

"Apparently your dad thought of everything. How he knew what size I wear I will never know. He packed a toothbrush, razor, and other bathroom items along with a few changes of clothes and some pajama pants."

Cassie's eyes widened at that bit of news. "I'm sorry, did you say pants? As in only the pants?"

Matt looked at her. "I'm afraid so. I think your dad was planning on playing matchmaker."

"Obviously." Cassie looked at the floor. Wow, Matt in her bed with nothing but pajama pants on. There was no way she was keeping her hands to herself!

Matt went over to her and placed his bag on the floor. He lifted her face. "If you don't feel comfortable sharing a bed with me, I can always camp out on the couch or make a pallet on the bedroom floor."

"No! It isn't that."

"Then what's wrong?" he asked.

Cassie looked at him incredulously. "You honestly don't know? Think about it Matt. You in nothing but pajama pants, me in my pajamas and us sharing a bed together. I'm not sure I can be a good girl like I promised."

Matt threw his head back and laughed. "Don't worry Cassie. I won't let you do anything you shouldn't."

Cassie sighed. "Part of me was afraid you would say that."

Matt smiled at her. "I love you."

"I love you, too. Why don't you get comfy on the couch and I'll go put your stuff away," Cassie said.

"Already acting like a wife and we aren't even engaged yet," he said affectionately.

"Well, don't get used to it. I'm planning on you putting your own clothes away at least part of the time," she told him.

Matt grinned at her. "I won't have a problem with that."

Cassie picked up the bag and went into their bedroom. She smiled just thinking of it being *their* bedroom. She put his neatly folded clothes in an empty dresser drawer and headed to the bathroom to put his toiletries away. Matt smiled at her as she walked through the living room.

"Almost done. Just let me put these things away and I'll be ready to watch the movie with you," she said as she walked into the bathroom.

"Okay. I'm waiting to start the movie so you won't miss anything," he replied.

Cassie put Matt's razor, shaving cream, and aftershave in the cabinet next to her makeup bag. She placed his brush and toothbrush next to hers on the counter and put his shampoo and shower gel in the shower. She took the empty bag back to their room and placed it on the floor by the dresser.

When Cassie entered the living room, Matt held his hand out to her. "Want to sit by me?"

"I'd love to." As she sat beside him, she leaned over and kissed him on the cheek. "Do you have any idea how happy you've made me?"

"Hopefully half as happy as you've made me." Matt smiled at her. "Ready to start the movie?"

"Sure. I chose it because... well, it was made in the nineteen-fifties."

"It actually came out right after I died. I never got a chance to see it, but I had looked forward to it going to the theatres. Thank you for selecting it today," he said with a smile.

Cassie smiled at him and laid her head on his shoulder. "Matt?"

"Yes, Cassie?"

"I know you don't want to make love to me until we're married, but I was just wondering about something."

"What's that?" he asked, looking down at her.

"Well, you're going to have a house all to yourself. Would you mind terribly if I sort of moved into it, too?"

Matt was quiet for a minute. "Do you have any idea how many bedrooms the house has?"

Cassie picked her head up off of his shoulder to look at him. Did he actual expect her to sleep in a different room?

"Three I think, but Daddy had been working on the attic. I think he was adding a master suite up there."

Matt nodded. "If your parents don't have an issue with it, then I don't see a problem. As long as you sleep in a separate bedroom until we're married."

Cassie sighed. "I guess I can agree to that."

Matt smiled as Cassie rested her head on his shoulder again. He knew that she found his ideas out-dated, but he would treat her with respect... even if it killed him. They sat in silence and watched the movie. About part way through, Cassie fell asleep. She'd had a very emotional day and needed the rest.

Matt had his arm around her and pulled her snuggly against his side to keep her from falling. He had a hard time believing that just that morning he had been a ghost with no hope of a future and this afternoon he was sitting on the couch with a beautiful woman by his side... not just any woman, but the woman that he loved. Life was definitely wonderful.

As the movie was ending, the front door opened and Cole stepped in. "I'm not interrupting am I?"

"Not at all. I'd get up, but Cassie fell asleep and I don't want to wake her."

Cole walked around the front of the couch and sat on the end opposite Matt and Cassie. "I guess it's been a pretty rough day for her."

"You can definitely say that," Matt agreed.

"I thought the two of you might want some time to yourselves so I hung out with Gabriel for a while, but it's getting close to dinner time and I wanted to shower before heading out," Cole said.

"I appreciate that, Cole. Our hike didn't last as long as we thought it would. We decided to watch a movie and relax. Or rather, I watched a movie and Cassie took a nap," he amended.

Cole grinned. "She's good at that."

Matt smiled in return. "Yes, she is. I can probably count on one hand the number of times she's stayed awake for an entire movie. It's like her body just can't sit still without going to sleep."

"Well, I'm going to jump in the shower. I won't be long if you need in there for anything," he said, rising from the couch.

Matt rubbed a hand over his stubble. He'd had it for fifty years and couldn't wait for a good shave. "I could use a shower and a shave."

"I'll be quick."

Cole went into his bedroom to gather some clothes. After Cole had gone into the bathroom and shut the door, Matt very carefully got up. He picked Cassie up and carried her into their room. After he gently laid her on the bed, he searched through the dresser drawers until he found the one that contained his clothes. He selected a pair of khaki pants and a navy sweater. By the time he went back into the living room, Cole was exiting the bathroom.

"There should be plenty of hot water left," he told Matt.

"Thanks, Cole."

Cole nodded at him and headed back into his room. Matt went into the bathroom and closed the door. He found a new toothbrush and Cassie's toothpaste on the counter and brushed his teeth. He started the shower and got undressed. When he stepped under the warm spray of the shower, he thought he was in heaven. After not having a shower for fifty years, it felt wonderful. He found the shampoo and shower gel Mr. Morgan had brought for him and quickly washed. Once he was done rinsing, he turned off the shower and towel dried himself. He wrapped the towel around his waist and turned on the bathroom sink.

Once the water was warm, he pulled his razor and shaving cream out of the cabinet above the sink as well as the aftershave. Using the shaving cream, he lathered his face and began shaving off the five o'clock shadow he'd been stuck with for fifty years. When he was finished, he rinsed his face and dried it with the hand towel beside the sink. He put on the aftershave and started to get dressed. Once that task was complete, he combed his hair and gathered his dirty clothes.

When he entered the bedroom, Cassie was still sleeping. He noticed her dirty clothes pile on the floor near the window and put his things with hers. He sat on the side of the bed and gently shook her awake. "Cassandra. Cassie, it's time to get up."

"Mmm?" Cassie slowly blinked herself awake. "Matt, is that you?"

"Yes, sweetheart. It's me. Time to get up and get ready for dinner."

Cassie yawned and sat up. "What time is it?"

"It's almost 5:30. I thought you might want to freshen up a little before dinner."

Cassie smiled at Matt. "You're so thoughtful." She noticed for the first time that he had shaved and recently taken a shower. "I've never seen you clean shaven before. I like it."

Matt smiled back at her. "I'm glad."

Cassie got up and looked through her drawer for a change of clothes. She wanted to look nice for Matt tonight. While she had already worn her fancy red dress, she did have a casual knit dress she could wear to dinner tonight. She pulled the black dress out of her drawer along with the matching panties and bra. She knew she didn't have a lot of time before they were supposed to meet Gabriel and Amber so she took a fast shower. When she got out, she put on her lacy string bikini panties and matching bra. They left little to the imagination and she planned on torturing Matt with them later. That man was going to be seduced whether he wanted to be or not! She slipped on her dress and dried her hair with the blow dryer. She turned on her curling iron and put on her makeup while she waited for it to get hot. Once her makeup was done and her hair was curled, she ran back to her bedroom to put on her thigh-highs and shoes.

She didn't see Cole or Matt anywhere in the cabin and figured they must be outside. She grabbed her jacket and stepped out onto the front porch. "Hi guys. Ready for dinner?"

Cole and Matt turned to face her. Matt couldn't believe how amazing she looked. "You look beautiful."

Cassie smiled at him. "Thank you."

Matt reached out with his hand to help her down the stairs. When she reached the bottom, she looped her arm through his. She smiled up at him and realized how lucky she was. How many women had the luxury of falling in love with their best friend?

Matt turned toward Cole. "We should probably head to dinner before your brother and Amber come looking for us. We're already a few minutes late."

"I'm afraid that's my fault," Cassie said with a sheepish look.

Matt smiled at her. "It was well worth it. You look wonderful."

"Thank you."

Matt and Cassie walked down the path arm in arm while Cole trailed behind them. She felt bad about how things had ended with Cole, but she couldn't be happier that Matt was in her life for good. As they approached the lodge, they saw Gabriel and Amber waiting for them on the steps.

"Sorry we're late. Guess we just aren't used to sharing a bathroom three ways," Cassie said.

"Quite all right. We haven't been here that long." Gabriel noted Cole's resigned expression. Things hadn't turned out the way he had hoped. He had been so sure that Cassie was the one for Cole. As leader of their pack, Gabriel should have been able to sense his brother's mate. Apparently he'd been wrong this time.

The five of them headed into the lodge and were greeted by a waiter who seated them by a window. They opened their menus to make their dinner selections. Cassie wasn't sure what she wanted to order so she asked Matt to order for her. He had yet to make a bad decision when it came to food.

Matt was having a hard time keeping his eyes off Cassie. She didn't dress up very often and he was fairly certain that he hadn't seen this dress on her before. He definitely would have remembered it! It hugged very curve of her body and had a low neckline. When she moved, the v-neck of her dress showed a tiny bit of black lace. Matt hoped that he was the only one who noticed. The thought of Gabriel and Cole seeing Cassie's black bra upset him.

Gabriel watched Cole. It was obvious that Cassie only had eyes for Matt, and vice versa. He knew this had to be hard on Cole. Before he could say anything, the waiter came over to take their order. After everyone ordered and the waiter left, they sat in awkward silence.

Amber could feel Gabriel's worry for his brother; Cole's broken heart; and Matt and Cassie's happiness. All of the emotions swirling around their table were a bit much for her to handle. She placed her hand on Gabriel's arm, both to comfort him and to help stabilize her emotions. He glanced at her and smiled.

Amber was about to say something to Cole when Kari walked over to them. "I noticed you had someone new sitting with you and thought I'd stop and say hi."

Kari smiled at Matt. "I'm Kari."

"Matt," he replied, barely glancing her way.

Cole and Gabriel looked between Matt and Kari. "You two haven't met before?" Cole found it hard to believe that Cassie hadn't introduced her boyfriend to her friends.

"No, should we have?" Kari asked.

Why would Cole think she had met Matt before? Kari definitely would have remembered him. He looked like a tall blonde god. In a word, yummy!

"I guess I just find it hard to believe that Cassie's friends wouldn't know her boyfriend," Gabriel said.

Kari looked shocked. "Boyfriend?"

Matt stood and shook Kari's hand. "It's nice to meet you."

"You're really her boyfriend?" Kari's eyes were wide as saucers.

Cassie looked at Amber for help. While Kari had seemed to finally give up on ruining Cassie's life, she wasn't sure she could trust her just yet. Cassie stood and faced Kari. "Yes, Matt is my boyfriend. He decided to surprise me by coming to the lake."

"But ... you've never seriously dated anyone in your whole life! Wait! That's the name you called out in the car on the way up here! You said he was just a friend," Kari accused.

Cassie blushed. "Actually, I have dated someone seriously. I just didn't announce it to the world. Then we broke up right before the trip. He came up here to get back together with me."

Kari looked closely at Matt. "How old are you anyway?"

Matt glanced down at Cassie and back at Kari. "I'm twenty-seven. Not that I see how that's relevant to anything."

Kari looked back at Cassie. "How long have you two been dating?"

"About three years," she said, sticking to the story she'd told Michael.

"So you were nineteen and he was twenty-four? No wonder you didn't want anyone to know!" She looked back at Matt. "What's wrong with you that at twenty-four you had to date a nineteen year old barely out of high school?"

"Technically, she was almost twenty and nothing is wrong with me. Cassie is mature beyond her years. Our fathers were friends and introduced us about five years ago. I wasn't quite sure what to make of her at first, but I quickly saw what a jewel she was. I had planned on asking her out when she turned eighteen, but I got caught up with work and didn't get a chance to visit much that year."

"Hmph."

Amber knew that Cole had told Kari he wasn't interested in her, but maybe if he knew that he couldn't have Cassie he would change his mind. "Kari, why don't you join us for dinner?"

Kari looked down at her tight navy dress. She looked at Cassie's snug black knit dress and Amber's plain pants outfit. "Well, I guess I'm dressed well enough to join you."

Amber wished that Kari would learn when to close her mouth. She was trying to extend the proverbial olive branch, but Kari wasn't making it easy. "We already ordered, but I'm sure one of the guys can get the waiter's attention. Why don't you sit by Cole?"

Cole looked at Amber to see what kind of game she was playing. He had already made it clear that he wasn't interested in Kari. Cassie having a boyfriend wasn't going to change that. Amber just smiled at him serenely. He could tell she was playing matchmaker, but it wasn't going to work.

Looking up at Kari, he pulled the chair next to him away from the table for her to be seated. Kari's smile was so brilliant it lit up her entire face. For the first time, Cole could see what the other guys had seen in Kari. She may not be the kindest of people, but she had a beautiful smile. It still didn't change his feelings toward her.

"Thank you." Kari sat in the seat by Cole. Gabriel waved at the waiter so she could order. Once Kari's order was placed, the group resumed their conversation.

Kari looked at Matt. "So, Matt. What do you do?"

"I'm an architect. I've been working for a small firm about an hour from here, but Mr. Morgan is helping me get started in Ashton Grove."

"That's very interesting. Where did you say you lived?" she asked.

"I've been living in Roseville, but I recently acquired a house in Ashton Grove," he answered easily.

"Oh? So I guess Cassie will be seeing a lot of you then," Kari asked, not sounding happy about that idea.

Matt smiled at Cassie. "I certainly hope so. We actually discussed the possibility of her moving in with me. Since I'll be in Ashton Grove and have a four bedroom house, it seems like a waste of space if I don't have someone to share it with." Cassie smiled back at him and reached for his hand under the table.

The waiter arrived with their food and everyone began to eat in companionable silence. Matt had ordered the stuffed salmon with a side of wild rice for Cassie. After the first bite, Cassie could see why he had ordered it for her. She had never tasted anything like it! While she had eaten fish on many occasions, she had never had stuffed salmon before.

During their meal, Kari continued to grill Matt on his past. "Where did you go to high school?"

"In a small town in Georgia. It isn't on most maps so I'm sure you've never heard of it."

"Where did you say you attended college?" she asked him.

Matt was getting tired of Kari and her questions. "At the University of Tennessee in Knoxville. You sure are full of questions."

Kari smiled at him. "Just trying to get to know you. After all, you *are* dating my friend."

"True. I guess I'm just not used to answering a lot of questions about myself," he relented.

"Did I hear correctly and your father is friends with Cassie's dad?" Kari asked him.

"Yes, he was. He passed away along with my mother. I'm the only one left in my family now," Matt replied.

"I'm very sorry to hear that," she said with false sympathy.

"Thank you."

Cassie had started to feel nervous when Kari was grilling Matt. They hadn't discussed his past much. She was glad that he was able to come up with answers so easily. She wondered how much of it was true and how much of it was made up. Cassie heard a faint ringing and realized it was coming from her purse. She dug her phone out and stood. Excusing herself from the table, she went into the lobby to answer her phone.

"Hello," she answered.

"Cassie? It's dad."

"Hi Daddy. Is everything okay?"

"Everything is fine. I've been doing a little research on Matt's family. It seems that he was the last of his line. Furthermore, his family owned most of a small town in Georgia called Spencer Falls. While you and I both know he's the real Matthew Spencer, we may be able to use a DNA test to at least prove he's a descendant. Your young man may be more well off than he knows."

"Really? What else did you find out," she asked.

"It seems that his parents died a year before Matt did. I don't know how to tell you this, but it was a murder suicide. It appears that his father was convinced his mother was cheating on him. He killed her and then killed himself. Matt was twenty-six at the time and was their sole heir. He was also unmarried."

"That's horrible about his parents," she said softly.

"Your young man got into a bit of trouble with an heiress a year later. A young lady by the name of Charlotte Beaumonde had set her sights on Matt. When he refused to marry her, she went into a rage. She told one of her suitors that Matt had stolen her innocence from her and refused to do the right thing. The young man killed Matt, thinking that he was defending Charlotte's honor. From what I gathered, her innocence was long gone before that. After Matt died, it came out that Charlotte had been sleeping around for several years. She died a few years later. Apparently she contracted a disease from her lifestyle."

"Oh my goodness!" Cassie was shocked to say the least.

"Has Matt not talked about any of this with you?" her father asked.

"No. Not a word," she replied.

"I imagine he's rather embarrassed over his past. I'm sure he'll tell you in his own time. Don't rush him honey."

"I won't. Thank you for calling me Daddy."

"You're welcome. I love you," he said with a smile in his voice.

"Love you too. Bye Daddy."

Cassie hung up the phone. She hurried back into the dining room and sat back down. When she looked at Matt, she realized that he was watching her intently. "Everything okay?"

She smiled at him. "Everything is fine. That was just Daddy checking in. I haven't called him since we've been here and he was getting worried. Guess I was just so caught up in everything that I didn't think about it."

Everyone finished their meals. When the waiter came around to take their plates, he asked if anyone wanted dessert. Matt waved him over and whispered something in his ear. The waiter smiled and left for the kitchen.

Cassie looked at Matt. "What was that about?"

He smiled at her. "You'll see. It's a surprise."

A few minutes later the waiter returned with the most delicious looking chocolate dessert Cassie had ever seen. It arrived in a large milkshake glass and was layered. The first layer at the bottom was chocolate pudding, the next was whipped cream. After that, there was a layer of chocolate cake with another layer of whipped cream. The pattern repeated all the way to the top of the glass.

"Oh my! It looks wonderful," Cassie said in delight.

"I hope you like it," he told her.

Amber looked at Cassie and Matt. She could feel that they wanted to be alone. "If the two of you don't mind, I think the rest of us will head back to my cabin. I thought we could watch movies and pop some popcorn. The two of you are more than welcome to join us if you wish."

Cassie looked at her friend and knew what she was doing. "Thanks Amber, but I think I'd like some time with Matt. Maybe tomorrow?"

"Sure, Cass. I'll see you tomorrow," Amber replied with a grin.

The group got up and left Cassie and Matt. Once everyone was gone, Matt took Cassie's hand in his. "Did your father really call because he was worried about you?"

"No, but he said that I shouldn't mention it," Cassie replied softly.

Matt sighed and looked at the table. "He found out about my family didn't he?"

"Yes, he did." Cassie looked at Matt. "It's okay Matt. We don't have to talk about it if you don't want to."

"I think it's past time that we had this discussion, Cassie. If we're going to get married, no matter how far down the road that may be, then you should know the truth about me and my family. You may change your mind after you hear my story."

"I'll listen if you feel like talking about what happened, but I don't want you to feel that you have to," Cassie assured him.

"It started when I was a small boy. My mother gave birth to a daughter when I was only eight years old. My sister's name was Marian and she was beautiful, but she died when she was ten. My parents were never the same after that. Marian's death was an accident, but I think my parents blamed themselves."

Cassie placed her hand in his. Matt looked into her eyes and saw nothing but comfort and love. It gave him the strength he needed to finish his tale. "After Marian died, my mother became distant. My father took her distance to mean that she was having an affair. I guess he figured that if she wasn't sleeping with him, then she must be going elsewhere. He couldn't understand that her grief kept her from wanting that type of relationship with anyone. He confronted her about it many times and she always denied it."

He paused and took a sip of his drink. "One night a few years later, he came home early. My mother's dearest friend was visiting. Unfortunately, her friend was a man. My father went into a rage and called her a whore. He threw Mr. Tenny out of the house and went after my mother. He chased her up to their room. I was down the hall in my bedroom when it happened. My mother had asked me to come home earlier that week for a visit. I had an apartment in town, but that wasn't close enough for her. I heard my mother scream right before I heard the first gunshot. Before I could run down the hall, a second shot was fired. I found them dead on their bedroom floor when I opened the door."

"Oh, Matt! I'm so sorry!" Cassie hugged him. She wished she could do more for him.

"I'm afraid that isn't the end of it. I was my father's only heir. We were pretty well off. Actually, we were very well off. We owned most of the town. Spencer Falls was smaller than Ashton Grove by about six hundred people. My graduating class in high school only had ten people in it. I was unmarried at the time. Even though the circumstances of my parents' deaths were less than honorable, it didn't keep the women from wanting to marry me. I was rich and had a lot of property."

"You're a very strong person, Matthew. I've always known that," she told him softly.

"I emptied my apartment and moved back into the family home. One of the neighbor's daughters came to see me the first week I was home. Her name was Charlotte Beaumonde. She was your age and very pretty. She also had the same temperament as Kari. It wasn't long before I realized that she had decided I would make the perfect husband for her... or rather, my family's fortune would. I tried many times to tell her I wasn't interested, but she wouldn't listen. The last time she came to visit me I told her that I was going to speak to her father about her behavior. She threatened to tell everyone that I raped her if I didn't marry her. I thought it was just the ranting of a silly girl."

"But she meant it didn't she," Cassie asked.

"Yes, she did. She was popular and had a ton of suitors. She told one of them that I had forced myself on her and refused to marry her. He came by my house later that night. Without even allowing me to say anything on the matter, he started a fight. I was holding my own and about to get the upper hand when he drew out a knife. I didn't even see it coming. One moment we were fighting, and the next I was dead."

"Do you know what happened to your home?"

"As far as I know, it was held for any future heirs. I left a few years later and roamed the state for almost fifty years. Then I found you... The moment I saw you I knew that you were special. I couldn't believe it when you could see me," he told her.

"That was the best day of my life," she told him with a smile.

"Mine too, Cassie. For some reason, once I met you, I wasn't able to leave Ashton Grove. I guess it was fate," he replied.

"My father has an idea. I'm not sure if you'll like it though," she said hesitantly.

"What's that?"

"He said that your estate is still being held in hopes that an heir exists. Apparently your father's lawyer had orders to hold the property for seventy-five years. If no one can prove they're a blood relation during that time, then the property will be auctioned off and the money will go to a charity. My dad said that DNA could show that you are related, well, to you. If that's the case, then the house, lands and any monies remaining in your accounts will be in your control," Cassie answered.

Matt was astounded. "I don't know what to say. I didn't even realize that was possible."

"You don't have to make any decisions today. Will you just promise me that you'll think about it? Even if you don't want your home and land, you might regret letting it fall into someone else's hands."

"I promise that I will think about. Before I make any decisions, I'll speak to you about it again. After all, this will affect both of us." Matt smiled at her. "Let's head back to the cabin. It's been a long day."

"Yes, it has," she agreed.

Matt stopped to pay their bill on the way out. When they left the lodge, Cassie turned to him. "There's something else I've been meaning to ask."

"What's that?"

She looked at him in curiosity. "How does a fifty year old ghost end up with current money in his wallet?"

Matt laughed. "Your father decided to 'loan' me some money when he gave me the ring. At the time I didn't think I could ever pay him back, but if what you said about my family's estate is true then I may have a way after all. I don't know how much all of its worth now, but it's more than I had this morning."

They walked back to the cabin in silence.

Chapter Eleven

When they entered the cabin, it was dark. No one had thought to turn on any lights before heading to dinner. Cassie flipped the light on as she walked through the front door. She wasn't surprised that Cole wasn't back yet. She figured that everyone was still at Amber's cabin watching movies.

Cassie and Matt both headed to the bedroom. While her Pooh jammies were comfortable and cute, Cassie was thankful that she had packed one other pajama set. She dug through her drawer and pulled out a green satin set of pajama pants with a matching camisole.

Matt took one look at what she was holding and gulped. "You aren't planning on wearing that, are you?"

Cassie gave him an innocent look. "I can't very well wear Pooh again. I've already slept in it for a few nights."

Shaking his head, Matt said, "Remind me to take you to town tomorrow for new pajamas. Preferably long, flannel ones with a high neck."

Cassie laughed at him. "It's not like you haven't seen me in these before."

"Yes, I know, but its different now."

Cassie stood on tiptoe and kissed his cheek. "It's still just the two of us in a bed. We've shared a bed hundreds of times before. Just because you're human doesn't make it different."

"The fact that I'm not a ghost anymore *does* make it different. I hadn't thought that it would feel different until I saw you pull those out of the drawer. Please tell me you didn't pack the long purple night gown! I don't think I could suffer through that one right now," he said in mock horror.

Cassie laughed. "No, I didn't pack that one."

She knew exactly which one he was referring to. It was the one nightgown she could wear and be guaranteed a Matt-free night. It had a plunging neckline, spaghetti straps, and a slit up the side that went almost all the way to her hip. It was also sheer. Every time she had worn it, Matt had disappeared for the evening.

He looked relieved. "Good. Do you want to change in here or the bathroom?"

"I think I'll take the bathroom so I can wash my face. If that's okay with you? Or do you want to change in the bathroom?" She got an impish look on her face. "Or we could both change here."

"Cassie!" When he saw her smile, he realized she was teasing him. "I can change in here."

Cassie gathered her pajamas close to her chest and left the bedroom. She closed the door behind her to give Matt some privacy. When she got in the bathroom, she turned on the light and closed the door. She pulled her hair back in a ponytail so she could wash her face and brush her teeth. Once she was finished, she changed into her satin pajama pants and matching camisole. Feeling a bit on the daring side, she decided to *only* put on her pajama pants and camisole. She gathered her dirty clothes and went back to the bedroom.

She knocked on the door before opening it. "Are you decent?"

"Yes, you can come in," Matt answered.

Cassie opened the door and saw Matt standing at the foot of the bed in nothing but his pajama pants. He was absolutely gorgeous! She had never seen him without a shirt before. He had every bit as much muscle as Cole had, but his hadn't come from a gym. The only way a guy looked like Matt back in his time was through hard work and physical labor. She wasn't sure why an architect would have done a lot of physical work though. There was a light dusting of blonde hair on his chest that Cassie wanted to touch. She felt her mouth go dry. Closing the door behind her, she walked past Matt to the window. She leaned over to put her dirty clothes in the growing pile under the window.

Behind her, she heard Matt draw in a deep breath. She stood and looked at him over her shoulder. "What's wrong?"

"Good God Cassie! Please tell me you're wearing something under those pajama pants!"

Cassie grinned at him. "I would, but I promised I would never lie to you."

Matt closed his eyes and groaned. She wasn't going to make this easy on him. When she had bent over, her pajama pants had left very little to the imagination. Just thinking of her lying next to him in that outfit made him grow hard. It was going to be a very long night, and an even longer week.

Cassie walked past him and crawled into bed. She drew the covers over herself and patted the empty side of the bed next to her. "Coming to bed?"

Matt sighed and headed around the other side of the bed. He climbed between the sheets, staying as far from Cassie as possible. Thankfully the covers were heavy enough to hide his erection. He hadn't reacted to a woman like that since he was a teenager. Then again, before Cassie he hadn't felt that way about a woman in a really long time. Even before he died he hadn't been interested in one particular woman. He had slept with quite a few women, but had never loved one. Not until now.

On the other side of the bed, Cassie sighed. "Matt?"

"Yeah?"

"Are you going to hug the edge of the bed all night?" she asked.

"Maybe," he replied stubbornly.

Cassie sighed again. She decided then and there to take matters into her own hands. She loved Matt, but he was being ridiculous. They were two grown adults and this wasn't the 1950s. She thought it was romantic that he wanted to wait until they were married, but he couldn't possibly expect them to sleep so far apart. Something had been awakened in Cassie during this trip, and she wasn't about to put it back to bed. A desire had been sparked and she was ready to let it burn.

Before Matt realized what she was doing, Cassie had moved over to his side of the bed and snuggled up next to him. She put her head on his chest and wrapped her arm around his waist. He felt her press her body against the length of his.

"Cassie?" Matt's voice sounded a little hoarse.

"Hmm?"

"What are you doing?" he asked.

"Going to sleep," she replied, a smile curving her lips.

"Over here?" he asked, sounding slightly panicked.

"Mmm-hmm. Is that okay?" she murmured.

"Uh... sure."

Cassie smiled in the dark. She sighed and pressed herself even closer to him. She heard Matt groan and tried not to giggle. She wondered what he'd do if her hand decided to go wandering. She waited several minutes so he would think she was asleep and decided to experiment.

Cassie slowly moved her hand from around his waist up to his chest. She curled her fingers into his chest hair and nuzzled her face against him. She could hear his heart beat increase.

She threw her leg over his and pressed her hips forward. That time she heard him gulp. Cassie was having a lot of fun, but she was starting to torture herself as well. She slowly slid her leg up his, until she reached an obstruction. Her knee came to rest against the underside of his erection. Now it was Cassie's turn to gasp. She hoped that Matt hadn't noticed and thought she was sleeping.

Cassie slowly moved her leg back down. At the same time, she let her hand wander from Matt's chest down toward his stomach. She stopped at the waistband of his pants. By this time, Matt was practically panting. Cassie murmured something against his chest, hoping he would believe she was dreaming. Very casually, her hand drifted down to his erection. Cassie had never touched a man before, nor had she ever seen a man naked. She was very curious about what he felt like and looked like down there. Her hand lightly brushed across him. He was hard and as her fingers caressed him, she felt his erection jump a little. Matt's body was tight as a drum. She half expected him to jump out of the bed at any moment.

Just when Matt thought he couldn't take a moment more, Cassie sighed in her sleep and rolled over onto her other side. He breathed a sigh of relief. Turning on his side, he watched her in the moonlight. Her long hair hung down her back in waves and curls, almost down to her waist. He wanted to know what it would feel like against his bare skin. It looked soft as satin.

Gently, he reached out and rubbed a strand between his fingers. It was even softer than he had imagined. Matt sighed and rolled onto his back. It was going to be a long, agonizing night.

On the other side of the bed, Cassie was disappointed. When Matt had touched her hair, she'd hoped that he would move closer. She would have loved to have fallen asleep in his arms.

Sometime after midnight, both Matt and Cassie fell asleep. Staying away from Cassie had been the hardest thing Matt had ever done. Never had he wanted anyone like he wanted Cassie. Just being near her made him wish he could reach out and touch her. Everything seemed almost dreamlike. He was afraid that when he woke up in the morning, he would find that it had all been a dream.

Chapter Twelve

Daylight streaming through the bedroom window woke Matt the next morning. As he swam back to consciousness, he slowly became aware of the warm, lush body pressed against him. Opening his eyes, he found Cassie pressed against the front of him. They had apparently turned toward one another during the night, instinctively seeking each other out.

Matt loved how Cassie felt in his arms. Waking up beside her had felt like the most natural thing in the world. Knowing that he would be able to hold her like this for the rest of his life made him extremely happy.

Cassie stirred in her sleep, moving closer to Matt. She had never felt more at peace than she did this morning. Stretching, she realized that she was wrapped in someone's arms. As she slowly opened her eyes, she saw Matt.

Giving him a sleepy smile, she said, "Good morning."

Matt smiled in return. "Good morning, beautiful."

Cassie ran her fingers down his cheek. Waking up in his arms had been a dream come true for her. She gently kissed him on the lips, savoring his warmth.

"I love you," she whispered.

"I love you, too. Very much," he told her.

Smiling at him, she asked, "What would you like to do today?"

"I don't care as long as you're with me. We can do anything you want to do," he answered.

Cassie snuggled into him, not ready to get out of bed and face the morning just yet. The events of yesterday seemed surreal. Even though she was lying in Matt's arms, she was having a hard time believing that he was human again. Secretly, she was afraid that the fates would be cruel and take him from her. For the past several years, all Cassie had wanted was to be with Matt. Now that she had the opportunity, she hoped it would last a lifetime.

"Why don't we get dressed and grab some breakfast? We can figure out plans for the day once we've had some food," she suggested.

"Very logical thinking for someone who hasn't eaten or had caffeine yet," he teased.

Cassie laughed. "It happens on rare occasions."

Matt hugged her tight. "As much as I would love to lie here holding you all day, I guess we had better get up."

Cassie sighed. "If we must. Although, I have to admit that I was also enjoying our morning."

Matt smiled at her. "Do you want the shower first?"

Already knowing his answer, she asked, "You know, we *could* conserve water if we took one together."

Matt blushed. The idea was extremely attractive, but he was standing his ground. He didn't want to take her innocence from her before their wedding night. He had a feeling that it was going to be an uphill battle. Maybe a quick wedding was a better way to go.

"You know my answer to that Cassie."

"Well, it was worth a try," she replied.

Matt shook his head at her, reluctantly letting her go as she climbed out of bed. Watching her stretch was a whole new form of torture. The material of her top stretched tight across her full breasts and rose up just enough to expose part of her stomach. Matt clenched the covers in his hands in an attempt not to reach out and touch her. She was the most beautiful, sensual woman he had ever known... and after being around for over seventy years he had seen a lot of women. None could ever hold a candle to Cassie.

Cassie finished stretching and started digging through the dresser drawer. She wasn't exactly running out of clothes. She was just running out of *sexy* clothes.

Perusing her options, she chose her undergarments and shirt with care. All of her jeans were about the same so that didn't take much thought. Selecting her last set of sexy black undies and her last lacy bra, she chose her lowest cut black shirt. After gathering all of her clothes, she headed for the bedroom door.

"I promise I'll be quick," she told Matt as she opened the door.

He gave her a lazy grin, "Take your time. We don't have to rush."

Cassie smiled back and headed for the bathroom. Turning on the shower, she brushed her teeth while she waited on the water to warm up. Once she was satisfied with the temperature, she stripped off her pajamas and climbed under the warm spray. She didn't want to hog all of the hot water so she washed as quickly as she could. After her shower, she towel dried her hair and threw on her clothes. Cassie pulled out her make-up bag and quickly applied a little mascara, blush and lipstick. When she was finished, she gathered her dirty clothes and headed back to her bedroom.

Matt was still lying in bed, but had evidently gotten out up for a minute since he had clean clothes laid out at the foot of the bed. He watched her put her things in the dirty clothes pile before climbing out of bed. Walking around the foot of the bed, he gathered her into his arms for another hug.

"I'm going to take a quick shower and then I'll be ready to go," he told her, placing a kiss on her forehead.

Cassie smiled up at him. "Okay. I'm going to put on my shoes and wait for you in the living room."

Matt left to take his shower and Cassie grabbed her shoes off the floor. She went into the living room and sat on the couch to put them on. Flipping on the TV, she sat back and watched the news until Matt was ready to go. In less than 10 minutes, he was showered, dressed, and ready to go. Cassie got up as he came out of the bathroom.

"Wow, that was fast," she said with a smile.

"I told you I'd be quick," he replied.

Matt held his hand out to her. Placing her hand in his, they walked to the front door. He opened the door and motioned for Cassie to go ahead of him. As they stepped out onto the front porch, Matt made sure the door was locked behind them. They walked in silence down the path to the lodge. The morning was cool, but sunny.

As they neared the lodge, Matt spotted Kari on the porch. She looked like a vulture waiting on its next meal. Matt had a feeling that next meal was Cassie. Feeling a bit devilish, he pulled Cassie to a stop and turned her to face him.

"Don't look, but Kari is on the porch. She looks ready to ambush you again," he told her in a low voice.

Cassie sighed. "Why won't she leave me alone?"

Matt gave her a wicked grin. "I normally wouldn't condone doing anything like this, but what do you say we give her something to watch?"

Cassie liked the way he thought! "Sounds wonderful. Maybe she'll get the picture and back off."

Matt pulled Cassie into his arms and brought his lips down on hers in a deep, passionate kiss that Cassie felt all the way to her toes. Matt grabbed a handful of her hair and pulled her closer. Cassie moaned, begging for more. For a minute, both of them forgot they were in public.

Gabriel walked up to the lodge at that moment. He noticed Kari on the porch, watching Cassie and Matt with steam practically coming out of her ears. Glancing back at Cassie and Matt, he realized they must have staged it for Kari's benefit, but things seemed to be getting out of hand. He cleared his throat, hoping to get their attention.

Matt heard Gabriel and lifted his head from Cassie's. A quick look in Kari's direction told Matt that she had seen their little public display of affection. However, she seemed even more pissed than before. What would it take for Kari to stop trying to steal guys from Cassie? It isn't like Cassie had dated a ton of men. Kari probably dated more men in one week than Cassie had in her entire life.

Gabriel walked over to them, "Good thing I showed up when I did. Looked like you had forgotten where you were for a minute."

Cassie blushed. "Good morning, Gabriel."

He grinned at her, "Morning Cassie. I take it y'all were about to get some breakfast."

"That was the plan," she answered.

"Then I'm afraid you're a few hours too late. In case you hadn't noticed, it's after eleven," he told them with an amused expression.

He knew that Matt had been through hell last night. Werewolf hearing allowed him to hear everything in the cabin. Both Cassie and Matt had tossed and turned all night so it was little wonder they had slept in. The brothers had been prepared to take a midnight walk if Cassie and Matt's reunion had ended up being a noisy one, but much to their amusement he had kept his word about just sleeping in the same bed as Cassie. Gabriel would bet good money that it wouldn't last much longer though.

Cassie looked shocked, "We slept until the early afternoon?"

"Yep, I'm afraid so. I started to wake y'all up, but I figured you'd get up when you were ready," he replied.

Matt shook his head, "I don't think I've ever slept that late before. Must have been more tired than I realized."

"Uh-huh," Gabriel said. Obviously not believing him.

Deciding to change the subject Matt asked, "Would you like to join us for lunch then?"

Gabriel nodded, "Sure. Everyone else is planning on eating around one o'clock, but I wanted to take one of the boats out before they're all gone today."

The three of them walked into the lodge. After being seated and perusing the menu, they ordered their food and chatted while they were waiting. Since it was still a little early for lunch, their food arrived in no time.

Later that afternoon, Cassie and Matt found themselves walking through the woods again. It was Cassie's favorite part of the lake. She really loved walking through the trees, listening to the birds, and enjoying the peaceful setting. A small stream ran through the woods to the lake. Cassie couldn't see the stream from the path, but she could hear the water.

They walked in silence for about an hour. Both Cassie and Matt were just enjoying each other's company. Even though they had spent time with one another almost daily for several years, it was completely different now that he was alive. Cassie had always cared about Matt and had most definitely desired him, but now she was able to act on those thoughts and feelings. Or at least she was trying to. Hopefully tonight she would be able to crack Matt's tough exterior. Regardless of his out-dated feelings about her virginity, she wanted to be with him; wanted to feel his hands and mouth on her body. Just thinking about it made her hot.

Matt was enjoying his time with Cassie. He loved talking to her, but he also enjoyed their quiet times together. Just being near her filled him with a contentment he had never experienced before. Cassie was beautiful, caring, intelligent, and so much more.

Pointing to a log on the side of the trail Matt asked, "Would you like to stop and sit for a few minutes?"

Cassie glanced at the log. "Sure, that sounds nice."

They walked over to the log and sat down. Matt reached for Cassie's hand and pulled her closer. He ran his free hand through her hair. Turning her face toward him, he lowered his head and covered her mouth with his. Cassie closed her eyes and leaned into him.

Wanting to feel her against him, Matt pulled Cassie into his lap. He wrapped his arms around her and pulled her close. Lifting his head, he looked down in her eyes. He saw her love for him and her desire. He could have easily been looking into a mirror as he was sure those same emotions were visible in his own eyes.

Matt cleared his throat. "Sorry about that. I have a hard time not kissing you when we're alone."

Cassie smiled at him. "Don't apologize. I'm glad you kissed me."

He grinned at her and caressed her cheek. Claiming her mouth in yet another kiss, his hands drifted down her back. Cassie reached down and pulled his hand up to her breast. Matt just about jumped off the log in shock.

"Cassie! What are you doing?" Matt demanded.

Cassie blushed. "Is it so wrong that I want to know what it feels like for you to touch me?"

Matt sighed. "No, it isn't wrong, but I told you that I wouldn't take your innocence from you unless we were married."

Cassie got up and started down the path again. Matt reached out and stopped her as she walked past him.

"Cassie, I didn't mean to hurt your feelings or to make you feel bad. I would never do anything to hurt you," he told her.

"I know, Matt. I think it's just best if we don't discuss it. This is one subject where we'll just have to agree to disagree," she replied.

Matt nodded his head, a little sad. He hadn't meant to upset Cassie, but he was doing what he thought was right. It didn't have anything to do with not wanting her... god knew he wanted her more than anything! If only he could make her understand, he released her arm and walked beside her. Leave it to him to ruin the afternoon.

Cassie wasn't really upset with Matt, but she would be lying if she said she wasn't a little miffed. She knew that he wanted her. Why couldn't he just admit it?

They walked until the sun started to set. As the sky turned pink and orange, Cassie looked at their surroundings. They had walked for miles today. Cassie hadn't been this far into the woods. Listening, she realized that she could no longer hear the stream, which meant that it must have looped back around to lake at some point. The air was getting chillier by the minute and Cassie shivered.

Matt saw Cassie tremble from the cold and put his arms around her. It was the first time he had touched her in over an hour. Hoping she wasn't still mad at him, he tipped her face up so that he could see her eyes. They were troubled, but she didn't appear to be upset with him any longer.

"What's wrong Cassie?"

"I didn't realize we had walked so far into the woods. It will take us hours to get back to the cabin," she answered.

Matt brushed her hair back from her face. "It's okay, honey. Even if it does take a while to get back, we'll manage."

"I'm sorry I was so upset with you. It just hurt when you didn't want me," she told him.

She was breaking Matt's heart. "How could you think I don't want you? Nothing could be further from the truth."

Cassie looked at him skeptically. "If you wanted me, why did you back away earlier?"

Matt sighed. "Just because I want you doesn't mean I should act on those feelings. We've been over this Cassie."

Cassie shook her head. She'd never understand him. "Let's start walking back to the cabin. We'll be lucky if they're still serving dinner by the time we get to the lodge tonight."

Chapter Thirteen

Several hours later, Cassie and Matt were seated at the lodge eating dinner. Michael, Cole and Gabriel had arrived at the same time so they were all sitting together. Before this trip, Cassie would have felt awkward being the only female at the table, but now it wasn't a big deal for her. She wished that Michael weren't sitting with them, but aside from that everything was fine.

Throughout dinner, Michael kept glancing at Matt's ring. The research he'd done had paid off. The ring essentially held the power to bring the dead back to life, or rather ghosts back to life. He had originally seen it in a book that one of his ex-girlfriend's owned. He had never told his brothers, but he had dated a wide variety of women not just in looks, but in other ways. This particular ex-girlfriend had been psychic. She not only shared Cassie's gift of seeing spirits, but she was also great at divination, palmistry and received psychic visions on occasion.

The dragon ring was passed down from generation to generation. It had last been recorded as being owned by a powerful family of witches who were believed to be descendants of Morgan LeFay, which would explain how Cassandra Morgan's family came to be in possession of it. Since Cassie had not mentioned Matt before, Michael was going to assume that he had been a ghost. From what Michael had gathered, Cassie declaring her love for Matt in the woods had made him human once more. The question was, should he tell his brothers about this or not?

Cole had been really upset when Cassie's boyfriend, whom no one knew anything about, had suddenly appeared. He had heard about his twin's lack of belief in witchcraft and wasn't sure if Cole would believe him or not. Gabriel probably would believe him. After dinner, he planned on having a talk with their pack leader.

Matt had noticed Michael's glances and wondered what was up. He seemed fascinated with the dragon ring. Matt had to admit that he preferred Michael's glances at his ring to Cole's glances at Cassie. It was obvious that while Cole had accepted Matt as Cassie's boyfriend, he still had feelings for her. Truthfully, Matt couldn't blame him.

As they finished their dinner, Michael stood and excused himself. He headed outside to wait for Gabriel. He stood in the shadows so that he wouldn't be seen by the others. Cassie and Matt were the next to leave. They were engrossed in a conversation and didn't notice his presence. Cole followed a minute later and headed for the lake.

Gabriel stepped out on the porch and stopped. Without turning his head, he asked, "Did you need something Michael?"

Michael grinned and stepped out of the shadows. "Just thought we could have a little talk, if you have some time."

Gabriel turned to face him. "Does it have anything to do with you staring at Matt's ring all through dinner?"

"You noticed, huh? I was trying to be subtle," he replied.

"You failed miserably then. What's up?"

Michael took a breath. How to start? "How much do you know about the spirit world?"

Gabriel raised his eyebrow, "What? You mean like ghosts?"

Michael nodded. "Yes. What do you know about them?"

Gabriel looked out at the lake. Deciding this conversation would be better elsewhere, he motioned for Michael to follow him. They started walking toward the lake, but Michael stopped him when he saw Cole.

"Wait a minute. I'm not sure you want Cole to hear this just yet," Michael said.

"Why not?"

"Because it involves Cassie. I wanted to share my information with you so you could decide the best way to handle this," he replied.

Gabriel had to respect his brother's answer. Maybe Michael was growing up after all. For the first time, Gabriel actually had hope for his little brother.

After they had walked a ways in the opposite direction of Cole, Gabriel asked, "Now, what is it you need to tell me about Cassie?"

"How much attention did you pay to her last name?" Michael asked.

"Morgan? It's a common enough name," Gabriel replies.

Michael shrugged. "Maybe, but if you add her name to the ring Matt is wearing it tells a story. The dragon ring is rumored to have belonged to Morgan LeFay, one of the most powerful women in history, and has been passed to her descendants over the years. It has the power to make a ghost human again."

Gabriel had a feeling he knew where this was going. It would definitely explain why Cassie's friends hadn't known anything about Matt. However, if Matt had been a ghost, then he and Cassie hadn't really been dating. What was the real story between them?

Michael took Gabriel's silence to mean he should continue, "Since Matt is wearing the ring and no one seems to know anything about him, I think it's safe to say that he was a ghost. Not to mention the flash of red light that came from the ring when I saw him and Cassie in the woods."

"Flash of light?"

Michael nodded. "Cassie told him that she loved him. The moment she said the words 'I love you,' the ring flashed. From what I read, the change to human form can only be permanent if the object of the ghost's affection declares their love."

Gabriel ran a hand down his face. "So Matt somehow or other got the ring and became human, which is now permanent because Cassie loves him. Is that about it?"

"That's it. I wasn't sure if Cole should know or not. Regardless of how Matt got here or who he used to be, Cassie seems to honestly love him. I'm not sure that Cole knowing all of this would help any right now," Michael told him.

Gabriel sighed. Some days being pack leader wasn't all that it was cracked up to be; part of him wanted to confront Cassie and Matt, but the other part believed they should have their shot at happiness. If Cassie really was descended from Morgan LeFay, then that would explain the feelings he'd had when he met her. Usually a pack member's potential mate would give off a psychic vibe of sorts, but if Cassie were a witch then that would explain away the feeling. If she wasn't destined to be Cole's mate, then what was the point of ruining her life with Matt?

Gabriel looked at Michael, "I have to sleep on it. I'm not sure what to do just yet, but I'll figure something out by the morning."

Michael nodded and left Gabriel to his thoughts.

Chapter Fourteen

Back at the cabin, Cassie and Matt were getting ready for bed. Cassie had already brushed her teeth and washed her face. Digging through her drawers, she didn't see any other pajamas. Sighing, she pulled the green satin ones from the pile of dirty clothes. She was either going to need a washing machine or a shopping trip tomorrow. Heading back to the bathroom, she quickly changed for bed. Once more, she decided to go without anything under her pajamas.

When she was back in the bedroom, she climbed into bed and pulled the covers up. Matt was already in bed on the opposite side, staying as far from her as he could. Figuring that they were going to have a replay of last night, Cassie pretended to go to sleep. Before she could move to his side of the bed, Matt gently moved closer to Cassie. He put his arm around her waist and pulled her closer to him. When her back was flush against him, she sighed in her sleep. Matt loved the feel of her against him. Her hair was silky against his chest. Her satin pajamas felt soft against his hand. He gently caressed her stomach.

Cassie was still pretending to be asleep, but Matt was making it difficult on her. She wondered if he was doing it on purpose to pay her back. Deciding to take full advantage of the moment, she wiggled her backside against him. Matt's quick indrawn breath was enough to show Cassie that she had struck a bulls-eye. She could feel the hard length of him throbbing against the back of her pajama pants.

Matt knew that he should turn away and go to sleep, but he couldn't seem to stop. Cassie had awakened something in him that had been dormant for a long time. Ghosts didn't sleep so he hadn't exactly been able to dream about her but he had fantasized more than once over the past several years. Over the years, they had shared a bed many times. Matt had often watched her sleep and had wondered what it would be like to hold her, to caress her awake... to make love to her. Even though she could feel him, he had never touched her in her sleep before. It hadn't seemed right since he wasn't alive and couldn't really offer her anything.

His hand slid from her stomach to her hip, pulling her firmly against his erection. His hand held her in place. When he realized she didn't seem intent on moving, he moved his hand back to her stomach. Her pajama top was so soft that he couldn't stop rubbing it. He rubbed his way up her stomach to her breasts. When he reached the underside of her breasts, he gently stroked the right one with his thumb. At Cassie's indrawn breath, he thought she had woken up. Matt became very still and waited to see what would happen. When her breathing returned to normal, he continued his exploration of her soft, curvy body. He palmed the underside of her breast and gently kneaded it. He loved feeling the weight of it in his hand. Cassie was very well endowed.

She moaned in her sleep and pressed even closer to him. He took her nipple between his thumb and forefinger and lightly squeezed. Cassie gasped and strained against his hand. It was obvious that she wanted more.

Matt's breathing was ragged. He wasn't sure why he was tormenting himself like this. He knew that he should stop, but it had been so long since he'd had a woman. He kissed the side of her neck and rubbed the palm of his hand over her nipple in a circular motion. Her nipple was hard and was clearly showing through her pajama top. Not wanting to neglect the other breast, he moved to the other side. He palmed the underside of her left breast while kissing her neck and her shoulder.

Cassie whimpered in her sleep. Matt lightly rubbed back and forth, working his way from the underside of her breast to her nipple. Her nipple was already puckered when he touched it. Cassie gasped and rolled onto her back.

Matt stilled, not sure if she was awake or not. When it seemed she was still sleeping, he looked at her in the moonlight. Her nipples were clearly outlined against the satin material. He rested his hand on her stomach and she arched against him. Matt slid down the bed a little ways so that he was face to face with her. After making sure she was still sound asleep, he slowly lifted the hem of her shirt. He watched as the shirt exposed inch by creamy inch of her skin. He paused when he reached her breasts, knowing that it wouldn't be right to expose her while she was sleeping.

The brain in his head was losing the battle with his *other* brain. He desperately wanted to see what Cassie looked like. She stirred in her sleep. Matt reached under her shirt and skimmed the surface of her right breast. Cassie moaned and arched her back. Matt threw his leg over hers and pulled her closer until her hip was nestled against his erection. He gently kneaded her breast and watched her face. He could see the desire etched on her features, even as she slept. Not able to stop himself any longer, he nudged her top up further and exposed her breasts. They were perfect, round mounds. Her dusky rose colored nipples were puckered from all of his teasing.

Matt continued to play with her right breast. He watched as his thumb gently rubbed her nipple. It didn't seem possible, but it got even harder. Moving to the left breast, he teased her nipple until both nipples were standing in perfect points. Unable to resist such a temptation, he lowered his mouth first to one breast and then the other. He flicked his tongue across her nipple and gently sucked it into his mouth. While he licked and sucked on one breast, he teased her other nipple with his hand. Gently rubbing the hard nub until Cassie was moaning softly.

He released her nipple, licking it one more time, before moving to the other breast. He had to shift his weight to allow his hand access to the breast closest to him, which brought the majority of his body across hers. He tongued her right nipple and massaged the underside of both breasts with his hands.

Cassie was writhing under him as he sucked and licked her nipple. He lifted his head and watched for signs that she might be waking up. Part of him wished she would, but the other part of him hoped she would continue sleeping. He wanted to give her pleasure without having to acknowledge that he was breaking his own vow to leave her untouched until their wedding night.

Realizing that her eyes were still closed, he trailed kisses down her chest and across her stomach. He lightly massaged the soft skin of her belly with his hand, dipping his fingers under the waistband of her pajama pants. He remembered seeing the outline of her when she had bent over last night and wondered if she decided against wearing anything under her pajama pants again. It took a great amount of restraint not to rip them off her.

Rolling back onto his side, he ran his hand from the side of her breast, down her rib cage, to her hip. Her body was seeking his warmth again so he pulled her close to him. He teased her, and himself, again by running his fingers just under the edge of her pajama pants... back and forth. Cassie arched her hips off the bed. Wanting to give her pleasure without taking her virginity, Matt slid his hand between her legs. Through the satin pants, he could feel how wet she was. Without removing her clothes, he gently parted her lips and used his thumb to massage her swollen nub.

Cassie gasped, arching off the bed. She wasn't sure how much longer she could pretend to be asleep. No one had ever seen her naked, much less had her breasts in their mouth. And no one had *ever* touched her where Matt had his hand now. She had never in a million years thought it would feel anything like this. There were no words to describe the sensations she was feeling.

Matt rubbed the satin of her pajamas against her. He wished more than anything that he could get rid of the pants and feel how soft and wet she was. He wanted to slide his fingers inside of her to bring her pleasure. He wanted to feel her convulse around him as she climaxed. Knowing that he couldn't do any of those things, he stayed his course, gently rubbing and teasing her through the satin pants.

Before he knew what she was doing, Cassie was pushing at the top of her pants with both hands, trying to get them off. Matt placed his free hand over hers. Instead of growing still as he had anticipated, she used his hand to pull one side of her pants down, exposing one hip. Matt visibly gulped. He realized that she wasn't going to take no for an answer. If she was this adamant in her sleep, he couldn't wait to see her when she was awake.

He paused in his love making long enough to lower her pants. Even though Cassie had never been with a man before, she apparently wore skimpy bathing suits and panties. She had shaved her bikini line and had trimmed the hair down really close. Matt felt as if he would explode at any moment. Women in his day hadn't done things like that, but from reading some of Cassie's magazines he knew that such a thing was rather common today.

Cassie arched her hips off the bed, wanting to feel those incredible sensations again. Matt ran a finger down her lips, gently parting them. Using his thumb, he teased her nub again. When he had her writhing and panting, he gently slipped the tip of his index finger inside of her. Cassie gasped and raised her hips, trying to draw him further in. Matt was helpless to do anything but watch. As his thumb flicked across her, his finger kept rhythm, sliding in and out.

When Cassie thought she couldn't take any more, Matt added his middle finger. He slid both fingers all the way inside of her, slightly curling them as he slid them out... stroking the inside of her. As he slid his fingers in again, she raised her hips. Matt increased his rhythm, sliding his fingers in and out faster and faster. Cassie thought she was going to die when suddenly she felt as if she were exploding. Her hips arched off the bed and she saw stars behind her eyes. It was her first climax. She opened her eyes and looked at Matt. He seemed embarrassed to be caught.

"That was absolutely amazing." Cassie's voice was husky.

Matt swallowed. "I didn't mean for things to go this far."

He removed his fingers from her and started to pull her pants up. Cassie stopped him with her hand. Instead, she pushed her pants the rest of the way off and lifted her top over her head. She sat on her knees in front of him, completely naked.

"What are you doing Cassie?" he asked, a little surprised.

"I don't care what you decided earlier. I want you to make love to me," she replied.

"I thought I just did," he said with a grin.

Cassie smiled. "That was wonderful, but I want you to really make love to me."

"Cassie, are you sure about this? Even though you climaxed, you're still technically a virgin," Matt said uncertainly.

"I'm sure. More sure than I've ever been of anything before," she answered quietly.

Cassie reached out and cupped his face in her hands. She kissed him softly on the mouth. Matt put his arms around her and brought her up against his body. The feel of her breasts pressed against him was almost his undoing. Matt teased her mouth open with his tongue. As Cassie kissed him, her hands drifted down his chest to the waist of his pants. She dipped her fingers inside of the elastic, but Matt placed one of his hands over hers to stop her. She leaned back to look at him.

"What is it?" she asked, unsure of why he'd stopped her.

"It's been a really long time since I've been with a woman. I can't promise that I'm going to be gentle or that I'm going to last very long. You deserve better for your first time," he told her.

Cassie gave him a small smile. "How could I deserve better? I'm making love with the man I love. What more could I ask for?"

Matt laid her down on the bed. He quickly stripped off his pants and lay down on his side by her. He lazily looked at her body in the moonlight. She was absolutely exquisite. He rubbed her breast until she gasped. Bending his head over her, he took her nipple in his mouth and gently sucked on it. Cassie ran her fingers through his hair and pulled his head closer. As Matt licked and sucked her nipple, his hand slid between her legs. She was still damp from before, but he wanted her slick and wet. He slid his fingers part way inside of her and rubbed her nub with his thumb. Cassie arched her hips off the bed, taking his fingers all the way inside of her.

Matt moved to her other breast, licking and sucking her nipple. Cassie had her fingers in his hair and held him to her breast. She ran one hand down his chest. She hesitantly moved her hand lower, until her finger tips brushed his erection. Matt groaned. He still had her nipple in his mouth and it made Cassie gasp. She tentatively wrapped her hand around his erection, curious about that part of him. She rubbed up and down slowly, and ran her thumb over the tip of him. For something so hard, his skin was surprisingly soft. Cassie had read enough romance novels to know that a man liked it when a woman took him in her mouth. She wondered what he would feel like against her tongue.

Not able to take a moment more, Matt pulled his fingers from her and rolled on top of her. He looked into her eyes and he placed the tip of his erection against her wet folds. Slowly, so he wouldn't hurt her, he slid into her inch by inch. He could feel her stretching to accommodate him, but knew that Cassie had to be hurting.

"Why did you stop?" she asked breathlessly.

"If I keep going, it's going to hurt. I promise it won't hurt this much the next time, but there isn't a way to stop the pain from coming the first time. You'll stretch enough for me to enter you all the way, but since you're body isn't used to having me inside it's going to hurt. Are you sure about this?"

Cassie nodded her head. Matt pulled out until just the tip of him was inside of her, then he thrust forward quickly. When he was all the way deep inside of her, he heard her cry out. He stopped and held as still as possible. When her whimpers quieted, he began to move again slowly. Before long, Cassie was raising her hips to meet him, stroke for stroke. Matt pulled almost all the way out, before sliding in as deep as he could go, making Cassie gasp in pleasure and lift her hips to meet him. Matt knew he couldn't hold out any longer. He thrust in and out of her, faster and faster. Ramming into her one last time, he felt her convulse around him as they climaxed together.

Afterward, he couldn't believe what he had done. It had only been forty-eight hours since he had been human again and he had already bedded Cassie. Pushing her hair back from her face, he leaned down and kissed her.

"Are you okay?" he asked.

She smiled at him. "I'm more than okay. I'm wonderful."

Matt smiled back at her. When he started to pull out, she wrapped her legs around him to hold him in place. It startled him for a moment, but he rolled onto his side pulling her with him. He knew he would eventually shrink enough that she wouldn't be able to hold him in. If it made her happy to stay joined with him for the moment, who was he to deny her?

He brushed her hair back from her face. "We should probably get some sleep. Thankfully, I don't think anyone else is back yet. These walls are probably pretty thin."

Cassie blushed. She hadn't even thought of Cole, Michael and Gabriel being in the cabin. The only thing she had thought of was Matt and the incredible sensations she had been feeling. While she was glad she hadn't been with anyone before, she was also happy that she had made love with Matt tonight. It had definitely been worth the wait.

With Matt's arms wrapped around her, Cassie quickly fell asleep. Matt held her against him as she slept. Sleep didn't come as easily for Matt, but he finally drifted to sleep with Cassie in his arms. At some point during the night, Cassie got cold. She reached down and pulled the covers over her and Matt. He was sleeping peacefully by her side. Trying not to wake him, she rolled onto her other side and nestled her back against the front of him. In his sleep, he put his arm around Cassie and pulled her close to him.

Cassie and Matt slept a deep, dreamless sleep until the morning sun came streaming through the window. Matt swam out of his deep sleep slowly. The first thing he realized was that Cassie's warm, naked body was pressed against him. His body had an instant reaction. Matt nuzzled the side of Cassie's neck and fondled her breast. Cassie murmured in her sleep and wiggled against him. Reaching between her legs, Matt felt how wet she was. He pulled her leg across his to open her up and gently pressed his erection into her hot, wet, center.

Cassie gasped and instantly woke up. This was definitely the best morning of her life. She was still sore from their activities the night before, but instead of the sharp pain of the night before there was just a dull ache today. Matt gently thrust in and out of her. He was extra careful with her, knowing that she would be very sore this morning. Cassie tipped her head back against his chest. She bit her bottom lip to keep from crying out.

Matt paused. "Are you okay? I'm not hurting you, am I?"

"No. It feels amazing. Please don't stop."

Matt rolled onto his back, pulling Cassie on top of him. He continued to thrust in and out of her. He used his hands to massage her breasts and tease her nipples. Cassie wasn't sure she could take much more.

"Matt, please..." she begged.

She didn't have to say anything more, Matt knew what she wanted. He moved his hands from her breasts to her hips. Holding her firmly in place, his thrusts came faster and harder until they both cried out in release. Matt could only hope that no one was home, or that they were deep sleepers.

Matt rolled them back onto their sides. Cassie pushed her hips back against him, holding him firmly in place. She loved the feel of him inside of her and wanted it to last as long as possible. Matt brushed her hair back from her face and kissed her cheek.

"I love you, Cassie," he whispered in her ear.

Cassie smiled. "I love you, too... so very much."

This was the second time they had made love without protection. Since Cassie had never been with anyone before, Matt knew it was a safe bet that she wasn't taking anything to prevent pregnancy. Being a ghost for fifty years meant that Matt didn't have any protection either. He had planned on waiting to ask Cassie to marry him for at least six months, possibly a year. He wanted to make sure that things were going to work out with her father's friend. Matt didn't believe in asking a woman to marry him if he couldn't provide for her, but if Cassie ended up pregnant that would change everything. It wouldn't be fair for him to take her future away from her like that. She still hadn't finished college.

"Cassie, I think we need to talk," he said.

Cassie sighed. His tone meant that he had bad news. "Please don't ruin the moment, Matt. Can't it wait?"

"No, Cassie. It can't wait. Do you realize that even now you could be pregnant? Neither of us thought about protection last night or this morning," he replied.

Cassie stilled against him. She hadn't really thought about it. "I guess I didn't think about that."

Matt sighed. "I'm not saying that I don't want to have children with you Cassie, but you haven't finished college yet. We aren't even married. I had always thought that when I had kids, they would be with my wife."

Cassie rolled over to face him. "Is that what's bothering you? My education and the fact we aren't married?"

"I guess that's the main part of it. I'm also upset with myself. Last night and this morning shouldn't have happened." At the hurt look in her eyes, he immediately regretted the words. "They were the most wonderful moments in my life, but it wasn't right for me to take advantage of you like that."

"Matt, you didn't take advantage of me. I wanted you just as much as you wanted me. We're both adults. I understand your concerns and I appreciate that you want me to finish college, but you need to understand something... if I have to put off the last two semesters of college because our love has resulted in a child, then that's what I'll do. I can always take a few semesters off," she told him.

"Cassie, you shouldn't have to do that."

"Shh. Whether you feel I should or not, is irrelevant. I love you and if we find out later that I'm pregnant then I'll love our child, too. Would it be better if we had a child after I finished college? Probably. But in all honesty, if we decide to have a family, I don't want to be a working mom. I want to stay home with our children," she said.

Matt sighed. "Your plans for your future shouldn't change because of me, Cassie."

"They haven't changed exactly. I always knew that if I found someone understanding of my gift and fell in love, that when we started a family I would give up my career to be home with the children. The only difference is that the children may come before the career. I will be happy either way as long as you're by my side and it's your children that I'm raising."

Matt hugged her to him and kissed the top of her head. She was the most wonderful, understanding, loving woman that he had ever met. Maybe it had been fate that he had been murdered all those years ago. If he hadn't been, he would never have met Cassie.

"Even if you are willing to give up your degree and your career, it would still be best if we went into town and picked up some protection. I would prefer that my children be born on the right side of the blanket so to speak."

Cassie laughed. "None of that matters today. You should know that."

He ran his fingers through her hair. "It matters to me Cassie."

"What if I don't want to go to town? What if I tell you that I prefer the feel of you inside of me without barriers?"

Matt swallowed hard. She wasn't making this easy. "Cassie ..."

Cassie wasn't going to budge. "No, Matt. You don't get to make all of the decisions for us. If you want to be with me, then we have to make some of the decisions together."

Matt knew that she was right and he knew what he had to do. He had wanted to wait, but if Cassie was insistent on their relationship continuing on its current footing then he wanted to know for sure that she was his and belonged to no one else. Matt slipped from the bed and walked over to the dresser. He opened the top drawer and removed the diamond ring.

He walked back over to the bed and sat on the edge. Cassie crawled over to sit beside him. She wasn't sure what he had pulled from the dresser drawer. Whatever it was, it was clenched in his fist.

"Matt? Is everything okay?" she asked hesitantly, wondering if she had pushed him too far.

Matt looked at her. She was beautiful even first thing in the morning. Her cheeks were flushed from their lovemaking; her hair was tousled; and her eyes were bright. Matt caressed her cheek and kissed her gently on the mouth. "Everything is fine. More than fine, everything is perfect."

Cassie smiled at him. "I thought maybe you were upset with me."

"No, Cassie. I'm not upset. You were just telling me how you felt and what you believed. I come from a time when men had the only say. I don't want that for us. I want a partnership, an equal partnership," he responded.

Without saying another word, he opened his hand and showed her the ring. Cassie gasped and looked at Matt. She hadn't expected this. "Matt, you aren't just doing this because I might be pregnant are you?"

"No, Cassie." Matt took a breath. "Cassandra Morgan, you the most beautiful, caring, loving, sensual woman I have ever known. You're my best friend and my life. I love you more than words can ever say. Would you please do me the honor of becoming my wife?"

"Oh Matt!" Cassie had tears of joy in her eyes. "Of course I'll marry you!"

Cassie held out a shaky hand for Matt to place the ring on her finger. The weight of the two carat-diamond felt strange on her hand. She watched it sparkle in the sunlight.

"I love you, Cassie."

"I love you, too." Cassie threw her arms around him in a bear hug.

Matt wiped the tears from her eyes and kissed her. "We should probably take a shower and get ready for breakfast."

Cassie looked at him bashfully. "Could we take one together?"

Matt threw his head back and laughed. "I would love nothing more, but I'm not sure we would ever get to breakfast. It's probably best if we shower separately... at least, this time. Why don't you go first?"

She shook her head. "I'll end up taking longer. You go ahead while I figure out what to wear today."

Matt groaned. "Let me guess, something tight with matching panties."

Cassie smiled. "Probably. Complaining?"

"No. I'm looking forward to seeing what you're wearing under your clothes. I *do* get to see what's under them later, don't I?"

Her eyes sparkled with mischief. "Of course you do. I wouldn't have it any other way."

Matt shook his head at her. He drew on his pajama pants and went over to the dresser. He got a pair of jeans and a gray sweater out of the drawer. He wasn't accustomed to underwear like they made today. They were form fitting boxers. He grabbed a gray pair to match the sweater and a pair of socks.

    Before he headed out of the bedroom, he looked over his shoulder to make sure Cassie had covered herself before he opened the door. When he saw that she had the covers over everything important, he opened the door and stepped into the living room. Closing the door behind him, he headed to the bathroom. It looked like everyone was either gone or still in bed.

Chapter Fifteen

Matt took a quick shower. When he was done, he brushed his teeth and shaved. Throwing on his clothes, he opened the bathroom door and headed back to the bedroom. He opened the door to find Cassie digging through the dresser. He quickly closed the door before anyone could see her. She hadn't bothered with her pajamas yet and was still walking around naked.

Slightly upset, Matt exclaimed, "Good God Cassie! What if someone had been in the living room when I opened the door?"

"Sorry, Matt. I wasn't thinking." She bent down and grabbed her pajamas off the floor. She slipped into them and gathered her clothes from the dresser. Turning to blow him a kiss, she hurried from the bedroom.

When Cassie closed the bathroom door, she leaned against it. She was a little sore and was looking forward to the hot water of the shower. Cassie put her clothes on the bathroom counter and turned on the shower. She stripped off her pajamas and stepped under the water. Standing under the warm spray, she let the water run down her face and body. She took her time lathering her hair and her body. After she rinsed, she stood under the water trying to relax her sore muscles.

Cassie smiled as she remembered last night and this morning. Matt had looked embarrassed last night when he realized she was awake. At first she had thought he was going to stop, but she was very glad that he hadn't. He had been so gentle with her, worrying that he was going to hurt her. And it *had* hurt at first, but after the pain ended there was nothing but pleasure.

She quickly finished her shower and turned off the water. Cassie towel dried her hair and wrapped the towel around her. She pulled her curling gel out of the cabinet and rubbed some through her hair. She only used it on special occasions when she wanted some extra wave and curl in her hair without using a curling iron. She moisturized her face and dried her body.

Cassie massaged lavender scented lotion into her skin. She noticed her breasts were tender this morning after all of the attention they had received from Matt in the past twelve hours. When she was finished, she put on her pink lacy boy shorts and matching demi-bra. She didn't wear it often because her breasts tended to spill over the top. She pulled on her jeans and her pink camisole. Over that, she wore a lacy pink stretch top. She quickly applied some lip gloss and mascara.

Cassie gathered her dirty clothes and opened the bathroom door. When she walked into the living room, she noticed Gabriel leaning against the kitchen counter. She wondered how long he had been there. Had he heard all of the noise she and Matt had made earlier that morning?

"Good morning, Cassie." Gabriel watched her over the rim of a cup of coffee.

"Morning, Gabriel. I figured that everyone would have already gone to breakfast by now," she replied.

"I gathered that," he said with a grin.

Cassie blushed. So he *had* heard them this morning. "I'm just going to put these in my room." Cassie dashed back into her bedroom.

Gabriel was still grinning after her bedroom door had closed. It seemed their little wall flower had spread her wings. He was happy for her and Matt, but he hoped that it wouldn't hurt his brother; he hoped this wouldn't set him back.

Cassie put her dirty clothes in the pile she had created in her room. Matt was already gone. She figured he was probably out front. She took a breath before opening the bedroom door. Thankfully, Gabriel was no longer in the kitchen. Cassie opened the front door and stepped out onto the porch. Closing the door behind her, she started down the steps. Where was Matt?

Cassie started down the path toward the lodge. She spotted Matt in the parking area by his Mustang. When he saw her, he started towards her. "I'm sorry I wasn't in the cabin when you finished your shower. I just wanted to check on the car."

"It's okay. I'm just happy I found you," she said.

"I didn't mean to worry you. I had planned on being back at the cabin before you were finished." Matt pulled her into his arms and kissed her. "I see you're trying to drive me insane with your wardrobe again. I don't remember you wearing this before."

"I normally wear it with my khaki pants and matching jacket."

Matt glanced down at her exposed cleavage. "And you decided to wear it like this because?"

Cassie smiled at him. "To torment you of course. I wanted to make sure that you were thinking of tonight for the rest of the day. Besides, if I'm wearing something like this on the outside, what do you think I'm wearing under it?"

Matt groaned and buried his face in her neck. "You're trying to kill me."

Cassie laughed and kissed him. "Let's go eat. I'm starving!"

"I wonder why." Matt took her hand and walked with her to the lodge. When they entered the dining area, the hostess took them to a table for two.

Before Cassie could look at the menu, she saw Amber across the room. She wanted to share her good news and asked Matt to excuse her for a minute. She knew that Matt would order something for her anyway.

When Cassie reached Amber's table, she noticed that Gabriel was heading their way. "I'm sorry, Amber. I didn't realize you were waiting on someone."

"Its okay, Cass. I'm just waiting on Gabriel."

"I'll leave you to your meal. We can talk later," Cassie told her.

"Wait, Cass. Is everything okay?" Amber asked.

Cassie smiled at her. "Everything is more than okay. I just had some news I wanted to share with you."

"Well, what is it? You know I won't be able to enjoy my breakfast if you leave me in suspense."

Cassie held out her left hand. "Matt and I are getting married."

Amber jumped up from the table squealing. She hugged Cassie tight. "That's so wonderful! I'm so happy for you!"

Cassie smiled. "Thanks Amber. I'll let you enjoy your breakfast with Gabriel." She turned to go, but turned back toward Amber before she walked away. "The guys don't know about it yet. I don't know how Cole will take the news."

Amber nodded. She understood Cassie's concern. "I understand Cassie. Now, go back to your doting fiancé before he comes over here to get you."

Cassie grinned at her and walked back to her table. When she sat down, their food was already coming out. Either Matt was starving or he thought she was. It looked like he had ordered one of everything. "Good heavens, Matt. Was there anything on the menu that you didn't order?"

Matt smiled at her. "I wasn't sure what you would like to eat this morning. I thought we could share. Just pick whatever you want."

Cassie smiled at him over her plate. She grabbed a pancake, some eggs and some bacon. She dug into her food with gusto. It seemed that staying up late and getting up early to make love had given her a large appetite. Matt grinned at her. She seemed really happy this morning and he was glad that he had been the one to put that smile on her face.

"What would you like to do after breakfast," he asked.

"I don't know. It's probably best if we find something to do outside of the cabin though."

Matt looked at her knowingly. "Would you like to go into town today? Or we could just take a drive through the countryside."

"I'd love to go into town with you. It's small though and there isn't much there. Oh! There's this great five n' dime type of store that has wonderful sundaes. I bet they serve lunch too," she replied enthusiastically.

He smiled at her. "Then it's settled. We'll drive into town after breakfast."

They finished their meal in silence. When they reached the lobby, Matt paid for the meal and escorted her outside. On the steps, he pulled her into his arms and kissed her. He couldn't get enough of this amazing woman.

"Are you ready to go? If you'd like to stay in the lobby a few minutes, I could go get the car and warm it up. You have to be freezing in that shirt," he said, looking at the low cut lacy top.

Cassie bit her lip. "It is pretty cold. Maybe I should just go and get my coat."

"I'll buy you a new one," he told her.

Cassie looked at Matt in surprise. For someone who had been so worried about not having a job this morning, he was being pretty free with his money now. "I thought you were worried about not having a job."

"Your father called on your cell phone this morning while you were in the shower. I spoke to him about my family's estate. The Medical Examiner in Whispering Lake has offered to take a DNA swab and send it to Spencer Falls. Apparently my small town still exists and so does the law firm my father used. Since we already know how the swab will turn out, it appears that I'm a very well off man. Your father still signed the Ashton Grove house over to me, but I also own my family estate in Spencer Falls as well as forty or so acres. My father had bought stock in some companies that have done very well over the years. The hundred-thousand dollars that my family boasted of has turned into a few million."

Cassie's eyes were huge. "Oh my!"

"Which means that I can give you anything you want. All you have to do is say the word, and I'll give you anything you could ever want or need. I also plan on finding a way to pay your dad for the car and house. I told him that over the phone, but he refused to accept anything," he told her.

Cassie shook her head. "That sounds like Daddy. I'll think of something we can buy for him that he's really been wanting. As for me, all I want is you Matt. But if you have all of that, you might want something more than just me. You could have any woman in the world."

"Maybe, but there's only one woman that I want. Since she agreed to marry me this morning, I'm hoping she plans on staying by my side. Don't the wedding vows say for richer or poorer? It just happens that I started out poor and ended up rich. Is that going to bother you?" he asked.

Cassie hugged him. "I would want you no matter how much or how little you had. All that matters is that I have you."

Matt kissed her and led her to the car. He opened the passenger door for her. Once she was safely inside, he closed the door and walked around to the driver's side. Matt slid into the driver's seat, buckled his seat belt and started the car. He hadn't driven in a long time, but he figured it would be like riding a bike. He put the car in reverse and backed out of the parking space. Within a few minutes, they were sailing down the road toward Whispering Lake. Matt had never cared much about what kind of car he drove, but he really loved this car! It handled like a dream.

Matt reached across the seat and put his hand on Cassie's leg. She looked over at him and smiled. He was definitely the luckiest man on earth. He had not only overcome death, but had found the woman of his dreams. He didn't know of anyone else that could say the same.

When they pulled into town, Matt found a parking lot in the middle of the square. He pulled the Mustang to a stop in the first parking space he found and turned the car off. He unbuckled his seat belt and stepped out of the car. Inside the car, Cassie unbuckled her seat belt and reached for her purse. She quickly checked her makeup in the mirror. Before she could reach for the handle on the door, Matt had opened it for her. He held his hand out to her and assisted her out of the car.

Once the car was closed and locked, he turned to face Cassie. "What would you like to do first?"

"I don't know. Want to just walk down Main Street and check out the different shops," she asked.

Matt held his hand out to her. "Let's go."

Smiling, Cassie placed her hand in his. They walked down Main Street for a few minutes before they came to a pet shop. Cassie stopped in front of the window to watch the kittens and puppies playing. They were so cute! Cassie's parents had never allowed her to have pets. Her mother was allergic to cats and her father was allergic to dogs. She had been allowed a gold fish once, but it had died after a few weeks.

Matt watched various emotions run across her face. "Would you like to go inside?"

Cassie shook her head. "No, that's okay. I just like watching them."

Matt had watched Cassie as she watched the animals play. She had looked at them with longing. He knew she didn't have pets at home, but they had never discussed why. Since she was going to move in with him, the first thing he planned on buying her was a pet. Any kind she wanted! If she wanted a larger animal like a goat or a horse, he would just buy some land to go with it.

Matt tugged her hand and led her further down the sidewalk. The next window Cassie stopped at was an antique store. Matt had an idea.

"Let's go in for a minute," he said as he tugged her to the door.

"Okay," she replied.

Cassie allowed Matt to lead her into the antique store. It was much larger inside than it looked. They passed by clothing, sports cards, old movie posters, and other vintage items. Some of the clothes looked like they were from the eighteen-hundreds. When Matt found a jewelry case, he stopped to look inside. On the top shelf, Cassie saw a beautiful emerald choker with matching earrings and ring. The tag said they were from nineteen-hundred. Pierced ears weren't common until much later so the earrings had apparently been altered at some point.

Matt noticed the set and saw Cassie's expression. He had stopped to look at a diamond bracelet. Before he could ask Cassie if she liked anything in the case, she wandered off toward some old books. Matt straightened and motioned for the store clerk. When the lady arrived at the jewelry case, Matt looked over his shoulder to make sure Cassie was still occupied. The sales clerk noticed that he was trying to keep his purchase a secret and leaned closer to him so he could whisper to her.

"I'd like to purchase the emerald set on top and the diamond tennis bracelet on the shelf below them. I'm going to have some money wired to me this afternoon.

Would it be possible for you to hold them until four o'clock?" he asked.

"Sir, you do realize that the emerald set is priced at seven-thousand dollars and the diamond bracelet is another five-thousand?" the clerk asked, taking note of his casual clothes.

"Yes, ma'am. I'm well aware of that. If you're able to hold the items until four o'clock, there will be a tip for you when I return to purchase them," he replied.

The clerk nodded. "Very well, sir. I'll place them behind the front counter once you and your lady have left."

"Thank you. My fiancé was looking at them a moment ago and I would really like to surprise her," he confided.

The sales clerk smiled at him and stepped back to her position behind the main counter. Matt walked over to Cassie. She was still looking at the old books. "Find anything, honey?"

Cassie looked at him in surprise. She wasn't used to hearing him call her anything other than her name. "I was just looking. Shall we head further down the street to another store?"

"If that's what you'd like," he held his hand out to her.

Cassie took his hand and led him out of the store. Everything in there had been really expensive. Matt may be rich, but there was no sense spending money when you didn't have to. She was fairly certain that he was used to buying whatever he wanted. She would have to teach him how to be frugal.

"Let's find a clothing store. You still need a coat," he said.

Cassie looked up at him. "Shouldn't we find the Medical Examiner first? So we can get your DNA test?"

"That's a good idea. Your father said that Dr. McKinney's office is off Main Street and Third. It should be just a little further," he replied.

They headed toward the ME's office. When they arrived, Dr. McKinney himself met them at the door. "It's nice to meet you, Mr. Spencer."

"Nice to meet you as well, Dr. McKinney. This is my fiancée, Cassandra Morgan," Matt said, motioning to Cassie.

Dr. McKinney nodded to Cassie. "Mr. Spencer, I have to say that I was honored when Mr. Morgan asked me to take your DNA swab."

"Why is that Dr. McKinney," Matt asked in curiosity.

"I grew up in Spencer Falls. My grandfather, Caleb McKinney was friends with the Matthew Spencer that was murdered in nineteen-fifty-one."

Matt was surprised. "I remember reading something of my grandfather's that mentioned Caleb. He considered him a true friend."

"I'm sure my grandfather would be happy to hear it. Now, let's get that DNA test completed. I can actually complete the test here and fax the results to the law office immediately. They should have everything within an hour, two at most."

"Thank you very much Dr. McKinney. What kind of test did the law office request," Matt asked.

"They said we could do either an oral swab or a blood test."

Matt wasn't familiar with the current technology for DNA testing. "Which will be more absolute?"

"Blood, though either will work," the doctor replied.

"Then let's go with the blood test." Matt looked at Cassie. "Honey, why don't you wait up here for me? I shouldn't be long."

"Okay. I'll just sit here and look through a magazine for a minute," Cassie said, motioning to a nearby chair.

Matt and Dr. McKinney walked into the back. A few minutes later, they both came back to the lobby. Matt shook Dr. McKinney's hand and helped Cassie up from her chair. "If you want to call the law office in about two hours, they should have the results."

Matt smiled at the doctor. "Thank you. I really appreciate this."

"It's no trouble. Nice to meet both of you! I hope you enjoy your stay," Dr. McKinney said with a smile.

"Have a nice day, Dr. McKinney," Matt replied.

The men shook hands and Matt opened the door for Cassie. They stepped out in the chilly October morning and went in search of a clothing store. Matt didn't want Cassie to get sick by running around without a coat. Cassie started to enter the same vintage shop she had been in a few days earlier, but Matt tugged her across the street to an upscale store.

"Matt, you don't have to do this. That vintage shop was just fine," she told him.

"Cassie, would you please just let me take care of you? I want to buy you a coat. May I do that one small thing for the woman I'm going to marry," he asked.

Cassie smiled at him. "Of course. I didn't mean to sound ungrateful."

Matt kissed her on the cheek. "You're not ungrateful. Just unspoiled."

Cassie walked over to the women's clothing area. She saw a beautiful black coat with embroidery on the lapel. She found one in her size and tried it on. Before she could look at the price tag, Matt had torn it from the coat.

"What are you doing?" she asked.

Matt grinned at her. "Buying you a coat of course. No sense in you taking it off."

"Matt, for all I know this coat costs a fortune. I don't need an expensive coat," she argued.

Matt placed his finger over her lips. "I'm buying the coat for you Cassie."

Cassie shook her head at him, but quietly followed him to the register. He handed the sales clerk the ticket.

When the coat was rung up, the total came to one-hundred-thirty-nine dollars. Cassie was astounded. She knew it was an expensive coat, but she hadn't realized just how expensive. Cassie did her best to hold her tongue as Matt paid for the coat. When they were back outside the store, she turned to face him.

"Thank you for my new coat," she said.

Matt smiled at her. "You're welcome."

They walked down to the five n' dime store Cassie had been to before. When they entered, Matt chose a small booth in the corner. He handed Cassie a menu and took one for himself. It didn't take them long to decide what to eat for lunch. It was still a little early so they had the place to themselves. The same man that had waited on Cassie before came to take their order.

"It's nice to see you again, young lady," the man said with a smile.

Cassie smiled at him. "Thank you. I told my fiancé about this place and we just had to stop for lunch."

"Well, I'm glad you did. What can I get for you?"

"I'll have a cheeseburger with everything and a side of fries. Do you have strawberry milkshakes?" she asked.

The man smiled. "Yes, ma'am, we sure do."

"I'll take one of those as well please," she replied.

Turning to Matt he asked, "And for you sir?"

"I'll have the same, but make my shake a chocolate one," Matt said.

"I'll have your order out to you in just a few minutes," replied the man.

The man went back behind the counter to start on their order. Once the cheeseburgers were started, he went to work on the milkshakes. He looked over at the young couple and smiled. They only had eyes for each other. He remembered those days well. His wife had passed on, but she had been the love of his life. When the milkshakes were done, he took them over to their table.

"Here you go. Y'all enjoy those and I'll have your cheeseburgers and fries ready in no time."

"Thank you." Cassie smiled at him. He was such a nice man.

Matt watched her. She was kind to everyone around her. "Have I told you lately how much I love you?"

She grinned at him. "Only a few dozen times, but I'd love to hear it a few dozen more."

Matt smiled at her. He reached across the table and took her hand in his. He loved seeing the engagement ring on her finger, knowing that he had been the one to put it there. It may not have been a ring he had purchased, but her father had given it to them as a family heirloom which made it much more special. Knowing that he had Mr. Morgan's blessing meant a lot to him. It was nice to be wanted for who you were and not for how much money you had.

"What time do you need to call the law office? Do you have their number?" Cassie asked.

Matt rubbed his thumb across her knuckles. "It was eleven o'clock when Dr. McKinney took my blood for the DNA test. He said to wait about two hours. So I guess I should call around one o'clock this afternoon. Your father gave me their number. Would you mind if I used your cell phone to call when the time comes?"

"Of course not," she replied.

Matt looked thoughtful for a minute. "That's something you can help me with. I'll need to purchase a cell phone. Maybe I should start with one of those 'pay as you go' phones they advertise on TV. If it looks like I'll use it a lot, I can set up a service contract with someone."

Cassie smiled; happy she could help him with something. "I'd love to help you. I bet the retail side of the five n' dime will have some. Or we can look for an electronics store. I'm sure they have one nearby."

Their food arrived at that moment, and it smelled wonderful. "Here ya go."

"Wow, this looks delicious. Thank you," she told the man.

"You're welcome, young lady. I hope you enjoy it. If you decide you want dessert, you just give me a shout."

Matt grinned. "Knowing my Cassie, we'll be shouting before too long."

The man chuckled as he went back behind the counter. Cassie looked at Matt.

"What is it Cass?" he asked.

"Nothing. You just know me so well," she replied.

Matt laughed. "After five years I'd better!"

As they were eating, Cassie's phone rang. She fished it out of her purse and managed to answer it before it stopped ringing. It was her dad. He had the worst timing on the planet. He either called when she was eating or when she was in the shower.

"Hi, Daddy."

"Hi, sweetheart. Is Matt around?"

"Sure, Daddy. Just a minute."

Cassie passed the phone to Matt. "He wants to speak to you."

Matt took the phone from her. "Hello."

"Matt! I heard from Dr. McKinney. The test results were faxed to the lawyers a few minutes ago. You can call them at any time. Do you still have their number?"

Matt was surprised. "Yes, sir. I can't thank you enough for all you've done."

"Just make my little girl happy and we'll call it even."

Matt smiled. "I'm doing my best, sir. We'll call you later tonight... hopefully with good news."

"You do that. Enjoy your afternoon. Tell Cassie I said bye and that I love her."

"Yes, sir. Goodbye."

Matt hung up the phone and gave it back to Cassie. "He said to tell you bye and that he loves you."

"Is that all?" Cassie asked, curious what the conversation had been about.

"He said the lawyers should have the DNA results now."

Cassie handed the phone back to him. "Call them. Let's get it over with and see what they say."

Matt took the phone from her and dug the number out of his pocket. He opened the phone and dialed the number. The secretary answered on the third ring.

"Mason, Gamble and Henry. How may I help you?"

"May I speak with Mr. Mason please," Matt asked.

"May I tell him whose calling?"

"Matthew Spencer."

"Oh my! Right away sir."

The secretary transferred him to Mr. Mason's office. If Matt had to guess, the Mr. Mason he was about to speak with was either his friend John Mason, or John's son. The elder Mr. Mason was sure to be dead by now. He had been in his fifties when Matt had passed away.

"This is Sam Mason."

"Mr. Mason, this is Matthew Spencer."

"Matthew! May I call you Matthew?" the lawyer asked excitedly.

"It's Matt actually," he said with a grin.

"Please call me Sam. I can't tell you how happy I am to hear from you. We received the DNA results from a Dr. McKinney in Whispering Lake, North Carolina, about ten minutes ago. Our office has been holding your property for quite some time in hopes that an heir could be found."

"I'm very grateful to your office. I assume this means that the property and funds are now legally mine?" Matt asked.

"There's some paper work that needs to be completed, but yes... essentially it's all yours."

216

"Could you fax the papers to me so I can get it taken care of today? I'd like to have some money wired to me in Whispering Lake, North Carolina. I'm vacationing this week with my fiancé," Matt replied.

"Congratulations! Mr. Morgan hadn't informed me you were engaged. If I may ask, who is the lucky woman?"

"Mr. Morgan's daughter, Cassie. We haven't told him just yet."

"I'm sure he will be thrilled with the news. He spoke very highly of you," Sam told him.

"Thank you."

"I can fax the required papers as soon as you give me a fax number. Once I have them, I can wire the money to the western union office on Main Street in Whispering Lake. You should have your funds within an hour of the fax coming through. Will that be soon enough?"

"Yes, that sounds great. I don't know where a fax machine is right now. Once I locate one, I'll call you back."

"Very well. I look forward to hearing from you again Matt."

"Thanks, Sam."

Matt hung up the phone and once more handed it back to Cassie. "Once we're finished eating, I need to find a fax machine. Sam's going to send me some papers I need to sign. Once that's complete, I can fax them back and my wire transfer should come through within the hour."

Cassie smiled at him. "That's wonderful Matt! I know you must be relieved to have that out of the way."

"It's good to know who you are and where you're heading," he admitted.

Cassie smiled at him. She had finished off her cheeseburger and was almost done with her fries. As much as she would love to have dessert, she wasn't sure she'd be able to eat any more. She was absolutely stuffed.

Noticing that she was almost done, he asked, "Want anything else?"

"No, thanks. I'm actually pretty full," she answered.

Matt stood and reached for the check. "I'm going to go pay our check while you finish your fries."

"Okay."

Cassie watched him walk up to the counter and sighed. He was just as wonderful to look at from behind as he was from the front. He paid their ticket, gave the sweet man behind the counter a tip, and headed back to their table. Cassie stood up and put her coat on.

"Ready to go find a fax machine?" Cassie asked.

"The man at the counter said we can find one at the electronics store around the corner. I can get my faxes taken care of and buy a cell phone all in the same place," he told her.

They left the store and headed around the corner. Half way down the block they saw a sign that said 'Smythe's Electronics.' They hurried the rest of the way there. When they entered the store, Matt noticed they were the only ones there. He rang the bell on the counter and a lady came out of the back room.

"May I help you?" the lady asked.

"Is it possible to have a fax sent here? And to send one back," Matt asked her.

The lady smiled. "Of course. It costs one dollar per page to receive one."

"That's fine. What's the number to your fax machine?" he asked.

He wrote the number down as the clerk gave it to him. He borrowed Cassie's phone once more and called Sam's office. After he gave Sam the number, he hung up and passed the phone back to Cassie. Within a few minutes, the fax machine started receiving the documents. Most of it was straight forward, but he wasn't sure what to put down for driver's license number, address and phone number. He borrowed Cassie's phone again and called her father. The clerk allowed them the use of the office since they were discussing confidential matters.

"Mr. Morgan? I hate to bother you again, sir, but I've run into a problem. The lawyers sent the paperwork to me, but they want my social security number, my phone number, my address and my driver's license number. I have the social security card you brought me, but I don't have anything else."

"Not entirely true. Apparently your father had some really high connections that have passed their loyalty to your family down through their generations as well. One of them is in a high position with the DMV. Have Cassie use her cell phone to take a picture of you against a solid blue background. Ask her to email it to me and your license will be ready in a few hours. He's going to overnight it to you."

Matt was a little relieved. "Thank you, sir."

"Son, as far as I'm concerned, you might as well be family already. Either call me dad or call me Stan. Either one works for me."

"I'd be honored to call you dad," Matt said, his voice tight with emotion.

Cassie looked at him. He could tell that she wanted to share their news with her father, but he would prefer to do it face to face. He shook his head at her. The timing wasn't right just yet. They would tell her parents when they got back to Ashton Grove.

"I'd like that, Matt. What else did you need?"

"Address and phone number. Although, I'm about to purchase a prepaid cell phone so that will take care of the phone number," Matt replied.

"That isn't necessary. Have Cassie take you to a cell phone store and add you to her plan. It would make sense for you both to be on the same one anyway, especially if she ends up moving to the Burberry house with you. Which leads me to your address problem... you already have one. Do you have a pen and paper for all of this information?"

"I'm ready."

Mr. Morgan gave Matt all of the information he needed. Matt completed the forms and he and Cassie went back out into the store. He temporarily had used Cassie's cell phone as his phone number. Once the documents were faxed back to Sam's office, they would locate the nearest cell phone store.

The clerk faxed the papers for them and rang up Matt's bill. It cost him thirty-five dollars between the thirty page fax he received and the five dollar charge to send everything back to Sam. The lady was even nice enough to tell them where they could locate the phone store, the western union and the post office.

When Cassie and Matt left the electronic store, they headed to the phone store. Matt would feel better once he had his own phone and didn't have to constantly use Cassie's. After he received his ID, he would check on getting a credit card and have the phones transferred into his name.

When they entered the store, Matt was a little overwhelmed. There were phones lining all of the walls and tons of rotating shelves in the middle with accessories. He ended up selecting something called a Razor. It was steel gray and light weight. Cassie talked him into a phone charger for the car, a carrying case and something called a Bluetooth. He figured she would explain all of it to him later.

Once his phone was activated, he called Sam's office and gave him the new cell number. Sam said that the western union transfer should have been completed so that's where they headed next. Part of the paperwork he had faxed had requested that fifteen thousand dollars be transferred for immediate cash access. He had also requested to have fifty-thousand dollars deposited into a new checking account for him. Sam promised to take care of everything.

Matt and Cassie found the Western Union place easily enough; it was three doors down from the phone store. Once Matt had his cash, they headed to the post office. He wanted to mail the original documents back to Sam's office. He used the copy machine out front to make a copy of the main page with his ID numbers, address and phone number on it. Then he put everything in an express mail envelope and had it shipped to Sam Mason's attention.

"I want to go through that antique store one more time. Do you mind?" he asked.

"No. We can go where ever you'd like. As long as I get to spend the day with you, I don't care where we go." Cassie threaded her fingers through his and they walked over to the antique store.

When they entered the shop, the lady behind the counter recognized him and welcomed them back. Cassie headed for the back of the store. She hadn't been that far before and wanted to explore a little while Matt looked around. Little did she know that Matt had already made his selections and just needed to pay for them.

Once the emerald set and diamond bracelet were paid for and packaged, Matt went in search of Cassie. He found her at the very back of the store. One of the cubicles held a bunch of baby items. There was a rocking horse from 1910, a cradle from the 1800s, and many other items. Matt watched her reverently run her fingers over the rocking horse and cradle. She hadn't noticed he was there yet and she gently touched her stomach. Matt knew that it would take at least a month before they would know if last night and this morning had resulted in a baby. He had spent most of the day hoping it hadn't, not for his sake but for Cassie's. Maybe he had been wrong to insist that she wasn't ready for a family.

"Do you like those?" he asked.

Cassie jumped in surprise. She hadn't heard Matt approach. "Oh! I was just looking."

Matt looked at her and asked again, "Do you like them?"

She sighed. "They're both lovely, but we don't need them."

"Maybe we do and maybe we don't at the moment, but eventually I'm hoping we will. Would you like to have them? I could have them shipped to the Burberry house," he offered.

Cassie shook her head. "They're too much, Matt."

"How much is too much?" he asked.

"The horse is three-hundred dollars and the cradle is almost a thousand dollars."

Matt smiled. "Let me talk to the clerk and see if she'll hold them until we return home. I should have a box of checks waiting on me when we get back to Ashton Grove. Why don't you wait here and I'll be back in a minute?"

"Okay." Cassie smiled at him. He was such a wonderful man.

Matt made his way back up to the front of the store. The clerk was on the phone so he patiently waited nearby and looked at some oil paintings on the wall. When he got to the last one, he couldn't believe his eyes. It was a family portrait of him, his sister and his parents in front of their home in Spencer Falls. He vaguely remembered his father commissioning it, but he hadn't realized it was no longer hanging in the hall of his family home. Apparently his home was not as intact as the law office believed.

The clerk walked over to him. "May I help you with something?"

He turned to look at the clerk. "Do you know where you got this painting?"

"I believe it was brought in about twenty years ago. I don't remember who sold it to us though," she told him.

"That's my family homestead," Matt said, nodding to the picture.

"You're related to the Spencer's of Spencer Falls?" she asked.

"Yes ma'am. My name is Matthew Adrian Spencer, III. The little boy in the painting is my grandfather," he replied, sticking to the story they had concocted.

The clerk look horrified. "Oh my! Well, I know it wasn't your father who sold it to us because the young man looked like he was still in college. I just feel terrible about this! I insist that you take the painting with you!"

"That isn't necessary, but I would be happy to purchase it from you. That is, if you could have it shipped," he asked with a hopeful expression.

She smiled at him. "Of course. I'll sell it to you for five hundred dollars."

"The tag on the painting says that it costs a thousand dollars," he told her.

"Consider it a family discount." The clerk smiled at him.

"That's very kind of you. If shipping items isn't a problem, I do have another request. My fiancé fell in love with an old rocking horse and cradle in the back of your store. The only problem is that after purchasing the jewelry, which she doesn't know about, I don't have enough cash left to buy them right now and my new checks hadn't arrived before we came here. We're heading home in a few days. Would you be willing to hold all three items and allow me to mail a check to you? I'd be happy to overnight it."

"I would be happy to. Just let me put some sold tags on the items and I'll write up an invoice for you. If you'll mail it back with the check, I would appreciate it. Makes my bookkeeping a bit easier."

"I understand. That won't be a problem. Thank you so much for working with me. Cassie really had her heart set on those baby items and I don't think I could have handled breaking her heart."

"Are y'all expecting?" she asked out of curiosity.

He smiled. "No, ma'am. I think she wouldn't mind if we were though. I have a feeling this will be a short engagement."

The clerk laughed. "I don't blame her. You seem like a wonderful, honest young man. There aren't too many of y'all running around these days."

"The world has definitely changed over the last fifty years," he agreed.

"Yes, it has. I'll be back there in just a moment with the tags if you'd like to go and give her the good news."

He nodded. "Thank you."

Matt headed back toward Cassie. On his way, he pulled out his cell phone and called Sam's office. He told him about the painting and asked to have photographs and an inventory of items be sent to his home address in Ashton Grove. Sam promised to get right on it and recommended that Matt make a trip to Spencer Falls as soon as possible. If he didn't plan on living in the house year round, some provisions would have to be made so this type of thing wouldn't happen again.

Cassie noticed his anxious expression and asked, "Are you okay, Matt?"

"I'm fine. Just a little shocked. I found a family portrait in the front of the store. It should be hanging on the wall at the house in Spencer Falls, but someone liberated it about twenty years ago and brought it here. The clerk is going to ship it with these two items after we return home. I promised to overnight a check to her."

"Oh, Matt. That's terrible about your painting! I'm glad you found it again though."

"Me too. I called Sam's office and they are going to inventory everything in the house and send the list, along with photos, to the house in Ashton Grove. Still, I'll have to make a trip there soon. I need to make sure that things like that don't continue to happen. Even if we don't live there, it would be nice to vacation there a few times a year and either retire there or pass it on to our children."

Cassie smiled at him. "I'd like that."

The clerk arrived with the sold tags and placed them on the rocking horse and the cradle. They thanked her and left the store. They had finished everything sooner than anticipated so Matt suggested they shop for clothes. He thought it would be nice to dress up for dinner. Cassie agreed, but only if he allowed her to shop in the vintage clothing shop. He was reluctant, but he finally agreed.

Inside the store, Cassie went straight to the dresses in the back. It had been a few days since she had found the red dress and she hoped they had gotten more items in since then. She found a stunning slate gray a-line dress that was knee length with spaghetti straps. It was thirty dollars, but that was a steal considering it was made by Jones New York. She found a pair of matching shoes that were her size and a beautiful wrap that was the same slate gray and had pink flowers embroidered on it. Once she had gathered all of her items, she went in search of Matt.

Matt was in the men's section. He had found a pair of tailored black slacks that had probably cost several hundred dollars new, but at the vintage shop they were only twenty dollars. When he saw her dress, he selected a gray shirt to match. He even lucked out in the shoe area and found a pair of black dress shoes that were still in their original box and had never been worn. Her father had already provided him with a brown belt and a black belt so he was covered in that department. They walked over to the register. When Matt went to grab his wallet, Cassie stopped him.

"It's my turn." She pulled out her credit card before he could argue. After she signed the receipt, they left with their purchases and headed for the car.

"You didn't have to do that Cassie," he told her.

She smiled. "I know, but I wanted to. Besides, knowing you, I'll get my next credit card statement and find out that it's been paid off."

"You know me so well!"

Cassie laughed at him. "I know that a million dollars is a lot of money, but what do you plan on doing to make sure you have some coming in all the time? If you keep insisting that we shop at expensive places, you'll be out of money in no time."

"I'm leaving most of it in the stock market. I sold some shares and cashed out a million dollars worth, but I have about another two million still tied up in Coca-Cola and some other companies that hit it big."

Cassie was stunned. She'd had no idea that Matthew's estate was worth that much. His father had invested his money very well. If Matt didn't want to, he wouldn't have to work a day in his life.

"I still plan on meeting with the architect your dad knows. It wouldn't hurt to get back into design work again. I kind of miss it truth be told," he said with a grin.

Cassie had even more respect for him than she had before. "You'd still work even though you don't have to?"

"Yes, I would. I don't have to work long hours like I did before though. I promise to make sure that I spend plenty of time with you, and later when we have a family, with our children."

Matt opened the trunk of the car and put their packages inside. Thankfully Cassie hadn't asked any questions about the small sack from the antique store. He was hoping she thought he had purchased something for himself. He wanted to give her the diamond bracelet tonight, but he would save the emeralds for another day.

Once their bags were safely stowed in the trunk, he walked around to the passenger side and let Cassie in. After closing her door, he walked around the front of the car and got in on the driver's side. He started the car and they headed back to the lodge.

By the time they arrived, it was already dark outside. Dinner would be served in about two hours, which gave them plenty of time to get ready. Matt parked the car and retrieved their bags from the trunk. When he and Cassie got to the cabin, all of the lights were on.

Cassie was the first to walk inside. Gabriel and Cole were on the couch watching TV, but Michael was nowhere to be seen. She and Matt started toward their room, but Gabriel stopped them.

"Hold up a minute you two."

Cassie turned toward him. "What is it Gabriel?"

"I had an idea today. When my brothers and I first got here, I took the master suite because I was the oldest. Since the two of you are sharing a room, not to mention that women tend to be in the bathroom longer than men when it comes to getting ready, I thought you might like to switch rooms. The master has a bathroom with a shower and a garden tub. It also has a closet and a larger dresser, not to mention a queen size bed."

"That's really nice of you, but you don't have to do that." It touched Cassie that he would be so thoughtful.

"It's no problem. Really. Do you want to switch?" he asked.

Cassie looked at Matt. It would give them more privacy and she certainly loved the sound of that garden tub! "What do you think?"

"Whatever would make you happiest is fine with me."

Cassie smiled. "Then we accept. It's so nice of you to offer to change rooms."

"It's not a problem. The maid came through an hour ago and changed all of the sheets. She also picked up everyone's laundry and promised to have it back in the morning."

"Thanks for letting me know. I was starting to get embarrassed over the mountain of clothes in my floor," she said.

Gabriel laughed. "Just give me a second to clear out my things."

While Gabriel was cleaning out his room, Cassie and Matt packed their clean clothes back into their bags. Cassie grabbed their things from the bathroom and headed toward Gabriel's room. Matt was still gathering their bags from their bedroom.

Once Gabriel was finished, Cassie went into their new room and started setting up their bathroom things. She heard Matt enter the bedroom and start opening drawers in the dresser. It was a little silly to change rooms with only a few days left of their trip, but Cassie was grateful for the privacy. The queen size bed was nice too.

After they had everything put away, they both collapsed on the bed. They'd had a long, exhausting day. Cassie rolled onto her side and snuggled against Matt. He put his arm around her and pulled her close.

"Think we have time for a nap before dinner? I'm wiped out from all of our walking today," she said.

Matt smiled. "I think we can manage an hour nap. Anything past that and you might not have enough time to get ready for dinner."

Cassie sat up. "I'll just set the alarm on my phone. That way we won't over sleep."

Once the alarm was set and the phone was placed on the night stand, Cassie snuggled against Matt again. He rolled onto his side, facing her. Pulling her close, he kissed the top of her head. Before long, they were both sound asleep with their bodies intertwined.

Chapter Sixteen

The alarm went off an hour later, startling them both awake. Cassie reached for the phone and shut the alarm off. It didn't feel like she had been asleep for an hour. For some reason, she was still really tired. Cassie groaned and sat up on the edge of the bed.

"Has it already been an hour," she mumbled.

"I'm afraid so, honey. Still tired," he asked, rubbing her back.

"A little," she admitted.

Matt kissed her on the cheek. "We better start getting ready for dinner. Unless you'd like to go into town for something instead?"

"No, eating at the lodge is fine. If we were at home though, I'd be sorely tempted to order a pizza," she replied.

Matt could sympathize. He had never eaten a pizza before, but he knew it to be one of Cassie's favorite quick meals. "We'll be home before you know it."

Matt realized that he was going to have to rethink his plans. When Cassie had first mentioned moving in with him, he had been adamant that she have a separate room until they were married. Since they had slept together twice now, and more than likely would again, there was no point in her sleeping anywhere other than in his bed. He had no idea what the house looked like or the type of furniture it had. Perhaps he would call Mr. Morgan later and inquire about it. He hated to wait until they arrived home to find out the master had a double bed or no bed at all.

Cassie went into the bathroom to start getting ready. She brushed her teeth, washed her face, and brushed her hair. Heading back into the bedroom, she got out her new dress and wrap. The dress had spaghetti straps, which meant that a normal bra wouldn't work. Unfortunately, Cassie had such a large bust that going braless was not an option. She dug through the dresser until she found her black satin strapless bra and matching panties. Cassie couldn't remember why she had packed them as nothing she had brought with her required them, but she was glad to have them.

Once she had gathered all of her clothes, she went back into the bathroom. There was no point in closing the door as Matt had already seen all of her there was to see. She took off the clothes she had worn into town and slipped on the satin panties and bra. Before putting on her new dress, she reapplied her makeup.

Instead of her usual bland eye shadow and generic looking blush, she applied a smoky gray eye shadow to her lower lid and followed it up with a sparkling silver one. She lined her eyes with black liquid eyeliner and used her long-lash mascara. She looked a little pale from a lack of sleep. Reaching into her makeup bag, she dug around until she found her iridescent plum blush. She applied a light layer to her cheek bones. Already she looked a hundred times better. To finish off the look, she put on a sheer plum lip gloss.

Cassie's hair was long and wavy, but after sleeping on it for an hour all of the curl had tumbled out of it. She turned on her curling iron and spritzed a little spray gel into her hair. While she was waiting on the curling iron to get hot, she climbed into her dress. She reached for the zipper, but there was no way for her to fasten it on her own.

"Matt? Could you help me a minute?" she called.

"What is it Cassie?" Matt stopped in the bathroom doorway and stared.

"Don't just stand there. I need your help," she said.

"What do you need help with?" He was hoping she needed help getting out of her dress. She looked beautiful!

Turning around, she asked, "Can you please zip me? I can't quite reach it."

Matt walked over and stood behind Cassie. He could see the top of her black satin panties and noticed her bra matched. Reaching down to grasp the zipper, he slowly zipped the back of her dress. When he was finished, he looked over her head at their reflection in the mirror. She was a little over a foot shorter than he was, so her head didn't even reach his shoulders.

"You look amazing."

Cassie smiled at him. "Thank you. Now scoot so I can finish my hair."

Matt grinned at her and went back into the bedroom. He quickly changed his clothes and put on his shoes while Cassie was working on her hair. He sat on the bed while he waited on her. It had been his experience that Cassie took at least an hour to get ready if she was 'going all out,' as she liked to say. She used to talk to him through the closed bathroom door when she was getting ready. He glanced toward the open door. Things had definitely changed for the better.

When Cassie was finished creating her spiral curls, she gathered one side and put a rhinestone barrette in it. Walking back into the bedroom, she slipped on the matching gray shoes. Opening the dresser drawer, she pulled out her jewelry box and put her small diamond earrings in. She also selected her diamond heart pendant that had belonged to her grandmother.

Turning to face Matt she said, "Now all that's missing is a bracelet. Since I don't have one to match, I'm ready to go."

"That's not entirely true." Matt walked over to her. Opening the other side of the dresser, he pulled out a long

231

white box. "I wasn't sure when I was going to give this to you, but I think this is the right moment."

Cassie took the box from him. When had he purchased jewelry for her? She'd been with him all day. Then she remembered that he had left the antique store with a small bag. All of the jewelry in the store had cost a fortune. She opened the box and gasped. Inside was a gorgeous diamond bracelet.

"Matt. I don't know what to say. It's beautiful!"

He smiled, happy that she liked it. "Not half as beautiful as you. I wanted you to have something to go with your engagement ring."

Taking the box from her, he removed the bracelet. He unclasped it and looped it around her wrist. Fastening it, he gently rubbed his thumb across the underside of her wrist. "I wanted to get you something special."

"Oh, Matt. I love it!" Cassie threw her arms around him.

Smiling down at her, Matt tipped her chin up. He bent down and gently kissed her on the lips. "I'm glad. Now, let's go to dinner, shall we?"

Cassie looped her arm through his. They grabbed their coats and headed into the living room. Gabriel, Michael and Cole had already left for dinner. Matt helped Cassie into her coat before putting on his own. He opened the front door and escorted her out on the porch. They made sure the door was locked and started walking toward the lodge. It was cold outside and Cassie stayed as close to Matt as she could.

When they got to the lodge, he held the door open for her. Cassie hurried inside, thankful to be warm again. She took off her coat and handed it to their hostess. The one thing Cassie disliked about cold weather was the necessity of a winter coat. They didn't go well with nice dresses. The hostess took Cassie's and Matt's coats and hung them up before escorting them to their table.

Once they were seated, the hostess handed them their menus and excused herself. Cassie placed her menu on the table and watched Matt. He was very handsome and looked very refined tonight. She could hardly believe that he was her fiancé. How had she ever managed to get so lucky? Not to mention that he was a wonderful lover. Granted, she didn't have anyone to compare him to, but she couldn't imagine being with anyone else.

Normally Cassie loved to eat and looked forward to dinner. Tonight she was looking forward to being alone with Matt – preferably in their bed, naked. She hadn't had a chance to explore that gorgeous body of his yet and fully intended to do so! Even though they had made love both last night and this morning, she couldn't seem to get enough of him.

Matt noticed Cassie was staring at him. "Something on your mind honey?"

Cassie blushed. "Nope, not a thing."

She picked her menu back up and opened it to the entrée section. She casually peeked over the top of the menu to see if Matt was still looking at her. Yep, he had sat his menu down and was watching her with one raised eyebrow. Guess he hadn't bought that 'nothing' comment after all.

Cassie sighed and put down her menu. "What?"

"What happened to not lying to me," he asked.

"Who said I was lying?" Cassie gave him a wide-eyed innocent look.

Matt crossed his arms and looked at her. "Try again."

"Um... Can I get back to you on that?"

Matt shook his head. "Cassie, just tell me what you were thinking."

"I can't!!"

"Why not," he asked.

"Because we're in the middle of a restaurant... and it was rather x-rated," she mumbled.

"Ah. That explains the blush." Matt smiled at her.

"Hmph." Cassie picked up her menu and did her best to ignore him. She still hadn't decided what to order when the waiter returned.

"Are you ready to order ma'am, sir?"

Cassie put down her menu and looked at Matt. "Would you mind ordering for me? I just can't decide what I want."

Matt grinned. He knew it had nothing to do with indecision and more to do with her mind being in the gutter. "Sure, honey."

He turned his attention to their waiter. "We'd both like to have the grilled chicken, steamed vegetables and rice pilaf. Could you also bring a glass of wine with dinner?"

The waiter wrote everything down. "Of course, sir. Will that be all?"

"I think that will take care of us until dessert."

The waiter headed toward the kitchen to give the chef their order. He returned a moment later with some glasses of water. "I thought you might like these until dinner arrives."

"Thank you," Matt said.

After the waiter left, he reached across the table for her hand. Cassie put her hand in Matt's. Her diamond ring sparkled in the candle light. Every time she saw it, her heart skipped a beat. It still didn't seem possible that Matt was really here with her and that they were getting married! She couldn't have asked for more.

Matt gently rubbed his fingers against her palm. "I love you, Cassie. I know I've told you that about a hundred times since I got here two days ago, but I feel like I'll never be able to say it enough."

Cassie smiled. "I love you, too. You can tell me that as many times as you want. I promise that I will never get tired of hearing it."

Matt lifted her hand to his lips and gently kissed the backs of her fingers. "I wish our food would get here. I'm rather anxious to get back to our room."

Cassie blushed. She was looking forward to that part too. "I couldn't agree more."

Matt's phone started ringing. "Honey, would you excuse me a minute? I think this might be Sam calling."

"Sure. I hope everything is okay."

"I'm sure it is. I'll be back in just a minute." Matt got up from the table and headed out onto the porch.

Once he was outside, he answered his phone. "Hello."

"Matt? It's Sam."

"Hi, Sam. What can I do for you?"

"I just wanted to let you know that I've processed all of the papers you sent to me. I noticed that on page twenty you said that everything should go to Cassie in the event of your death. Are you sure you want to do that before you're married? What about your family?" Sam asked.

"I don't have any remaining family. Cassie and I may only be engaged, but as far as I'm concerned she's my wife. She plans on moving in with me once we return to Ashton Grove," Matt replied.

"If that's how you want it, then we'll honor your wishes. Not that we want anything to happen to you! It's just that most men of your wealth generally obtain a prenuptial agreement in the event of a divorce. I noticed you declined that on the papers."

"Cassie is a very special lady. I can honestly say there isn't another like her in the world. Nothing is going to come between us, now or ever. Actually, we just recently decided to make one of the spare rooms into a nursery. We aren't expecting yet, but I think Cassie wants to start a family soon," Matt told him, hoping to ease the lawyer's mind.

"Well, it sounds like you have the real thing. I'm happy for you both."

"Thanks, Sam. I appreciate your concern."

Matt closed the phone and headed back inside. Around the corner of the lodge, Michael had been listening to Matt's conversation. So, if anything happened to Matt, Cassie became a very rich woman. He knew that he screwed up with her so it wouldn't matter if he were the last man on earth... but if Matt were out of the picture maybe she would give Cole another chance.

Michael headed back to the cabin. He had some planning to do. Cole had been moping ever since Matt had shown up. Everyone could tell that Matt and Cassie were really in love with each other, but Michael knew that she had been happy with Cole. It seemed reasonable that she would be happy with him again. All he had to do was remove Matt from the equation.

Back at the lodge, Matt was sitting back down to dinner with Cassie. Their food had arrived, but she had waited on him to return before eating.

"You didn't have to wait on me," he told her.

"I wanted to. Is everything okay with Sam?"

"Everything is fine. He just wanted to double check on the papers I had faxed to him. He said they should all be processed by the time we're done eating."

She smiled at him. "That's wonderful. I know you'll be happy to get everything settled."

Cassie dug into her food. It was delicious! Matt always did such a great job at selecting things she liked. He was absolutely perfect for her. She couldn't imagine being with anyone else. Even though she still felt bad about Cole, she was so happy that Matt was here.

Chapter Seventeen

After dinner, Cassie and Matt went back to the cabin. No one else was home. They smiled at each other and headed to the bedroom. Since they were alone, they wouldn't have to worry about the brothers hearing anything. Cassie couldn't wait to get Matt behind a closed bedroom door!

Matt followed Cassie into the bedroom and shut the door. He turned her to face him and kissed her. He gently moved his lips over hers. Cassie wrapped her arms around Matt and pressed her body against his. Putting his hands on her hips, he pulled her closer.

Outside a wolf howled. Cassie gasped and jumped back. "What was that?"

Matt looked perplexed. There shouldn't be wild wolves around here. "It sounded like a wolf."

"In the woods? Where I hike?" Cassie shivered. "Remind me to never go in there again!"

Matt rubbed his hands up and down Cassie's arms. "It's okay honey. Why don't you go climb into a hot bubble bath and I'll step outside for a minute just to make sure the wolf isn't near the cabin."

She looked at him with slightly frightened eyes. "Is this really the time for a bath?"

Matt gave her a sexy grin. "I was kind of hoping to join you when I got back."

Cassie smiled. "Well, why didn't you just say so? Why go check on that wolf? Just follow me into the bathroom now."

"I would, but I know that you're going to worry about that wolf all night."

No sooner had the words left his mouth, than not only one wolf, but two wolves howled. There must be a pack that lived nearby. Matt was a little surprised. Wolves were supposed to be shy and should want to be far away from civilization.

Cassie was really scared. "Matt, I'd really rather you didn't go out there!"

Matt looked undecided. If they were wild wolves, she may have a point. Obviously if they were this close, they weren't typical ones. Looking at Cassie's worried face, he made up his mind. He held his hand out to her.

"Let's go take that bath."

Cassie smiled and threw her arms around him. "Thank you! I would have been so worried about you!"

"I know. That's why I decided to stay with you instead of going outside."

Cassie took Matt's hand and led him to the bathroom. She started filling the tub with hot water and added bubbles. Turning to face Matt she had a devious thought. She smiled at him and stepped closer.

She trailed her fingers down the front of his shirt, stopping at the waist of his pants. Cassie looked at Matt from under her eyelashes. She had a devilish grin on her face as she untucked his shirt. Walking her fingers up the front of his shirt, she started unfastening his buttons one at a time. When Matt's shirt was completely unfastened, she pushed it off his shoulders.

Matt had never been with a woman who was so brazen in the bedroom. He knew it was the two-thousands and not the nineteen-fifties, but the last time he had been with a woman she would have never thought of taking his shirt off of him. For that matter, she had just laid there and let him do all the work.

Matt stepped forwarded. Wrapping his arms around Cassie, he unzipped her dress. Slowly pulling the straps down her arms, he watched the dress slide off her body. She was left standing in nothing but her high heels and black satin bikini panties strapless bra. Matt felt his mouth go dry. Her breasts were swelling out of her bra. If she bent over, she'd probably spill out of it.

Cassie turned around. Leaning over the tub, she turned the faucet off. When she turned back around, Matt was staring at her. Or rather, he had been staring at her butt. Grinning, she walked over to him and started unfastening his belt. The belt slid from the loops easily and dropped to the ground with a thud. Cassie unfastened the button on his pants. As she reached for the zipper, Matt reached down and stopped her.

"Uh-uh. My turn."

Matt turned Cassie around. He lightly ran his hands up her back until he reached the band of her bra. Unhooking the clasp one hook at a time, he let it fall to the floor. Before Cassie could turn around, he slid his hands down her back and around to her stomach. Pulling her body tight against his, he reached up to cup her breasts. They were definitely more than a handful. Matt kissed her neck and flicked her nipples with his thumbs.

Cassie gasped and arched against him. Suddenly, he stopped and took a step back. She looked over her shoulder at him in bewilderment. It had felt so wonderful. Why had he stopped?

"I think it's your turn again," he told with a raspy voice.

Smiling, she stepped forward and reached for his pants. She slid the zipper down and pushed the pants off his hips. Kicking his shoes off, Matt stepped out of his pants and stood before her in nothing but his underwear. Cassie reached for the gray silk boxers, but he placed a hand over hers and stopped her.

Going down on his knees, Matt very slowly slid the black satin panties down her legs. He carefully removed them without taking off her shoes. He couldn't explain it, but there was something very sexy about her standing before him in nothing but a pair of three inch heels. As he stood, he slid his hands up her legs, trailing his fingers along her inner thighs. He let his fingers barely touch the curls at the junction of her thighs before drifting up her belly.

Cassie was so turned on she wasn't sure she could stand much more. She grabbed Matt's boxers and pulled them down. Before he realized what she intended, she was on her knees in front of him. Gazing up at him, she licked the tip of his erection before sucking it into her mouth. Matt groaned and grabbed a handful of her hair. He'd never had a woman do that before and it was exquisite torture.

Cassie sucked him all the way into her mouth until she felt him against the back of her throat. She loved the feel of his silky flesh sliding against her tongue as she pulled back until the just the tip of him was in her mouth. She loved both the taste and the feel of him. Having never done this before, she hoped she was doing it right. She sucked him all the way into her mouth again, stroking the length of him with her tongue. Matt briefly pulled her head closer, shoving himself further down her throat before quickly pulling all the way out of her mouth.

"If you don't stop that, I won't last another minute. No one has ever done that before."

Cassie looked up at him, "Didn't you like it?"

Matt pulled her to her feet. "More than anything."

"I wasn't doing it wrong?" she asked uncertainly.

"Honey, I haven't had that done before, but from where I'm standing you did everything right."

She smiled up at him. Cassie glanced over her shoulder at the tub then back at Matt. "I think the water can wait a minute. Since I'm still in these heels, there's something I want to try."

"And just where do you get all of these ideas?"

"From those romance novels I'm always reading. I just didn't think I'd ever get a chance to try them out personally," she replied.

Matt followed her to the bedroom. "And you're wanting to try what exactly?"

Cassie slipped his hand between her legs so he could feel how wet she was. "Since I'm ready for you, I figured that just this once we could skip the foreplay."

"Baby I hate to tell you this, but that's what we've been doing in the bathroom."

"You know what I mean," she grinned at him.

"Then why don't you lie back on the bed."

She shook her head. "Uh-uh. I want you take me from behind."

Cassie turned around and without taking off her heels, she leaned over the foot of the bed. Matt was shocked that his sweet, innocent Cassie was so bold, and yet he was absolutely amazed at the beautiful sight in front of him. Cassie spread her legs and looked over her shoulder at him.

"Why don't you come over and slide something inside me?"

She certainly didn't have to say it twice. Matt walked up behind her. The heels she had on put her at the perfect level for him to slip right inside of her. Reaching down, he spread her lips and thrust inside as far as he could go. She was tight and very wet.

"Cassie, I don't think I'm going to last long right now. I promise we'll do this again tonight though."

"I don't care. I just want you and I want you now," she told him over her shoulder.

Matt began thrusting fast and hard. He gripped her hips to keep her steady. Cassie gasped each time he slid all the way inside her. He continued thrusting until he knew he was going to climax. He rammed into her three more times fast and hard. He felt her convulse around him and knew that she had found her release. Feeling her muscles clamp down on him was enough to send him over the edge. With one final thrust, he spilled his seed inside of her.

He moved his hands from her hips to her breasts. Cassie gasped and arched again his hands. He was still inside of her and semi-hard. He started to pull out of her, but Cassie backed up into him... firmly keeping him in place. Apparently she already wanted more.

"Honey, as much as I would love to go again right this very moment, I just don't think I'm up to the task. You have to give an old man a break."

Matt pulled from her and gently ran his fingers down her back. He leaned over to kiss her on the shoulder. "I love you."

Cassie turned and kissed him. "I love you, too."

"Let's go enjoy that bath before the water gets cold," he told her.

Out in the woods, Michael and Gabriel were in wolf form. Michael had changed in hopes of luring Matt outside. If he could get him into the woods alone, then he could set things right. Unfortunately, Matt wasn't the one who had come into the woods to investigate the howling... Gabriel had, in his wolf form.

Gabriel growled at Michael and nudged him back toward the cabin. This was something that needed to be discussed in human form and not as a wolf. He wasn't entirely sure what his little brother was up to, but he figured it wasn't good. The two wolves headed back toward the cabin. When they got closer, they changed back into human form. Gathering the clothes that were stashed nearby, they quickly dressed.

Michael looked at Gabriel. "You're going to give me a lecture aren't you?"

"Yep. But I have a few questions first."

Michael sighed. It was going to be a long night. He knew that Gabriel wouldn't understand. He was almost scared to ask what his punishment would be, but he had a fairly good idea. The last time he had royally screwed up in a werewolf related matter, Gabriel had forbidden him to change for at least a week. It was the worst punishment you could ever give a werewolf.

Ashton Grove was small and didn't have any werewolves in the area except for their family. The nearest large town was Atlanta, which was several hours away. The pack master of Atlanta covered not only Atlanta, but all of the cities within an hour of the big city. All of the outlying areas were on their own. Gabriel being the oldest was the pack master of their family, and therefore the pack master of Ashton Grove. His word was law in the local werewolf community... what they had of one.

When they were back at the cabin, Gabriel ushered Michael into his room. It looked like everyone else was still out, but they couldn't be sure. Gabriel closed the door and turned to face Michael. He had a feeling this was going to be interesting.

"So, would you like to explain to me why you were howling in the woods near our cabin?"

"I was trying to right a wrong," Michael told him.

Gabriel shook his head, "I'm almost scared to ask, but what wrong would that be?"

"Cassie."

"And what exactly is wrong with Cassie," Gabriel asked him.

"She's with the wrong guy! You know as well I do that she should be Cole's mate!"

"No, I don't know that. I sense something about her, but it could be anything. It doesn't mean she's destined to be one of our mates," he told his little brother.

Michael gave him an exasperated look. "What else could it be?"

"Maybe she has an unusual ability. She might not even be aware of it."

"What? You mean like being psychic or something?" Michael asked, remembering what he had read about the dragon ring Matt wore.

"Something like that. All three of the girls have something interesting about them. I'm not sure what it is, but I can honestly say that I don't think they're our mates."

Michael sighed. "I'm sorry I fucked up."

"Thankfully Matt stayed with Cassie. If he had gone into the woods and you had harmed him or killed him, do you really think Cassie would have been in a romantic mood?"

Michael hung his head. "No, I guess not."

"Besides, haven't you seen the way she and Matt look at each other? They were clearly meant to be together. Our mates are out there somewhere, and we *will* find them one day... or they'll find us, but they aren't here at Whispering Lake."

Michael nodded that he understood. "So what's my punishment to be?"

"I thought about it on the way here, but then you surprised me. What you were planning was very wrong, but you were trying to do it for Cole. That being the case, you can't change into wolf form for the remainder of the trip, which is far better than the two weeks I had in mind."

"Okay." Michael looked at him. "Thanks for understanding."

"Just don't get any other ideas like that into your head! The next time you get a brilliant idea, try sharing it with me first."

"Sure. Am I free to go now?" Michael asked.

Gabriel looked at him skeptically. "I guess that depends on where you plan on going."

"There are two girls sharing a cabin on the other side of the lake. One of them looked pretty hot. Thought I'd go check it out."

Gabriel just shook his head. "Go ahead."

After Michael left, Gabriel went into the living room and settled on the couch to watch TV. This vacation hadn't been as relaxing as he had hoped it would be. He would give anything to be back in Ashton Grove, riding through the countryside on his Harley. Even working in the garage wasn't as stressful as this week had been!

Things had been going pretty good with Amber, but he knew she wasn't his mate. There was no sense letting things go further if he knew there wasn't a future there. It wouldn't be fair to Amber. Every wolf had a mate, his just hadn't come along yet. He imagined she was out there somewhere. Since he was only twenty-four, he wasn't in a huge rush to find her just yet. There was still plenty of time. However, if other werewolves moved into the Ashton Grove area, having a mate would have its benefits. Pack masters with mates weren't challenged as frequently as single pack masters.

He wasn't sure what to do about Cole. His brother hadn't been the same since Cassie and Matt had gotten back together. It was clear the couple belonged together, but Cole was taking it hard. This was the first time in a year that he had seemed really interested in a woman. It was starting to look like he had gotten over April only to start the process over again with Cassie. Gabriel just hoped that his brother would snap out of it.

Gabriel turned off the TV and headed to his bedroom. It was only ten o'clock, but he was worn out. His brothers were going to be the death of him. If he didn't find their mates soon, they were going to drive him insane. He figured that if they were married their wives could help keep them in line.

Cole wasn't really a problem. Mostly Gabriel was worried about his emotional state right now. Depression in werewolves was even more dangerous than in humans. It could either make them lethal to themselves or to other people. He didn't think Cole had it in him to harm another person, but he wouldn't put it past him to harm himself. And that is what terrified Gabriel.

On the other side of the cabin, Cassie and Matt were exploring each other's bodies. After making love in the bathtub, Matt had dried Cassie off and taken her to the bedroom. She was lying underneath him on the bed looking up into his eyes. She was so trusting and loving. Matt didn't think he would ever get enough of her.

"Matt?"

"Hmm?"

"Would you kiss me?" she asked.

Matt smiled at her. He leaned down and did as she requested. He gently kissed her on the lips, then he trailed kisses down her chin, down her throat and further. When he got to her breast, he trailed kisses down to her nipple. Cassie gasped when he flicked his tongue across her nipple, making it harden. She arched her back, silently begging for more.

Matt raised his head and briefly looked into her eyes before capturing the other nipple in his mouth. He licked and sucked on it until she was panting for more. His erection pressed against her and he could feel how wet she was. Returning to the other nipple, he sucked it into his mouth and lightly grazed it with his teeth.

Cassie could feel him pressing against her. She was hot, wet, and desperately wanted him. She lifteded her hips off the bed until he slipped inside of her. Taking him all the way inside of her, she wrapped her legs around him to hold him in place. There was not another feeling in the world like having Matt inside of her. When they were joined together like this, she felt as if they were two halves of a whole. It was almost like they were puzzle pieces that fit together perfectly.

Matt gasped and looked at Cassie in wonder. He hadn't anticipated her doing that. "You just get more and more amazing each time we're together. I think I created a monster."

Cassie smiled at him. "I don't hear you complaining."

"Never!"

Cassie eased the grip she had on him and he began a steady rhythm, thrusting in and out of her. She raised her hips to meet each of his thrusts. It hadn't taken her long to figure out that by meeting his thrusts she could take him further inside of her. He went deeper when he took her from behind, but she loved being able to look into his eyes as he thrust into her.

She grabbed his shoulders and held on for dear life. Matt was thrusting faster and faster. Cassie felt like she was going to burst if he didn't finish it soon. Every nerve in her body was on fire. She was breathless from the pleasure that he gave her. As Matt pounded into her even harder, she climaxed. Feeling her hot, wet folds clench down on him sent Matt over the edge. He thrust into her one last time before reaching his release.

Afterwards, he didn't even try to pull out. He just rolled onto his side, pulling Cassie with him, and held her. He smoothed her hair back and kissed her. How had he ended up with this beautiful, remarkable woman? Cassie was everything he had always wanted in a woman. He was the luckiest man on earth that she was soon going to be his wife.

Cassie snuggled into Matt and closed her eyes. After making love to him for the past few hours, she was exhausted. It was definitely time to sleep. She threw her arm around his waist and draped her leg over his. Apparently three times in three hours was her limit. She felt boneless and satiated.

Matt watched her drift off to sleep. He was beyond tired after pleasing her, and himself, three times. Feeling her warm naked body next to his was incredible. It was a sensation that he would never tire of. Within minutes, he was asleep.

Chapter Eighteen

Matt woke to the sound of a wolf howling. Looking out the window, he saw that it was morning. He frowned when the wolf howled again, even closer than before.

He glanced at the woman lying next to him and saw that Cassie was still asleep. Pushing the covers aside, he got out of bed and walked to the window. A movement at the edge of the woods caught his eye. A flash of red fur stumbled through the bushes. Peering closer, he saw two blue eyes staring back. He wasn't sure if it was wolf, a husky, or some combination of the two.

Matt turned from the window. He grabbed his clothes and got dressed quickly. Regardless of whether or not the animal was wild or domestic, it appeared to be injured. He'd always had a soft spot for animals and couldn't stand the thought of one suffering.

Once he was dressed, he slipped quietly from the room, closing the door behind him. When he was certain he hadn't disturbed Cassie's sleep, he crept through the living room and out the front door. He cautiously walked around the cabin, not wanting to startle the wounded animal.

As Matt approached the woods, he had a sense of foreboding. Something wasn't right. It was quiet – too quiet. What had happened to the chirping birds? And where was the wolf dog?

Stepping into the wooded area, he scanned the trees and shrubs for signs of life. A pounding began behind his eyes, the pain taking him to his knees. He cradled his head in his hands as a vision overtook him.

A sinister Michael standing over a body, bloody knife gripped in his hand. The vision sharpened and focused on the body. *Matt lay on the ground, fighting for his last breath. Blood gurgled in his throat and seeped from the gash in his neck. Breathing his last breath, his sightless eyes stared up at the sky. A triumphant Michael grinned, a look of accomplishment on his face.*

As the vision broke, Matt groaned. Shaking his head, he climbed to his feet unsteadily. He'd never received visions before and knew it must be the power of the ring. It had apparently magnified whatever psychic abilities he'd had in his former life.

Coming to the woods had been a mistake. He backed up a step, ready to return to the cabin when the cold, sharp edge of a knife was pressed to his throat.

Cassie woke to sunlight streaming through the window. She reached over to Matt's side of the bed, but it was empty. Looking up, she realized he wasn't in the room. Stretching lazily, she crawled out of bed and headed to the bathroom. Peeking around the door, she didn't see Matt. He must have already showered and dressed. What time was it anyway?

Digging through the stuff on the counter, she found her watch. It was already 10:00 in the morning. She had slept most of the morning and had missed breakfast! Last night's activities must have worn her out more than she realized. Walking over to the shower, she started the water. While it was heating up, she went to get her clothes.

As Cassie selected her outfit, she realized her period was late and wondered when precisely it should have started. She dug her planner out of her bag. Looking at the calendar, she realized that she should have had her period before the trip. She was sometimes late, but it gave her hope that maybe her time with Matt had already resulted in a little Spencer.

Smiling, she went back into the bathroom and took her shower. Since it was so late in the morning, she rushed through washing her hair and body. She quickly shaved and got out. Once she was dried and dressed, she applied a little make-up and headed back to the bedroom. Matt still hadn't returned. Cassie threw on her shoes and headed into the kitchen.

Looking around, she didn't see anyone. It was really strange that she would have been left alone in the cabin. Maybe Matt had just gone to the car to get something. She grabbed her cabin key and her purse before heading out the door. Once outside, she walked toward the parking lot.

Matt's Mustang was still in the same parking place. She didn't see him so she decided to check the lodge. Cassie couldn't think of any other place he would have gone. Of course, he could be taking a walk. If that was the case, it could be a while before he returned.

Cassie entered the lodge and looked around. The dining room was empty and the servers were clearing away the dishes. Even the hostess stand was empty. Turning, Cassie headed back down the stairs and toward the cabin. She couldn't very well sit around all morning waiting on someone to show up. She would leave Matt a note and get the car keys.

When she returned to the cabin, it was still empty. Finding a piece of paper in the kitchen drawer, she quickly wrote a note letting Matt know she went into town to pick up a few things for their return trip the next morning. She went into the bedroom and dug through Matt's drawers, searching for his car keys. After a moment of searching, she grabbed the keys to the Mustang and headed back to the parking lot.

Within minutes, she was zipping down the road toward the town of Whispering Lake. Cassie had partially been telling the truth in her note. She did want to pick up some sodas and snacks for the trip home, which she planned on making with Matt instead of her friends, but she also wanted to stop by the pharmacy. She knew it was really early to tell anything, but she was hoping they would have an early warning pregnancy test. Not that she needed a warning. Far from it! She would be ecstatic if she were already carrying Matt's child.

Matt tensed. "What do you want?" he asked in a voice that was calmer than he felt. His heart was pounding and all he could thing about was Cassie.

Michael stepped closer, keeping the knife firmly against Matt's throat. "I want you to walk."

"Where?" Matt asked, scanning the trees for any other people, anyone who might be able to help him.

"Just do as I say," Michael growled.

Matt decided it was best not to argue. He'd already seen his fate in his vision, but maybe he could find a way to change it. Why else would he have had the vision? It seemed cruel to show him events that were set in stone.

They walked in silence, deeper and deeper into the woods. They kept off the trails, walking through the dense trees and shrubs, their feet crunching on the dried leaves littering the ground. As they approached a clearing, Matt swallowed his fear. It was the place from his vision, the place where he had died.

"Can you at least tell me why you're doing this?" he asked.

Michael growled. "Shut up and get on your knees."

Matt dropped to his knees, every nerve in his body at attention, waiting to see what would happen next. He tried to keep his breathing even. He wouldn't give Michael the satisfaction of knowing how terrified he truly was at that moment.

Pulling into the parking lot on Main Street, Cassie parked the car. After locking the doors, she headed toward the pharmacy. She knew she would be on pins and needles until she had the test in her hands. Upon entering the pharmacy, she headed for the isle that said feminine hygiene.

Cassie reviewed the many choices and finally found what she was looking for. Luckily, they also had some drinks and snacks so she was able to buy everything in one stop. After making her purchases, she headed back to the car. She noticed it only had half a tank of gas and drove to the BP station she had passed on her way into town. Once the car had a full tank, she headed back to the cabin. Part of her was hoping Matt would still be gone. Another part of her was anxious to see him.

What would normally be a thirty minute drive, Cassie made in twenty. She was anxious to take the pregnancy test and see the results. She parked the car, locked it, and headed to the cabin with her sack of goodies. When she got to the cabin, everyone was still gone. Her note was still on the counter so she knew Matt hadn't returned.

Cassie hurried into the bedroom. She put the snacks and sodas on the dresser and took the pregnancy test to the bathroom. Closing the door, she locked it for privacy. If Matt came in, he would probably want to know why she had locked herself in the bathroom, but she would worry about that later. She read the instructions and decided to take the test while everyone was away. Taking a deep breath, she peed on the little stick. The instructions said to lay the stick down on a flat surface for one minute to await the results. It was the longest minute of Cassie's life. One line would mean she wasn't pregnant and two would mean her life was about to change forever.

As the seconds slowly ticked by, Cassie paced back and forth in front of the bathroom counter. Once the minute was up, she looked at the stick. Two lines! Her hands flew to her abdomen in amazement. She was pregnant! Now, how to tell Matt? He would want to get married immediately if he found out. Buying herself some time to think things through, she put the stick and box back into the sack. She started to put the sack in the bathroom trash, but stopped herself. If she put it in the bathroom trash, Matt might find it. Instead she left the cabin and deposited it in the larger trash can near the lodge.

Cassie was starting to get worried about Matt and the others. She decided to walk to Amber's cabin and see if anyone was there. On the first knock, Amber answered the door.

"Cassie? What are you doing here?"

"I was hoping that you might know where Matt or the guys had gone. I haven't seen any of them all morning," she told her.

Amber looked surprised. "No. I mean, they aren't here now. Gabriel came by this morning to talk, but I haven't seen anyone else."

Cassie sighed. "Maybe they're all getting along and went off to do guy type things together."

"Would you like me to help you look for him?" Amber offered.

Cassie smiled at her. "That would be great! I wasn't too worried when I got up this morning, but it's been over an hour and I still haven't seen anyone."

Amber locked up the cabin. "Think they could have gone for a hike in the woods?"

"It's possible. Want to take a walk with me? Maybe we'll run into them."

"Sure. Let's go," Amber said.

The two women walked down the path to the woods in silence. Amber was lost in her thoughts. Gabriel had come to the cabin this morning with bad news. Well, to her it was bad news. She had thought things were going really well, but he had told her it was better if they were just friends. Maybe if she were patient, he would change his mind. He said that he enjoyed spending time with her, but he didn't think she was 'the one.' Gabriel had told her it didn't seem fair to let things go any further if he thought his soul-mate was still out there somewhere.

Cassie was also lost in her own thoughts. She wanted to share her news with her friend, but knew it wouldn't be right to tell Amber before she told Matt. She wasn't sure if she should wait until they returned home or tell him today. On the one hand, she wasn't sure how long she could contain herself. She was so excited she was bursting at the seams! But she also knew Matt and knew that while he would be excited, he would also drag her off to the nearest church to get married. She loved him and wanted to marry him more than anything, but she wanted to know he was marrying her because of her and not because she was pregnant. It was silly of her and she knew that. After all, he had said he wanted to marry her the first day he arrived. He obviously loved her and she loved him. It shouldn't matter when they got married. The important thing is that they *were* going to get married and they were going to be a family.

"Cassie, are you all right?"

"I'm fine Amber. Why do you ask?"

"You just seem quieter than usual," Amber responded.

"I'm just worried about Matt. It isn't like him to be gone so long without letting me know where he is."

Amber smiled at her. "I'm sure that he's fine. If we don't find him out here, then he's probably boating or fishing or something. Maybe he went into town."

"His car is still in the parking lot. I borrowed it this morning to pick up a few things in town."

"Don't worry, Cassie. We'll find him," Amber said, trying to reassure her.

Amber looped her arm through Cassie's. She knew her friend was upset because she could feel it too. There was something else though... part of Cassie seemed happy about something. Amber wondered what her friend was up to. Then again, she was engaged to a handsome guy that she apparently loved so maybe that's where the feeling of happiness was coming from.

The women walked in silence, enjoying nature. Being in the woods was starting to make Cassie feel more relaxed. She loved hearing the birds and watching the wildlife. Taking a deep breath, she breathed in the scent of the trees and fresh air. The longer they walked, the better Cassie felt. After thirty minutes, they came to a log and decided to sit down for a minute.

"Cassie, if something was bothering you, you'd tell me right?" Amber asked.

"Of course I would Amber! Right now, I'm just worried about Matt. This isn't like him."

Amber rubbed Cassie's arm in comfort. "We'll find him. Everything will be fine."

Cassie sighed. "I know I'm being dramatic and probably worrying over nothing. Let's head back. It will be time for lunch soon. Since I missed breakfast, I'm starving."

They got up and headed back down the trail the way they came. Going back didn't seem to take quite as long and they arrived at Cassie's cabin in twenty minutes. Cassie headed up the steps. When she realized Amber wasn't following her, she turned to her.

"Would you like to come in?" Cassie asked.

"Are you sure?"

"Please. I don't want to be alone right now."

"Okay." Amber walked up the steps and went inside with Cassie.

When they entered the cabin, everyone was still gone. Cassie walked over to the couch and turned on the TV. Amber sat beside her and they flipped through channels. There was absolutely nothing on so they selected a movie from the cabin's DVD collection. Cassie let Amber pick since she wasn't sure she would be able to focus on it anyway.

Leave it to Amber to pick something like Center Stage. Cassie still felt bad about Cole without watching a movie that had a love triangle in it. Maybe it would at least distract her until Matt came back. If he wasn't back by the end of the movie, she didn't know what she would do.

A few minutes into the movie the front door opened. Cassie practically jumped off the couch. When she turned around, she saw that it was Cole. Her face must have shown her disappointment.

"Everything okay, Cassie?" Cole asked.

"Yeah. Everything's fine," she said with a wan smile.

She didn't look very convincing. Cole looked at Amber in hopes that she would elaborate. Something was apparently wrong and Cassie wasn't talking. Was there trouble in paradise already? The fact that he felt happy just thinking that Cassie might be free again was sad.

"Amber, what's going on?" he asked.

"Cassie woke up this morning and Matt was gone. He didn't leave a note and he's been gone for several hours. We checked the woods and the lodge. Cassie said his car is still here. We hoped maybe he was with you and your brothers," she explained.

"I haven't seen him today. When I got up, Gabriel and Michael were already gone. I don't know if Matt was still here or not."

"Do you know where your brothers are? Maybe he's with them?" Amber asked.

Cole shook his head. "I haven't seen them all day."

Cassie sat back down on the couch. If Matt didn't show up soon, she was going to start crying. Her day had started out so wonderful and now it was turning bleak. What good was finding out you were pregnant if the man you loved had vanished?

Cassie sat straight up. Vanished? What if her father had been wrong? What if Matt hadn't exactly disappeared, but had turned back into a ghost? Without realizing she was doing it, Cassie started to cry. Tears slid silently down her cheeks. The thought of losing Matt was more than she could bear.

Cole couldn't stand seeing her so upset. He walked around the couch and sat down beside her. He looked at Amber at a loss as to what he should do. Was it okay for him to comfort her? Or should he just leave her with Amber?

Amber gave him a nod of encouragement. Cole put his arms around Cassie and hugged her. He gently rubbed her back and whispered comforting words in her ear. Amber sat on the other side of him feeling her friends anguish. All of Cassie's despair, concern, fear, and agony were washing over her. If Cassie didn't stop soon, Amber would also be crying.

Cole picked Cassie up and carried her to her room. She hadn't made the bed so the covers were still pulled down. He gently laid her down and pulled the covers over her. Sitting beside her, he held her hand and rubbed her palm with his fingers. Looking at the doorway, he saw Amber.

"Why don't you get her some water? It might make her feel better," he suggested.

Amber nodded and turned to the kitchen to do as he requested. Cole smoothed Cassie's hair back from her face. Her tears had finally stopped and he wiped the few remaining ones from her cheeks. He hated to see her so upset. Once she was settled and hopefully sleeping, he would go look for Matt. If Gabriel were here, then they could search for Matt in wolf form.

Amber returned with the water and a sleeping pill. She thought it would do Cassie a world of good to take a nap. "Here, I thought this might help her sleep."

Cassie took the water, but refused the pill. "Cassie, you should take it. Amber's right, you need to rest."

"I can't take it," she told him.

Cole looked concerned. "Why? Are you allergic or something?"

Cassie looked back and forth between Cole and Amber. "I just can't take it. I'll be fine."

Cole looked worried, but a light went off for Amber. "Cass, if you can't take the sleeping pill, what about your anxiety medication? Would you like one of those?"

Cassie shook her head. She didn't want to tell them she was pregnant because she wanted Matt to know first. She also knew she needed to stay calm for the baby's sake.

"I can't take those either," she mumbled.

Cole's eyes widened in comprehension. "You're pregnant!"

Cassie blushed. "I didn't want to tell anyone until I had told Matt. I just found out this morning."

Amber smiled at her. "That's wonderful Cass! I'm so happy for you!"

Cassie smiled in return. "Thanks."

She glanced uncertainly at Cole. She knew that this news wasn't what he wanted to hear. Cole looked stunned and a little sad, but he still held her hand and sat by her side. It wasn't fair for him to find out like this. She had planned on telling him, if she ever saw him again in Ashton Grove, but she had planned on breaking the news gently.

Cole leaned down and kissed her cheek. "I'm happy for you Cassie."

"Thank you, Cole."

He gently squeezed her hand. "Why don't you try to rest? I'm sure Amber will stay here with you while I go out and see if I can find Gabriel. If Matt isn't with him, my brother can help me locate him."

"Thank you for taking care of me," Cassie said.

Cole gave her a bittersweet smile. "I enjoy taking care of you. Now rest. I'll be back soon with your fiancé in tow."

Cole got up and headed out of her bedroom. Amber was close on his heels. Once they were in the kitchen, he pulled the door closed. He figured Cassie would like some quiet time.

Cole turned to Amber. "Would you mind staying for a while? Until I return?"

"No, I don't mind," she told him.

Cole smiled. "Thanks. I don't think she should be alone right now. I'm hoping she'll rest."

Cole grabbed his keys and headed out the front door. He knew that Gabriel loved the lake. He would start there and then head into the woods if he hadn't found him yet. When he was twenty minutes from the cabin, he saw someone standing on the lake shore ahead of him. As he got closer, he realized it was Gabriel. Unfortunately, he was alone. Cole had hoped Matt would be with him.

"Gabriel, we have a problem."

Gabriel groaned. "What's Michael done now?"

"Nothing that I know of. It's Matt. He's missing," Cole told him.

Now he had Gabriel's attention. "For how long?"

Cole shrugged. "Cassie said he was gone this morning when she woke up. She hasn't seen him all day and she's really worried about him. Amber is at the cabin with her. I think we convinced her to rest."

Gabriel could tell there was more. "What else?"

Cole shook his head. "It's nothing. I was just hoping you could change into your wolf form and locate Matt. I

260

told Cassie that I would have him with me when I returned."

Gabriel knew there was more, but he wasn't going to press Cole. Whatever it was, he would share it when he felt the time was right. "Let's go into the woods."

The brothers walked deep into the woods. When they were sure they were safe from prying eyes, Gabriel shifted into his wolf form. Cole gathered his brother's clothes and followed him. It wasn't long before Gabriel caught Matt's scent. When they found them, Gabriel and Cole were both shocked. Michael was with Matt and their brother had a knife to Matt's throat.

Gabriel growled low in his throat. Michael froze and looked in their direction. He knew he was caught. He immediately dropped the knife and dropped to his knees. Gabriel stepped forward, growling.

"Is that a wolf?" Matt asked, not sure what to believe after investigating a phantom wolf earlier.

Cole wasn't sure how to answer that. He looked at Gabriel, unsure what to do. Gabriel turned and looked at him. He swung his head around and looked at Matt. Coming to a decision, Gabriel changed back into his human form.

Matt was stunned. After being a ghost for fifty years, he shouldn't have been surprised to learn that werewolves existed, but it was still mind boggling to say the least. "Are all of you werewolves?"

Gabriel regarded him silently. After a minute, he responded. "Yes, we are."

Matt nodded, not really sure what else to do. "That explains the howling wolves we heard last night near the cabin. Thank you for coming to find me."

Cole handed Gabriel his clothes and looked at Matt. He looked terrified and was a little shaken up. "Cassie is resting at the cabin. She's been really worried about you."

"Is she okay?" Matt asked.

"She's fine. Amber's with her."

"Good." Matt wasn't sure what else to say.

Cole walked over to him and put a hand on his shoulder. "Are you ready to head back?"

Matt nodded. All he had been able to think of was not ever seeing Cassie again; not holding her close to him; never being able to tell her again how much he loved her. Unless he was lucky enough to come back as a ghost the second time around... but then, how likely was that?

Gabriel was walking beside Michael. He wasn't sure what do with his brother. Technically, the crime had been committed in human form, which meant that if Matt wanted to press charges there wasn't anything they could do. If Michael had been in wolf form, then Gabriel would have been the one to decide his punishment. He already knew if Matt called the cops he wouldn't stand in the way. Michael had been warned repeatedly and yet he'd still defied Gabriel's orders to stay away from Matt.

As if sensing his thoughts, Matt looked at him over his shoulder. "You're their leader right?"

Gabriel nodded. "Yes, I'm the pack master, or alpha."

"So you punish them when they've done something wrong?"

"Only when they're in wolf form. Since Michael assaulted you in human form, it's your right to call the local authorities. Honor binds me to bear witness that your testimony is true should you decide to press charges," Gabriel told him.

Matt looked straight ahead again. "If I don't involve the authorities, can you guarantee that he won't come near me or Cassie ever again?"

"I don't know. I already punished him once and told him to leave you alone," Gabriel replied honestly.

Matt stopped and looked at Gabriel. "What do you mean by that?"

Gabriel sighed. "It was Michael who started howling near the cabin. He was trying to lure you outside last night." He looked at Michael with disgust. "My brother had it in his head that if you were out of the picture Cassie would go back to Cole. He thought that she was destined to be Cole's mate, but he was wrong."

Cole looked at Michael in alarm. "You were going to kill Matt because you thought Cassie was my mate?"

"Yes. It wasn't right that he should show up and take her from you. You know as well as I do that she smells different. If she isn't your mate, then explain that one to me," Michael said.

Cole shook his head. "She isn't my mate. I care for her, but she isn't my mate. She smells different because she's psychic."

Michael was ashamed of himself. "I'm sorry. I really thought she was your mate. I was trying to right a wrong, or at least I thought that's what I was doing, righting a wrong."

"Dammit, Michael! The only wrong here is the one you committed! Leave Cassie and Matt alone! Can't you see how happy they are together?" Cole demanded.

Michael looked at Cole. "I see how happy they are. I also see how miserable you are. It's been over a year since you actually lived life. The moment you laid eyes on Cassie you changed into the Cole you used to be."

Cole was taken aback. He didn't know what to say. "Have I been that bad?"

Michael looked at Gabriel. He didn't want to hurt his brother, but Cole needed to hear the truth. Both Michael and Gabriel had been worried about him. That was a large part of why they had come to the lake.

Gabriel decided to end this. "Yes, Cole. You've been pretty bad off since April left last year. She wasn't your mate, but you were close to each other. It's like part of you left with her. You go to class, you come to work and you go home. It's like you're drifting from one day to the next without really living any of them."

Cole looked at the ground. "I'm sorry you've both been worried about me, but you have to let me work through this on my own. You're right. Seeing Cassie that first day lit a spark inside of me that I haven't had in a while. You're also right in saying that I've been miserable since Matt got here, but you didn't count on one thing."

"What's that?" Gabriel asked.

"The fact that her happiness means the world to me. If she has that with Matt, then they have my blessing. As long as Cassie is happy, then I'm fine. She loves Matt and it's obvious that he loves her," he answered.

Matt stepped closer to Cole. "I wish there was a way to make things better, but there isn't a way for both of us to be happy. You're right when you say I love Cassie. I love her more than life itself. The whole time Michael had that knife to my throat all I could think of was that I wouldn't ever get to hold her again or tell her how much I love her. Death itself didn't scare me, but the thought of leaving Cassie *did*."

"Let's get you back to the cabin. It will be dark soon. I promised Cassie that I wouldn't return unless you were with me. She doesn't need any extra stress right now," Cole said, regretting the words the moment they left his mouth.

Matt looked at him oddly. "Extra stress? What else is she worried about?"

Cole realized he'd said too much. "She isn't worried about anything but you. Let's just get you back."

Matt stopped him. "You know something. What is it?"

Cole sighed. "Cassie has something to discuss with you. She didn't tell me what it was, but I guessed. If I tell you before she does, she'll kill me."

"You're starting to worry me, Cole. Just tell me what it is," Matt insisted.

Gabriel figured it was the least they owed him after Michael had tried to kill him. "I know you were keeping something from earlier when you found me by the lake. Just tell him whatever it is. If Cassie is upset with you later, we'll deal with it."

Cole rubbed a hand down his face. "Cassie's pregnant."

Matt looked stunned. "She's what?"

"She's pregnant. She didn't tell me, but I figured it out. When I was trying to get her to rest I offered her a sleeping pill. She said she couldn't take it. Amber offered her one of her anxiety pills to help ease her stress and she said she couldn't take that either. I figured the only reason to not take medication that was prescribed to you, at least if you're a woman, is if you're pregnant. She made me promise not to tell you," Cole replied.

"Wow. I'm going to be a dad." Matt had a deer in the headlights expression. "Isn't it too soon to tell though?"

Cole shook his head. "Apparently not. She seemed pretty definite about it."

Gabriel and Michael were just as stunned. If Michael had killed Matt like he'd planned, then Cassie would have been left alone and pregnant. He couldn't believe he had almost done that to her. He looked at Gabriel.

Gabriel grabbed Michael's arm. "We'll discuss this at home. Better yet, we may let Mom discuss it with you at home."

Michael gulped. "Mom? You don't really want to involve her in this do you? I mean, hasn't she been through enough already?"

"Guess you should have thought of that before you almost left a pregnant woman without her mate," Gabriel told him.

Michael groaned. "Shit. Mom's gonna kill me!"

"Yep, now let's get Matt back to Cassie," Gabriel told him.

The four of them walked the rest of the way to the cabin in silence. It was almost dark outside when they arrived.

Matt and Cole walked through the front door together, with Gabriel and Michael on their heels. Amber jumped up off the couch at the sight of them.

"Oh thank god! Cassie's been so distraught I thought she was going to make herself sick," Amber said, rushing over to them.

Matt hurried through the kitchen and opened the bedroom door. Cassie was lying on the bed sobbing her heart out.

"Honey?"

Cassie lifted her head. "Matt? Is that really you?"

Matt quickly walked to the bed and sat down beside her. "Yes, baby. I'm here."

Cassie sat up and threw her arms around her neck. "I was so worried about you! Where have you been?"

"I got into a little trouble out in the woods, but Gabriel and Cole found me and brought me back to you. I'm safe and I'm never leaving your side again," he reassured her.

Cassie sobbed against his shoulder. She had never been more terrified in her life. "I was so scared."

Matt's heart was breaking. "I'm sorry honey. I didn't mean to scare you. Please say you forgive me."

"Of course I do! I was never angry with you," Cassie told him.

Matt kissed her hair and held her close. "I love you so much Cassie."

Cassie looked up at him. "I love you, too. I had wonderful news for you this morning, but it doesn't seem that important right now. Not half as important as you being back here with me."

Matt looked down into her worried eyes. "Whatever it is you wanted to tell me, I could certainly use some good news today."

Cassie wiped the tears from her face. "This isn't how I wanted to do this. I had thought I could tell you over breakfast or even lunch."

"What is it Cassie?" Matt asked, even though he already knew the answer.

"I'm pregnant," she blurted.

Matt smiled. "That is the best news I've had all day. I couldn't be happier!"

"Really? You really are happy about it?" she asked, not sure if he was being serious or not.

"Why wouldn't I be?"

Cassie looked down. "I don't know. I guess after your whole speech about being married before sharing a bed I wasn't sure how you would take the news."

Matt lifted her head. "Honey, I'm sorry I ever made you think I wouldn't be happy about this. It just means we'll get married a little sooner than we had originally planned."

Cassie knew he would say that. "But…"

"No, Cassie. Think about it. Do you want to be far enough along that you're showing on our wedding day? Or do you want to be the size you are now when you walk down the aisle?" he asked her.

Cassie sighed. "You're right. When I look at my wedding pictures twenty years from now, I'd prefer to be this size and not the size of a small cow."

Matt chuckled at her. "You're going to be beautiful even when you're nine months pregnant. Now, how do you think your father is going to take the news when he not only finds out he's gaining a son-in-law but also a grandchild?"

"I think he already knows about the first part. Mom will be completely in shock, but I know Daddy will be happy about being a grandpa."

Matt grinned. "That's good to know. At least I won't have to worry about him coming after me with a shotgun."

Cassie laughed at the idea of her father holding Matt at gunpoint. Her father was the most passive person she knew and had probably never held a firearm in his life. Her mother was the one she was most concerned about. She was always telling Cassie how important it was to finish her degree. Cassie sometimes wondered if her mother didn't regret not having a career. Her mother didn't act unhappy, but Cassie suspected that at times she felt unfulfilled.

"I wanted to tell you first, but I'm afraid that Amber and Cole kind of guessed. I was really upset and they kept offering me sleeping pills and anxiety medication. When I refused and told them I couldn't take anything, they both figured it out."

"It's okay, Cassie. Don't upset yourself over it."

Matt kissed her and walked over to the dresser. He pulled out a clean change of clothes and headed into the bathroom. After taking a fast shower, he got dressed and went back into the bedroom to check on Cassie. She was sitting on the edge of the bed putting on her shoes.

"Just let me wash my face and brush my hair. Would you check with Amber and the guys and see if they want to join us?" she asked.

"Sure," he replied.

As Cassie headed into the bathroom, Matt walked into the kitchen. It looked like everyone was still here. Matt hadn't told Cassie about Michael's part in the day's events and he didn't intend to. She didn't need the stress.

"Is everyone ready for dinner?" he asked.

All of them turned to face Matt. They hadn't even heard him come out of the bedroom, which was fairly amazing considering that three of them were werewolves. His hair was still wet from his shower and he had changed his clothes.

Gabriel walked over to him. "Are you sure you want all of us joining you for dinner tonight?"

Matt nodded. "Cassie wants to make her special announcement and would like everyone to be there. I didn't give her any details about what happened. It's more than she could probably handle right now."

"We won't say a word," Gabriel assured him.

Cassie came out of the bedroom and looped her arm through Matt's. "Are we ready for dinner? I'm starving!"

Amber smiled at her. "Probably because you haven't eaten all day. Let's go fill that bottomless pit of yours."

Cassie smiled back at her. Amber had a point. Cassie ate non-stop already, but now that she was pregnant it was going to get worse. Just the thought of shopping for baby things and maternity clothes was exciting. She knew that she was still young, but her fairytale had already come true.

Matt and Cassie followed everyone out of the cabin and over to the lodge. They told the hostess they would need a table for six. Amber had insisted that Kari wouldn't want to join them. Matt figured she was just trying to keep Kari away from Cassie. He appreciated it too.

Once they were seated and had menus, Cassie looked at Matt. Should they wait until after they ordered or until they had their food. Matt shook his head for her to wait. He didn't have the heart to tell her that everyone already knew she was pregnant. If she wanted to make a big announcement, then he wasn't going to stop her.

Everything on the menu looked wonderful to Cassie. After not eating all day, she was ravenous. She decided that instead of just ordering an entrée tonight she would also order a side salad and a cup of soup. Hopefully she would still have room for dessert. That was the best part after all.

After everyone had placed their orders, Cassie took Matt's hand in hers. She looked at everyone and took a deep breath.

"I have an announcement to make. You already know that Matt and I are engaged, but I found out some other news this morning. We're also going to have a baby," she told them with a big smile.

Everyone smiled and congratulated them. They talked for a while about baby things and about Cassie's plans for school. She would finish the semester, but she wasn't sure if she would be able to make it through the whole spring term or not. She shouldn't be due until sometime in July or August, but she didn't want to stress herself out either.

Cassie's side salad and soup arrived and she attacked them with gusto. Amber was the only other person who had ordered a salad. Cassie felt a little strange eating in front of everyone, but she was so hungry that she didn't really care. By the time their dinner had arrived, Cassie had cleaned both her salad plate and her soup bowl. You would think that would have filled her up at least a little, but she still felt like she was starving when her dinner was placed before her. She not only managed to clean her plate, but she polished off a large slice of coconut cake as well.

After dinner, everyone went back to their cabins. They were leaving the next morning and needed to get most of their things packed.

Cassie filled the tub with warm water. She was still a little stressed over Matt missing for most of the day and thought the warm water would relax her. He hadn't really told her what happened yet, but she was glad he was back by her side safe and sound. As soon as the tub was full, she turned off the faucet. Taking off her clothes, she stepped into the warm water and sank up to her neck. It was very soothing and she started to feel better almost immediately.

Matt peeked in the bathroom and saw Cassie relaxing in the tub. He went and knelt beside the tub and watched her. She had her head tipped back against the side of the tub and her eyes were closed. She had pulled her hair into a knot on top of her head to keep it from getting wet and her face looked freshly scrubbed.

Matt stripped down to his underwear and knelt by the tub again. He tenderly reached under the water and placed his hand on her stomach. It amazed him that there was a tiny life growing inside her. Not just any life, but their child. Matt honestly didn't care if it was a son or a daughter; as long as the baby was healthy he would be happy.

Cassie opened her eyes and quietly regarded him. She covered his hand with her own and smiled at him. "My stomach might be flat now, but in a few more months it will start getting bigger and bigger."

"My mother started showing with my sister when she was about four or five months along. Or at least that's when her clothes couldn't hide it any longer," Matt told her.

"Do you think a month would give us enough time to prepare a small wedding? I don't really have that many people I would invite other than my family," she said.

Matt grinned. "Trust me, with money all things are possible. If you run into a road block, let me talk to them. You will have everything you want for your wedding. That much I promise you."

Cassie rolled her eyes at him. "I don't plan on spending a fortune on this wedding. But I do know where I want to have it... if you'll agree that is."

"Where's that?" Matt asked cautiously.

"I'd like to have it in Spencer Falls in your childhood home."

Matt had trouble swallowing. "I'd really like that."

Cassie thought for a moment. "You know that I'm a Wiccan, but my parents don't. We'll have to get a minister to perform the ceremony."

"Honey, at this point I don't care if we just jump over a broom. I want you to be my wife no matter what it takes."

Cassie sat up and kissed him. "Why don't we head to the bedroom?"

Matt smiled. "I can think of nothing I'd love more."

Cassie reached down and removed the stopper from the tub. She stood up and stepped out of the tub. Matt was waiting for her with an open towel. He wrapped it around her and gently dried her off. After he was done, he picked her up and carried her into the bedroom, carefully laying her on the bed.

He removed his boxers and joined her. Leaning over her, he lightly kissed her stomach, looking at it in wonder, still amazed his child was in there. He kissed his way from her stomach up to her lips. The kiss started out soft and gentle, but Cassie grabbed his hair and deepened the kiss.

Matt pulled away and looked at her. "You had a really rough day today. Are you sure you want to do this? I'd be just as happy holding you while you sleep."

Cassie placed her hand on his cheek. "I want to feel you inside of me. You can hold me as long as you want afterward."

Matt rubbed his erection against her and felt how wet she was. "How much foreplay were you thinking of tonight?"

"None. I want you inside of me this very minute."

Matt slowly slid into her inch by inch until he was completely filling her. "Is that what you wanted?"

"Oh yes." Cassie closed her eyes from the pleasure.

Matt started a slow gentle rhythm. Cassie was arching her hips to meet him stroke for stroke. Her nails were digging into his shoulders. He was keeping a slow and steady rhythm that was driving her crazy. It felt like there was a storm building and she was waiting for it to be unleashed.

Matt watched her expressions. He could tell she was close, for that matter so was he. He started moving just a little faster and she gasped. As he slid all the way inside of her, he felt her muscles clench down on him as she climaxed. The moment he felt her release he allowed himself the same pleasure.

Afterward, he held her close to him. He lightly rubbed her back until her breathing became even and deep. She may have napped at some point today, but the stress of not knowing where he was had taken its toll on her body. Matt held her as close as he possibly could, afraid of letting her go.

This had been the most amazing week of their lives. Matt knew it was just the beginning, but he was sad their time at Whispering Lake had come to an end. In the morning, they would head back to Ashton Grove. It would be Matt's first time officially meeting Cassie's mom and he was terrified of how she would react to the news of their engagement and pregnancy. He knew that Cassie's dad would be excited about their engagement, but he had placed his trust in Matt to do right by Cassie. In that, Matt had failed him... it hadn't been his intention to get Cassie pregnant, but she had been far more tempting than he had bargained for.

Matt's nerves about the coming day kept him from falling asleep immediately. As he wondered about what tomorrow would bring, he watched Cassie sleep. She looked so peaceful lying beside him. He smoothed her unruly curls back from her face and kissed her. Cassie snuggled closer to him. Holding her in his arms, Matt eventually fell asleep... happy and optimistic about his future for the first time in fifty years.

Epilogue

Nine months later, Cassie was watching her newborn daughter, Elizabeth Marian Spencer, sleep peacefully in her crib. Matt watched them from the doorway. It amazed him at how perfect his life had turned out. He had a wonderful job at a local architecture firm that allowed him to work from home three days out of the week; a large inviting house; a beautiful, loving wife; and now a perfect baby girl. A year ago if you had told him that all of this was possible, he would have laughed.

Cassie looked over her shoulder and saw Matt in the doorway. She smiled and walked over to him. Wrapping her arms around his waist, she stood on her tiptoes to kiss him. Cassie never tired of kissing this wonderful, sexy man that she was lucky enough to call her husband.

When they had left Whispering Lake and returned to Ashton Grove, things had been stressful and uncertain. Her mother had freaked when she found out Cassie was engaged and *both* of her parents freaked when they found out about her pregnancy. After a month of awkward visits to her parents' house, things had returned to a semi-normalcy. Her mother helped her decorate the nursery and her father had started spending more time with Matt. In the end, both of her parents had been very supportive of their hasty marriage and unborn child.

Even though Mari had only been home from the hospital for a day, her grandparents had already stopped by to see her twice. Cassie could tell that her parents were going to dote on her daughter and spoil her rotten. Her life could not be more perfect... well, except for Mari's two hour feedings, but that would change soon enough.

Cassie and Matt had found their happily-ever-after at last.

Notes from the Author

If you aren't familiar with Wicca and would like to learn more, I highly recommend Scott Cunningham's *Wicca: a Guide for the Solitary Practitioner*. It's very informative on Wicca as a whole, giving an overview of the various branches of Wicca, the Sabbats, Initiation, and many other aspects of the religion.

The Wiccan Rede is mentioned in this tale. The Rede is similar to the Christian Ten Commandments, a set of laws, or guidelines that should be followed to live your life well. A copy of the Rede is included in this book.

Matt's dragon ring does not exist, nor does the line of super witches it belongs to; it's simply a made-up design and part of Cassie and Matt's story.

To my knowledge, there is no such town as Whispering Lake, North Carolina. However, the town itself was inspired by two very real places – Dahlonega, Georgia and Mt. Airy, North Carolina.

I hope you enjoyed *Whispering Lake* as much as I enjoyed writing it! If you're upset over Cole not getting his HEA, be sure to look for *Moonlight Protector*, the first book in the Ashton Grove Werewolves series – available from Wild Horse Press.

Jessica Coulter Smith

Wiccan Rede

Bide within the Law you must, in perfect Love and perfect Trust.
Live you must and let to live, fairly take and fairly give.

For tread the Circle thrice about to keep unwelcome spirits out.
To bind the spell well every time, let the spell be said in rhyme.

Light of eye and soft of touch, speak you little, listen much.
Honor the Old Ones in deed and name,
let love and light be our guides again.

Deosil go by the waxing moon, chanting out the joyful tune.
Widdershins go when the moon doth wane,
and the werewolf howls by the dread wolfsbane.

When the Lady's moon is new, kiss the hand to Her times two.
When the moon rides at Her peak then your heart's desire seek.

Heed the North winds mighty gale, lock the door and trim the sail.
When the Wind blows from the East, expect the new and set the feast.

When the wind comes from the South, love will kiss you on the mouth.
When the wind whispers from the West, all hearts will find peace and rest.

Nine woods in the Cauldron go, burn them fast and burn them slow.
Birch in the fire goes to represent what the Lady knows.

Oak in the forest towers with might, in the fire it brings the God's
insight. Rowan is a tree of power causing life and magick to flower.

Willows at the waterside stand ready to help us to the

Summerland.
Hawthorn is burned to purify and to draw faerie to your eye.

Hazel-the tree of wisdom and learning adds its strength to the bright fire burning.
White are the flowers of Apple tree that brings us fruits of fertility.

Grapes grow upon the vine giving us both joy and wine.
Fir does mark the evergreen to represent immortality seen.

Elder is the Lady's tree burn it not or cursed you'll be.
Four times the Major Sabbats mark in the light and in the dark.

As the old year starts to wane the new begins, it's now Samhain.
When the time for Imbolc shows watch for flowers through the snows.

When the wheel begins to turn soon the Beltane fires will burn.
As the wheel turns to Lamas night power is brought to magick rite.

Four times the Minor Sabbats fall use the Sun to mark them all.
When the wheel has turned to Yule light the log the Horned One rules.

In the spring, when night equals day time for Ostara to come our way.
When the Sun has reached it's height time for Oak and Holly to fight.

Harvesting comes to one and all when the Autumn Equinox does fall.
Heed the flower, bush, and tree by the Lady blessed you'll be.

Where the rippling waters go cast a stone, the truth you'll know.
When you have and hold a need, harken not to others greed.

With a fool no season spend or be counted as his friend.

Merry Meet and Merry Part bright the cheeks and warm the heart.

Mind the Three-fold Laws you should three times bad and three times good.
When misfortune is enow wear the star upon your brow.

Be true in love this you must do unless your love is false to you.

These Eight words the Rede fulfill:

"An Ye Harm None, Do What Ye Will"

About the Author

Jessica Coulter Smith was born in Tennessee, but travelled all over starting at the age of ten. Having lived in Georgia, California, Texas, and Louisiana, she has once again made her home in Tennessee... for now. A wife and mother, she often finds herself chasing small children around the house. An avid animal lover, she has two cats, two dogs, a bird, and a horse.

Her first book was publishedin 2008. However, this wasn't the first attempt Jessica made at writing. She still has a YA novel that she started when she was thirteen, which she recently began working on once more. In addition, she has received several awards for poetry and has five published poems in various anthologies, the first of which was published when she was sixteen.

You can find her on Facebook, MySpace, and at her website: www.jessicacoultersmith.webs.com.

Made in the USA